The Predicament

A novel by

Phil Thomas

Foundations Book Publishing
Brandon, MS 39047
www.FoundationsBooks.net

The Poe Predicament
By Phil Thomas

ISBN: 978-1-64583-047-4
Cover by Dawné Dominique Copyright © 2021

Edited and formatted by: Steve Soderquist

Copyright 2021© Phil Thomas

Published in the United States of America
Worldwide Electronic & Digital Rights
Worldwide English Language Print Rights

All rights reserved. No part of this book may be reproduced, scanned or distributed in any form, including digital and electronic or mechanical, including photocopying, recording, or by any information storage and retrieval system, without the prior written consent of the Publisher, except for brief quotes for use in reviews.

This is a work of fiction. Names, characters, businesses, places, events, and incidents are either the products of the author's imagination or used in a fictitious manner. Any resemblance to actual persons, living or dead, or actual events is purely coincidental.

The Reviews Are In!

"A page-turning, edge-of-your-seat tale certain to delight fans of Edgar Allan Poe. The Poe Predicament spins a fantastic, mesmerizing tale of dark spirits and cross-time calamities. Don't dare miss it!" –

-James Chambers, Winner of the 2016 Bram Stoker Award

"A delightful mix of time-travel and twisty mystery, *The Poe Predicament* will appeal to all Edgar Allen Poe fans who wish to step back in time and meet the man himself. An entertaining read!"

-Lydia Kang, author of *A Beautiful Poison* and *Opium and Absinthe*.

"Dark as a raven's wing, The Poe Predicament rushes at you like a cutpurse only to snatch the rug from beneath your feet. A smashing combination of mystery and time travel, this debut novel from Phil Thomas is a compulsive read."

-John C. Foster, author of *Mister White* and *Baby Powder*.

"Heartfelt, innovative, and imaginative, Phil Thomas delivers a tour-de-force first novel with *The Poe Predicament*. Featuring a seamless blend of historical fiction, mystery, and science fiction, this unique creation is sure to vault to the top of every genre lover's to-read pile."

-Daniel Braum, author of *Underworld Dreams*.

Acknowledgments

Rome wasn't built in a day, and neither is a book. It takes hard work, planning, resources, and many life-cycles. It starts with an idea, even if it's a glimmer, and with some luck and dedication, that idea results in the end product you now hold in your hands: a published novel. There's a lot that happens in between—edits, rewrites, and the always inevitable and often unpleasant process of killing your darlings. Along the way, there is an army lurking in the shadows, coaxing the ink and paper towards the light of day.

It is often in the form of an agent or an editor or a marketing manager. Other times, it comes in the form of support from family, friends, and peers. This is my first novel, and it wouldn't have been possible without the encouraging words from the people closest to me. First and foremost, I would like to thank my parents, to whom I've dedicated this book. My middle school teacher was the first to bring to their attention that I could (kind of) write. My craft wasn't perfect, and it still isn't, but it sparked a lifelong interest in writing. They acknowledged and encouraged my work, and for that, I will always be grateful.

Thank you to my first writing partner, Matt Brooks. Many a night was spent at the bar with a spiral notebook, a pen, and several beers, jotting down and fleshing-out ideas for our screenplays. It was a fantastic journey seeing that blue ink transform into finished celluloid. And to my friends that I worked with writing and working on those films, including Ryan Maginley and Jamey McCarney, thank you. Your contributions were priceless.

Thank you, my cohort in crime, airwave maestro and fellow author, T. Fox Dunham—we've spent the last five years hosting our show, *What Are You Afraid Of?* It was a blast, and I look forward to the next five. I love your books, and you did a fantastic job editing the Pink

Floyd anthology, *Coming Through in Waves*. The end result is nothing short of amazing. And to think, I would never have met you if my laptop hadn't died at Barnes and Noble. I'm glad it did. Thanks for the outlet...and the shine box. Luckily I didn't have to go home for it.

To my lady, Colleen, for being an amazing cheering section for my writing and giving me the confidence I probably don't deserve. You're a sweet, caring, and wonderful person. I love you, babe.

On the business side: I would like to give my sincere gratitude to the wonderful and talented folks at Foundations Book Publishing. Thank you so much for taking a chance on this novel. I hope it makes you proud. Steve Soderquist and Laura Ranger, I appreciate your enthusiasm for the book and your great attention to detail when editing and formatting the manuscript. To Susan James Pierce, thank you for putting together a thorough and effective promotional strategy. Let's market the hell out of this thing.

A picture is worth a thousand words, but in this case, you've captured all seventy-thousand of them. Dawné Dominique, you did an incredible job with the cover. I still remember the first time I saw it; my jaw dropped. I didn't know what to expect, but you exceeded my expectations.

And to you, the reader, for buying my book. I sincerely hope you enjoy it, and if you like it, please leave a review. And even if you don't like it, let me know why. I can take it.

To Eddie and Richard and Lynn and Drake and London and Ava and Lilly—I'm sorry you're not here to read this, but that zombie was gaining quickly.

Thanks,

Phil

For my mother and father, Patricia and Ronald Thomas. Both of which have always been there when I needed them…

Table of Contents

Prologue 1

One 3

Two 9

Three 12

Four 15

Five 23

Six 27

Seven 41

Eight 46

Nine 49

Ten 55

Eleven 60

Twelve 64

Thirteen 69

Fourteen 76

Fifteen 79

Sixteen 87

Seventeen 95

Eighteen 102

Nineteen 112

Twenty 126

Twenty-One 133

Twenty-Three 150

Twenty-Four 157

Twenty-Five 165

Twenty-Six 176

Twenty-Seven 184

Twenty-Eight 191

Twenty-Nine 208

Thirty 214

Thirty-One 229

Thirty-Two 234

About the Author 238

Prologue

The flea market overflowed with patrons, filling the venue with wall-to-wall bodies. Rows of tables lined the isles with everything from cheap trinkets to expensive artwork. The vendors haggled to keep the prices high, while the buyers did their best to part with as little cash as possible.

A young woman looked on in silence, waiting for an opportunity to squeeze through the crush of people, hoping no one would notice the pair of emerald earrings she had spotted on a center table. They were perfect, just what she'd been looking for. Of course, she would have to get her ears pierced, something she'd never gotten around to doing.

When a small gap opened up, she pressed through the nest of bodies and approached the table. "What do you know about these?" she asked, immediately pointing to the opened tin box.

The chubby vendor shrugged, choking on his cigar. "Only that they once belonged to the wife of a wealthy nineteenth-century businessman."

"How much do you want for them?" she added, digging through her purse and doubting the story. She looked up at the man when she sensed his hesitation.

"For you, three-hundred."

She opened her wallet and quickly leafed through the money. "Just one moment," she stalled. After counting the cash again, she closed her purse and held up her Visa card. "I don't seem to have enough. I'll have to charge, it if that's okay?"

"I'm sorry, we don't take credit cards. Now step aside."

"Wait," she said.

"Next!"

"I have two-hundred and sixty-one dollars and," she continued counting silently, "fifty-three cents."

The vendor stubbed his cigar in a cheap tin ashtray, his serrated eyes staring back. "Fine. They're yours if you want them," He held out the box in one hand and opened his palm with the other. She smiled wanly and placed the folded money in his hand.

The man hesitated, pulling the earrings from her reach, squinting at her. "Are you sure that's all you have on you?" he croaked in a raspy cigar-tainted voice. "You wouldn't be holding out on me, would you?"

"No, I swear. You can check my purse if you need proof."

He grunted and placed the box on the table, maintaining eye contact. The woman snatched the earrings before he changed his mind and immediately felt a disjointed connection; an odd sensation she'd never experienced before.

She shook away the feeling. "Thank you for your generosity. You have no idea how much I wanted these." She turned and pushed through the crowd, making her way toward the sliding glass exit with a mixture of joy and uneasiness.

One

Metallic red streamed down Richard Langley's face as he reached the front of his apartment complex. His heart jumped under his oversized parka, his legs numb. He'd never stolen anything in his life. A perfect record now shattered at the age of thirty-five. He wasn't sure what to make of the recent events. It all happened so fast.

He made his way up the concrete stairs and into his apartment building, ignoring the doorman's concerns for his appearance. The front door key clicked the lock, and he felt a rush of relief as he entered his one-bedroom apartment. Everything looked familiar; comfortable. Not like outside.

He placed the book on his bedroom nightstand and fumbled the bathroom light on to assess the damage done to his face. It was worse than he expected. His eyelid had sustained a deep gash and his eyeball had ruptured some blood vessels, prompting a fiery reflection.

His room was unexplainably frigid. He kept his coat on, flopping on the bed with a cold compress to his face. He thought about Jenkins and Sarah and wondered if they were all right. They were his friends, and he'd wronged them. Shit. It wasn't like he'd meant to do it!

Something occurred while he was in that bookstore. Something he couldn't rationally explain.

He had started his day like any other, completing his calculated daily routine of showering, brushing, flossing, two bowls of corn flakes, one glass of orange juice, then brushing and flossing again. After greeting the doorman, he appeared outside into the blustery New York City winter and headed to the corner bookstore.

He placed exactly twenty dollars into his pocket and left his credit cards on the night table. Being an over-spender had forced him into this new budgeting method and from what he could tell, it was working so far. He'd given his car up years ago, preferring public transportation. Today, he decided to skip the subway and walk the ten blocks.

As he waited for the light to change, he zipped up his parka to the bottom of his chin and examined his phone for any missed calls or text messages. There were none.

The small golden bell on top of the door announced his arrival as he entered the bookstore. A large sign hung above his head that read: Bookworms. An appropriate name, considering most of their dead-skin binders housed them. It had only been one week since he'd been there but the monotony of his post-marriage life made it seem much longer. The store was empty except for a man crouched on his knees, stacking books in the self-help section.

"Hello Jenkins," Richard said. "Isn't this your day off?"

Jenkins and his wife owned the bookstore for close to fifteen years. They were on the wrong side of forty-five, but Jenkins had two things Richard wanted—companionship and happiness. Their relationship reminded him of much better days with his wife.

Jenkins smiled and continued to neatly restock the books next to him.

"Have anything interesting there?" Richard asked.

"Most of this is crap, well, unless you want to unlock the secret to happiness or make a million dollars in three weeks," he said with a sigh. "But, I do have some new arrivals if you want to look through them."

Richard nodded and spotted the stack on the counter. Not many books came into the store and when they did, it was usually something he had little interest in.

"Have you looked through any of these yet?" he asked.

"Nope," Jenkins replied.

Richard picked up the stack and began to search through them. Nothing caught his eye. In fact, he wasn't familiar with anything he saw.

After scouring through two dozen books, he was down to the last one. It looked old, in fair condition with a bit of yellowing and a few tears, but acceptable. He opened the front cover and read the inside description aloud.

"Tamerlane and other poems, 1827. Copy two of fifty."

Without noticing the signature, he looked up to ask Jenkins how much he wanted for it.

"Hey, Jenkins..." Looking back down at the book, he asked, "Do you have any information on this book here? It's by some author named A Bostonian."

Jenkins might've answered, but Richard heard nothing. His breathing slowed, and his head felt heavy. The sensation grew intense and the room began to spin rapidly. He stumbled sideways and braced the edge of the counter.

"Are you all right, Rich?" Jenkins asked. He sounded far away.

"Yeah, yeah, I'm fine."

"Do you need to sit down?"

Richard wiped his forehead, unable to process his onset condition. But when his ears started to ring, that's when it became real.

"Do you hear me?" A silky woman's voice seeped from the plaster walls. She continued, this time speaking forcefully. "We don't expect you to understand what's happening, but I already feel you know what to do."

The voice had become so deafening that it rumbled the already unstable structure. But Jenkins went on his way, oblivious to the phenomenon as a bright, circular ring manifested around the book. Richard sensed several invisible hands restraining his wrists when he tried to place it back on the pile.

"This is bigger than you," the voice persisted. "Leave here, as quickly as you can." Richard's actions became mechanical; not his own.

As he looked over at Jenkins, who was still intently stocking his books, he struggled against the force that guided his hand, attempting to place the book inside his parka. He was being controlled, much like a puppet on a string.

Sarah appeared from a side room and leaned on the front counter. "I think most of the inventory is sorted. I don't believe there's anything else for today." Jenkins stared at the pile of books that Richard had rummaged through.

"You can log that pile into the database and stock them if you want," he suggested.

"Oh, I already logged those yesterday when you weren't here. Most of them are worthless, except for one."

"Leave now!" the voice insisted. But Richard resisted the urge. He wasn't about to steal from his friends, no matter what some disembodied voice told him.

Richard didn't initially hear Jenkins calling his name but after snapping out of his daze he noticed Jenkins staring at him, eyebrows raised.

"Rich, didn't you hear me?" Sarah frantically searched through the book pile, her face sunken. "Did you happen to see a book entitled Tamerlane, or something like that?"

"Yes, I have your book," was what he attempted to say. But what came out was, "No, I don't think so."

"Weren't you asking about a book by someone called A. Bostonian?"

Sarah chimed in. "That's it, A Bostonian. Did you see it?"

Richard swallowed and attempted to say, "Yes," but again, that wasn't what came out. "I have to get my dry-cleaning," is what he said. "I'm sorry, but I need to leave."

As he involuntarily stepped toward the exit, something dropped from under his coat. It felt like an eternity for the object to hit the ground, but when it happened, the look of astonishment on Jenkins' face could only be matched by Richard's frustration. A warm rush of unwarranted embarrassment and shame fell over him like a cold blanket. It didn't matter. For whatever reason, he wanted the tome more than ever, and he didn't have a clue why.

He reached down and grabbed the book, pushing Jenkins out of the way but not before Jenkins grabbed his legs, causing him to lose balance and smash his face against the corner of the bookcase. A painful rush surged from his eyelid, immediately blinding him with a thick, reddish obstruction.

Sarah yelped like a frightened puppy while Jenkins collapsed on the floor. Richard kicked his leg away and ran out the front door as he heard Jenkins yell, "Thief!"

Richard's faculties returned to normal by the time he flopped on his bed, but not the unexplainable desire for the book. The room felt colder, so he pulled his coat tighter across his chest, unable to explain the temperature change, even after noting the seventy-one degrees on his bedroom thermostat.

He shook off the recent events and opened to the first page. And that's when he noticed it...

Something scribbled in light ink, just underneath the author's name. It was slightly faded yet still legible. But it couldn't be correct. He looked closer just to be sure, and immediately Googled the signature to see if the pattern matched. It did. Edgar Allan Poe. He also noticed a message written on the back page:

To my Emerald Lady. I will never forget you. 1831

Richard wasn't sure if the words had any historical significance yet but he suspected it could only add value to the book.

Assuming this was a legitimate signature, Jenkins and Sarah had somehow acquired something significant. He became drowsy after reading the eighth poem and closed his eyes for only a moment...

But it was enough to change his life forever.

Two

A horse galloped past the window, startling Richard awake. He frantically jumped to his feet, expecting an intruder, or worse, the cops, here to give him more free time than he wanted. When the gallop quieted in the distance, he sighed and sat quietly on the edge of the bed, realizing night had fallen.

As he stumbled to find the light switch he wondered how long he'd been asleep. It was still morning when he'd arrived back home. Had he slept all day? In the cloak of darkness, he tripped over the nightstand, prompting an invisible object to tip over and crash to the wooden floor.

A moment later, a door opened down the hallway and echoed into his room. Footfalls started toward him. He froze, wondering how someone gained access to his locked apartment.

The cops, they've found me.

He thought for a moment about telling the truth but quickly understood how insane he'd sound. "No, officer, it wasn't me. It was the voices in my head."

Richard slowly raised his hands, awaiting the inevitable. His bedroom door slammed open and a dark silhouette stood before him, holding a single candle that shadowed off the bedroom walls.

"Is everything all right?" a raspy voice asked. "I heard something break." Richard lowered his hands and adjusted his sight on the shadowy figure. He reached for his nightlight but caught dead air. "I didn't think you'd be back so soon," the figure continued, walking closer to Richard with the candle outstretched. "I thought you were going to the Skinned Calf for a nightcap." The figure noticed Richard's faint silhouette against the dull candlelight. "Wait," he announced, stepping backward. "You're not my houseguest. Who are—"

"I live here, I think," Richard interrupted, wondering if he'd stumbled into the wrong apartment. It didn't seem logical, but neither was hearing voices that weren't there.

"I'm giving you just ten, no wait, five seconds to get out of here before I notify the authorities," the confused voice announced. Both men stood in the darkness for a few moments, neither one saying a word. Richard stared at the figure and couldn't remember being more frightened, not even in the bookstore earlier that day. Well, five seconds had already come and gone, and Richard had yet to see a glimmering cell phone light or an emergency call placed.

Between glances of the figure in front of him, he began to identify the glow on the surrounding walls. These weren't his walls. Nothing was his: the ceiling, the bed, nightstand, the hardwood floors, the doorway...all were unfamiliar.

The man didn't move.

Richard finally nodded and rose slowly from the bed. When the bleak shape stepped aside, he couldn't initially assess the man's expression. Maybe he was just as frightened? And then Richard caught its embossed frown in the sharp candlelight. It was cold, but like a child's whimper, attempted to appear more menacing than it was.

Richard nodded and raised his hands slightly. "I'm leaving now, okay?" he said. "I apologize for the mix-up." As he carefully eased past the figure into the darkened hallway, he waited for an attack from behind, maybe a bludgeoning over the head? But nothing came.

Moonlight speared through the row of windows, leading him down the stairwell to the front exit. As he reached for the barely visible handle, he understood the figure was listening and wanted to make as little noise as possible. After the lock clicked and sounded throughout the living room area, he rumbled the heavy door sideways and stumbled outside into the moonlight.

Three

The sidewalk was an ice rink. He lost his footing on the slippery steps and reached for a nonexistent railing, propelling him into a partially frozen mud puddle. The bottom half of his coat sleeve dripped with the brown liquid, along with his pants and sneakers.

There was a hole in the knee of his pants where he scraped the skin, producing a laceration. After brushing the mud off his coat the best he could, he slowly raised his head.

He forgot his misfortune when he heard the faint echo of atonal violin music rising in the distance along with some laughter and indecipherable conversations. Richard blinked and wiped his eyes, just to be sure he hadn't imagined it. The images remained.

Old-fashioned gas lamps lined both sides of the cobblestone street. The road widened with rows of quaint structures, belching black smoke from their rooftops. Redbrick pubs, restaurants, residential homes, and a playhouse theater greeted him. Each commercial building had its own hitching-post where parking spots should've been, and while some were vacant, others were occupied by faithful companions, awaiting their owner's return with great patience.

It was nothing like he'd ever seen in real life. But he held his composure and began to make his way down the unfamiliar street toward the inspiring scenery. Horse carriages sounded in the distance along with the cacophony of soft night owl hoots.

Each step was an act of will. Richard hoped his bloodied knee wasn't fractured and needed to relieve the fresh sheet of pain somehow but doubted they sold aspirin in any of the corner stores.

From the bedroom window, the shadowy figure directed his gaze at Richard, wondering who he was and baffled as to why he had been in the guestroom. He turned away from the window, picking up the book the intruder had abandoned and paged through it. It was in pristine condition, with no yellowing of pages or tears. The figure placed the book on the bed and extinguished the candle with a single breath.

The longer Richard walked, the more he wanted to see. Attempting to dissect his situation would be fruitless. Instead, he focused on finding shelter. After noticing a crossroad, he stopped for a brief moment and set his sights upon a three-pointed intersection where traffic in the form of horse-drawn carriages came and went. He noticed the passengers and drivers decked out in fancy attire, with long flowing pastel-colored garments for the ladies and black top-hats and elegant evening suits and bow ties for the men. Richard stopped at the intersection to marvel at the beautifully detailed carriages, their handcrafted images extenuating the look and appeal of a vehicle long since vanished. The gaslamps which lined the sidewalks cast sinister shadows along the winding streets. He recognized that he might be standing on the site of New York City's upper-class district, possibly Fifth Avenue.

When pedestrians began to give him strange glances as they walked by, Richard looked down at his attire, realizing how out of place he must look.

I stick out like a whore in a church, he thought.

While looking to the corners of the intersection he noticed a pub on the right side of the street. Its bright, interior light spilled out through its many windows, beckoning him. It looked magnificent.

"The Skinned Calf," Richard said as he read the overhead sign. He recalled the anonymous figure mentioning it while in the bedroom. It seemed like a pleasant enough place. He had always imagined buildings and antiques looking old and beaten, forgetting they were once new. To him, everything seemed as though it had recently been constructed. Richard limped along the dirt road toward the golden lights of the pub. To his left, he noticed a large clock in the middle of the crossroads that read 10:20. It wasn't as late as he thought.

Four

When he reached the two front steps he stopped for a moment to admire the antiquated porch. Two rocking chairs displayed themselves neatly on either side of the carved cherry-wood door, with four strategically placed cherubs etched into the grain. Each held a violin and sat upon a Pegasus. A round steel doorknob was molded into the head of a calf. Mesmerized by the detail, he flinched when the knob turned and a thin bean-pole materialized from the saloon. The stranger brushed past him and sneered.

"Excuse me, sir," Richard said.

"Wha tha' hell are you wirin'?" the man slurred, eying Richard's beige and blue winter parka, which sported the Outdoor Adventure caption on the right side.

"I'm…not from around here," Richard said delicately.

"Well, id luks ridilulous to me," the man said. Richard felt a tinge of offense at the man's insults and wanted to point out the drunk's mussed greasy hair and disheveled appearance. His shoes had multiple splits on the front where his toes hung freely, and his thin cloth pants appeared to be held up by a long cord that wrapped around his waist.

"An what are ya wirin' on your feet?" the drunk asked through hiccups.

Richard was hoping he wouldn't notice his Nike cross-trainer running shoes.

"Are ye a spaceman?"

"Uh, no," Richard said, wondering how the day he woke up to could so ludicrously wind up to the here-and-now of this weird reality. "I've had an accident that requires some medical attention. My leg is wounded, and my vision is getting worse from a prior injury."

The man swayed back and picked some food from his teeth. Richard put his hands in his pockets and began to walk away. "Never mind," he said.

"I know who cin help you," the drunk belched.

Without another word, the man turned and re-entered the pub, motioning to Richard, who apprehensively followed the man through the large wooden door into complete chaos.

The interior unfolded like a ticker tape. A sprawling ornate bar announced itself in front of him surrounded by round wooden tables, layering the main floor in no discernable order. The bar was crowded with patrons, passed out on the tables and floor. A pianist sat in a corner, diligently playing an unfamiliar tune, seemingly oblivious to the madness around him. The carved high-rise ceilings gave everything a much-needed dose of class and elegance.

The thick cigar and filterless cigarette smoke infiltrated Richard's eyes and caused them to tear. Squinting to relieve the sting, he noticed intense poker games at a few of the tables where winners celebrated, and losers accused them of deceit.

The drunken man grabbed him by the coat sleeve and started leading him to the bar area. No one noticed him and that's the way he wanted it. As far as he was concerned, he was a ghost. Everyone appeared dressed as though they were attending a funeral. He'd never seen so many shiny gold pocket watches or top hats in his life.

"C' mon. The bartender will have ya fissed up in no time. He's also a practisin' physician and tens to wounds whenever bar fights brick out."

Richard wondered what other professions this "Dr. Bartender" might be involved in. "So, is this bartender also a barber?" Richard smiled.

The drunken man turned around and ran his fingers through his crop. "Who do ya thin cuts my hair?" Richard's smile faded as they continued pushing through the crowd.

"I hope he's a better doctor than a barber," Richard mumbled to himself. The drunk plopped in one of the few open seats and greeted the bartender by calling him Dr. Nate. The two men continued to speak but Richard couldn't hear them over the high octaves in the joint. He saw the bartender toss an apron at someone, giving some standing orders, and then turned to Richard. He motioned for him while leaving the bar area. It was difficult to see the doctor through the thick wall of bodies.

"Go follow Dr. Nate," the drunk spouted. "He's agrid to help ya out. Hyurry!"

Richard wondered why this guy hadn't been flagged yet, but he thanked the drunken man and started wading through the sea of people. He noticed a few inquisitive glances directed toward him as he carefully nosed through the crowd, making sure not to spill anyone's beer or whiskey, which seemed to be all they served.

Upon emerging from the sea, he noticed the bartender sitting at a large occupied table, staring in his direction. He was a balding middle-aged man with a potbelly and a double-chin. Richard sat and extended his hand.

"I appreciate you doing this for me, sir."

"I'm a doctor, not a sir," the bartender insisted.

"My apologies, doctor."

Richard could sense the bartender assessing his attire from where he sat, but luckily he remained silent.

"Emery told me you'd been hurt."

Richard propped his leg on the table and lifted his pant leg. "Yeah, my knee is in bad shape, and my eye is even worse."

A person dressed in a dirty white apron abruptly approached the table with a medical bag and a bottle of whiskey. The bartender took the bag and began to lay items on the table. They appeared primitive, nothing like any kind of medical equipment he'd ever seen. Pulling a short saw from the bag, the bartender finally spoke up.

"That leg is going to have to come off."

Richard frowned and slowly stood, holding onto the uneven chair for support. "What are you talking about? Just what kind of a doctor are you?" he asked.

The bartender burst into a belly laugh. "Calm down! I was just having a little fun with you." Richard didn't share his enthusiasm but somehow managed a nervous chuckle. "Anyway, I think a bandage should take care of that knee. Prop your leg back up so I can wrap it," he instructed.

Richard did as requested and allowed the bartender to clean the wound and apply an unidentified liquid. After the bartender wrapped it with some cotton terry cloth, he began work on Richard's eye using the same routine.

When he finished, a man at the table spoke up. "Just out of curiosity," he said, "what kind of a coat is that anyway?"

"It's just a regular coat," Richard said. The men sat silently for a moment. It sounded eerily quiet, even with the surrounding noise. Just as Richard was about to say his goodbyes, a young man dressed in a plain dark-blue military uniform approached the table.

"Do you mind if I sit here, gentleman?" Not waiting for a response to his question, the man sat down before anyone could answer. He removed his brimmed hat and placed it in front of him. "Much obliged. I just lost a quite unsettling amount of savings to that louse at the poker table over there. I swear he's using a trick deck. Anyway, I was just wondering, since you're the active bartender, would it be possible to comp me for just a few drinks this evening? I will gladly stop by tomorrow to settle up." The man clutched his empty rocks glass, trying not to look desperate.

"I don't remember seeing you in here before," replied the bartender. "How do I know you'll keep your word?"

"I don't have much in the way of collateral, but maybe you could hold on to my watch for ransom," the man offered, pulling a shiny gold watch from his pocket and unhooking the chain link from his vest. The bartender palmed the watch and examined it for a moment.

Richard remembered the twenty dollars in his pocket.

"Excuse me, sir," he interrupted. "That won't be necessary. I'll cover your drinks tonight."

The man smiled. "Are you sure? I don't want to be a burden."

"It's no burden at all. Give him back the watch, and I'll cover his expenses."

"Fair enough," The bartender said, handing the watch back. The man thanked Richard and began eying the bottle of whiskey on the table.

"Doctor, how about you pour us some of that whiskey?" Richard said.

"Now you're talking." The doctor poured two large glasses of the pungent-smelling booze.

After toasting their glasses, the nameless man gulped every drop before Richard even smelled his. "If it's all the same, I think I prefer to sip mine."

The other men shrugged as if to say suit yourself. While the men knocked back their drinks, Richard wondered about the military man and his agenda. After taking a small sip of the atomic cocktail, he decided to find out.

"So what's your story?" he asked the man.

"Ah! I apologize, where are my manners? The name's Eddie."

"I'm Richard," he said, shaking hands.

The bartender chimed in. "I hate to break this party up, boys, but I have to get back to the bar. There's a lot of thirsty people and my assistant can only handle so much." Richard expressed his gratitude once more as the bartender left the half-full bottle of whiskey.

"Well, I suppose this is ours," Eddie said, pouring another drink. Richard was astonished at how much this man was consuming. Aside from some slight speech impairment, he seemed to be firing on all cylinders.

So much had happened in the last twelve hours that Richard had a brief reality check as he looked around the room at the people, the poker games, and the drunks passed out on the floor. He wanted answers. He needed them if he was to figure this crap out. It was growing late and soon the bars and pubs would all be closing, sending their patrons on their way.

Richard paused and grasped the bottle from off the table.

"Hey Eddie, how about we have one more drink before the place closes tonight?"

"You read my mind," Eddie replied, tapping his index finger against his temple.

While he poured the round, Richard tried thinking of ways to ask Eddie for help without sounding too desperate. He hated begging for handouts, but he had no place to go and nowhere to sleep. It was too damn cold to be alone on those desolate streets. That realization overcame his pride, which had to be swallowed, along with the shot of whiskey.

"So Eddie, do you live around here, or just traveling through?

"I just arrived this afternoon from West Point. It was a tiring journey, but I'm planning on bunking with some close friends tonight just a few blocks from here. I have, however, arranged my lodging elsewhere for the remainder of my stay."

"I'm also from out of town," Richard lied. "I had a room booked in the city for tonight, but unfortunately, I mixed up the dates and my room has been rented out. So I now find myself, for lack of a better word, screwed."

"Screwed?" Eddie asked, perplexed.

"Yes, sorry, I'm not from around here. What I meant to say was, I'm in trouble."

"Oh, that's a shame," Eddie replied, nodding. "Where will you go after you leave here?"

Richard knew this was his chance to gain sympathy. He'd be sleeping with the stray mongrels if he blew it. "I noticed a sweet spot behind the back alley that might be a suitable place to catch a nap. If I pile the trash bags high enough, they should give me just the cushioning I need."

Eddie cringed. He sat silent for a moment, sipping his drink. "Hmm, I won't hear of it," he finally said. "I'm sure accommodations could be made for you to stay with us tonight. I'm certain I glanced upon an extra room in the upstairs hallway as I unpacked earlier."

Richard smiled. "Are you sure it won't be any trouble?"

"No trouble at all. I'm sure Mr. And Mrs. Stockton would be more than happy to help you in your time of need. They are, after all, good people." Eddie pulled out his pocket watch to check the time. "Yes, it's getting late. We should be heading out. We'll bring the bottle with us."

Both men abandoned their table and waded through the now thinning crowd towards the door. Just as he was about to exit the pub, Richard remembered he hadn't paid the tab. "Wait one minute," he said. "I'll meet you outside."

Eddie walked out and took a seat on a rocking chair that occupied the porch area, synching his pocket watch with the gigantic clock across the way and gazing upon the vacant forked intersection.

The horse carriages ceased to occupy the streets, and their counterparts seemed to have retreated home for the night. As Eddie finished his watch sync, the porch doors sprung open and Richard stumbled out. "Don't come back!" exclaimed a hulking man by the doorway.

"I've already told you my money is real," Richard replied.

"It's obviously not! You're trying to pull a fast one, and you're lucky I don't have you arrested!" Richard struggled to his feet, still in agony from his wounds. "I never want to see you in here again!" The bouncer slammed the door in Richard's face. Eddie appeared confused at the outburst he'd just witnessed.

"What happened in there?" he asked.

After brushing the dust off his pants and coat, Richard replied, "We should probably be on our way before anything else happens. I'll explain while we're walking."

Richard, not being accustomed to this way of life, almost asked Eddie if he thought the bouncer had called the police. He began to think about all the luxuries he took for granted that had been instantaneously ripped from his reach. No cell phones. No Internet. No computers, cars, airplanes, credit cards, movies, recorded music, and, worst of all, no Netflix. And no way to curb the searing pain from his wounds. Aspirin didn't exist, and he left his prescription medicine on his dresser somewhere in the future.

He was lost.

Five

As they walked on, Richard explained that the bar incident was just a misunderstanding and assured him that the money was real. Eddie appeared to accept this and didn't ask for any proof.

The main road they walked along narrowed and transformed into a small cobblestone street that looked vaguely familiar. The dark alleyways of the residential neighborhood seemed appropriately out of place within the tranquil scenery surrounding them. On occasion, a vagrant would stumble out from the darkness to set their envious gaze upon Richard and Eddie before returning to feast on whatever scraps of food they had acquired. The full moon and carefully spaced gas lamps continued to light their path.

Eddie watched the ground as he walked. Neither man said much, prompting an uncomfortable silence. Nonetheless, they had approached the fourth block of the street and were closing the gap on their destination.

"We're here," Eddie said as he pulled the keys from his pocket. As he toiled through his key ring, Richard noticed a detail that further sunk his spirit.

"Excuse me, but is this where you're staying?" he asked.

"Yes, it is. Is there something wrong?"

Richard couldn't move. All he could do was glare up at the same house that he'd awoken earlier that night. Knowing once the owner recognized him, there'd be trouble. But a single fact remained…he had nowhere else to go.

"Nothing is wrong. I'm just admiring the structure of the home."

Eddie nodded, and both men entered the darkness of the first-floor living room. It was pitch black, and Richard found himself tripping over variously placed objects.

"Maybe we shouldn't wake Mr…what did you say his name was again?"

"Stockton," Eddie replied. "Don't worry. He won't mind. I'll just explain the dilemma and everything should be fine."

Richard doubted his traveling companion's optimism but kept up his façade. He pulled the parka hood over his head and yanked the strings tight, concealing most of his facial features.

After locating a portable oil lamp on one of the nearby tables, Eddie struck it lit and began guiding their ascension up the narrow staircase. Richard sensed his courage fall away as they reached the top, and even more so when Eddie gently knocked on the bedroom door.

"I don't want to scare them," he said while knocking again, this time a bit louder.

A muffled movement sounded from the bedroom interior. The door slowly opened, revealing the same ominous shadow that Richard had previously encountered. The man silently stared back at them.

"I regretfully apologize for having to wake you, friend," Eddie said with a touch of fear in his voice. "But, we currently seem to have a small dilemma on our hands."

"What time is it?" Mr. Stockton asked.

"Oh, I'm not quite sure, but I believe it's getting on somewhere near the two o'clock hour."

"I see. Couldn't this have waited until morning?"

Eddie swallowed hard. "An emergency has arisen," he added. "My friend here has had a terrible mix up with the local hotel and has no place to stay. It's awfully cold outside, and I wanted to ask your permission for him to stay the night."

Up until this point, Richard had been hiding behind Eddie but decided to make his presence known by stepping forward. He extended his hand, hoping the parka hood would do its job effectively.

Stockton didn't return the gesture, but took pity on the journeyman and informed Richard that he could stay in a spare bedroom. Exhausted, and with nothing else to say, Stockton shut the door on his two guests and navigated through the darkness back to the warmth of his bed where his young wife stirred gently between the abundance of sheets and fluffy blankets. He watched her uncomfortably.

As Richard stood in front of the bedroom's gold-plated mirror, he wondered how much money the owners actually had. It must've been a shit-load, even by *his* early twenty-first century standards. His eye had stopped bleeding but the cloth had been soaked-through and was in desperate need of changing. After pulling the bandage off, he felt the hair ripped from its follicles, figuring it more sanitary to keep it off. He remembered it tinged with rust-colored stains, and a musty odor when first applied. It disgusted him.

Accompanied by his oil lantern, Richard sat on the king-size bed. He remembered it from earlier and couldn't believe the irony. As he peeled the covers to climb into bed, something dropped onto the floor. After reaching down beside the bed, he felt around and retrieved the object. His eyes struggled to see in the blanket of darkness. He held his lantern up, noticing the familiar book and title: *Tamerlane and other poems, 1827. Copy two of fifty.*

It looked like his book. It felt like his book. But in much better shape than he remembered. This particular copy looked like it had been printed yesterday. Upon closer inspection, he noticed the absence of any signature and no inscribed message was present. He struggled to recall what it said, something about an emerald lady. He hid the book underneath the mattress, concluding that it could be his ticket home and blew out the candle, wondering if he might awake in his own bed.

Six

He awoke to a younger sun. It was nine o'clock, and he did the same thing he did every morning no matter where he was. He pulled the picture of his wife from his wallet and raised it to eye level. It hurt to look at her, but the pain reminded him that he was alive. The blonde highlights in her hair and eternally frozen smile subtly interrupted the faded print and eroded edges of the photo. It was all he had left of her, and it was the way he preferred to remember her: happy, content, and full of life.

He sighed and placed the picture back.

Having failed to sleep much, he was exhausted and disturbed by some nightmarish images that tormented him through the twilight hours, but he became even more disheartened by the realization that he wasn't in his room. He stared at the prism chandelier suspended above the bed, attempting to shake the images from his mind. He continually dwelled on them and he wondered if this might be some sort of side effect.

After sitting up in bed to get an accurate look around the guest room, he admired the beautifully colored porcelain sculptures that rested on top of the elongated bureaus. In addition to the black lantern oil lamps that hung from the four white walls, a stone fireplace slept next to one of the bureaus. Out of habit, he reached for some Mega Men multi-vitamins that usually sat on the nightstand before remembering where he was. He needed to get home, if anything, to patch things up with his ex-wife.

Another reason to find a way out of—

And then he remembered the book under his mattress. A smile broke across his face. He quickly retrieved it and noticed how different it looked in the light of day, but still no signature or message. He closed his eyes and held the tome tightly in his grasp, hoping to see his familiar bedroom. He squeezed hard.

He slowly opened his eyes and looked around the room.

Shit.

He slid the book back to its hiding spot and decided to address the rumbling in his stomach. Having slept in his clothes, he slipped on his Nike cross-trainers and proceeded to the kitchen to find something that might resemble breakfast.

There were multiple hallways in the upstairs of the house, and Richard tried remembering which one led to the staircase. In the process of navigating the hall he came upon Eddie's room, noticing that the door was open and his suitcase sprawled across the bed. He decided not to investigate further and proceeded to find the stairs.

While traveling down the hallway, a doorway opened behind him. After glancing over his shoulder, he witnessed a beautiful blonde-haired woman exiting one of the rooms wearing only a white paper-thin nightgown that left little to the imagination. Richard subtly blushed and pretended not to notice, just as her sensual voice from behind beckoned.

"Excuse me, but are you our new guest?"

He turned, noticing her curvy figure underneath the transparent gown. If she was aware that he'd snuck a peek, she didn't seem to mind. Richard cleared his throat and replied, "Well, I guess you could say that."

"I'm Mrs. Stockton. My husband and I own the house."

"Well, it's nice to meet you," he said, feeling his cheeks growing warmer. "Could you point me in the direction of the staircase? I think I'm lost."

"Yes, it's right there," Mrs. Stockton said, pointing to her right.

He felt like a fool for not noticing the steps down the corridor. He thanked her and took the stairs down as fast as his injured leg could carry him. When he reached the bottom, he noticed how different the living area looked in the daylight. It was incredible. The glimmering chandeliers projected caustic refractions onto the oil paintings of the famous generals and military soldiers that lined the towering walls. But one painting, in particular, caught his attention. It was a familiar image from the nightmare he'd had the previous night; a muddy-black translucent phantom, holding a pitchfork and a decomposed head.

As he absorbed the details, he noticed sapphire flames surrounding the apparition and an unsettling landscape of volcanic mountains and caverns and fiery skies in the background.

He sensed a strong presence behind him, inducing a cold chill. After sensing its hot breath on the nape of his neck, he was about to turn to confront his voyeur when a familiar voice spoke out.

"How do you like it?"

Richard turned to see Mrs. Stockton standing directly behind him. This time dressed more appropriately in a long crimson gown. "How do I like what?" Richard asked, wondering how she'd changed so quickly.

"The painting. It's incredible, isn't it?"

After wondering how anyone could have something so sinister in their living room, Richard focused his attention back on the painting and immediately noticed details he'd missed the first time. As he analyzed the unfortunate victims lynched on blackened trees, noosed by their own disemboweled intestines, he wondered what kind of person would display such crap.

"Incredible isn't the first word that comes to mind," he replied. "It's horrifying."

"Horrifying? What do you mean?" Mrs. Stockton asked. Richard examined it once more and shrugged. "Sometimes, if I'm having a bad day," she continued, "I'll turn the throne toward the fireplace and sit for hours, admiring its beauty. I love how the stream flows directly past the small cottage there. I can almost hear it."

Richard hoped she was attempting a bad joke because there was no stream, no cottage. "That's not what I see," he replied, startled by the woman's admission.

"My husband picked it up from Samuel the peddler about a week ago," Mrs. Stockton replied. "Well actually, he's not really a peddler, that's just a nickname I've given him. He's more of a craftsman and artist. However, I do believe he painted this particular piece."

"Maybe he should look for another line of work," Richard said, shifting his focus to the rest of the room. He noticed an assortment of medieval tapestries, knight's armor, various torture devices, and an oversized throne placed strategically before the fireplace. It was apparent that Mr. Stockton had a fondness for hoarding macabre collectibles from the Renaissance era.

Engrossed as he was by the makeshift museum, he noticed a pleasant aroma creeping from the kitchen area accompanied by laughter and muffled voices.

"Well, it was very nice speaking with you again, but I really need to—"

He stopped mid-sentence when he turned and noticed the eerie absence of Mrs. Stockton. He glanced around the room to see where she could've gone.

He filed the disturbing event to the back of his mind and proceeded to follow the delightful essence. Upon peering into the kitchen, he noticed Eddie and a young woman whispering and preparing what seemed like an extravagant breakfast buffet. He struggled to hear the conversation, but their whispers were too soft to be deciphered over the bustling outdoor resounds. He casually strolled through the double saloon-like doors, which creaked abrasively against the poorly oiled hinges, announcing Richard's presence to the kitchen's occupants.

"Well, good morning, Richard," Eddie greeted him. I didn't hear you approaching us, and might've mistaken you for a church mouse had you not been more significant." Since Richard had no idea what Eddie was talking about, he mustered a compliant smile.

"Yes, it wouldn't be the first time that happened."

"That's alright friend, why don't you sit down and have breakfast with us. We're just about to dish it out."

He took his seat in one of the wooden chairs that circled the table like something in a medieval castle. It struck Richard as odd that Mr. Stockton was such a devout collector of that particular time-period, when here he was living in an era most people only read about. He thought about his own little piece of history and wondered what it was all about, especially the voice that gave him instructions to obtain it. And how did it have authority to commandeer his actions to the point of helplessness? But in this place, it was not a sophisticated piece of literature, just an ordinary book.

The woman placed a metal plate in front of Richard, overflowing with a delectable arrangement of fruits, grains, and a few unidentifiable morsels of food that resembled something that might've once been stuck under someone's shoe.

Eddie glared at Richard and slowly rubbed his hands together in preparation for the meal he was about to devour. "I trust you had a rested night's sleep?"

"Uh, yes, very rested," he lied.

"Good, that's what I like to hear," Eddie replied, pouring some thick, cloudy liquid into their metal goblets. As reluctant Richard was to eat some of the food presented to him, he decided to begin sampling his breakfast.

He tried the gritty textured concoction of dark lumpy meat, which he followed with some grey porridge-like substance. It didn't taste quite as bad as expected, but it was a far cry from the type of cuisine he was accustomed to in the modern New York City restaurants. Needing something to wash the questionable taste from his mouth, he examined the beverage on the table.

"Can I ask what this is, Eddie?" Richard asked, raising the glass to test it.

"What do you mean?" Eddie looked at him, puzzled.

"I mean, what is this?" he asked, taking a subtle whiff. "It smells like beer, am I right?"

"You've never had small beer? Why I have it every morning, I thought most people did."

"Beer for breakfast?"

"Give it a try. I think you will find it quite delectable," Eddie insisted. Richard took a small sip and was surprised at how tasty it was. The unknown woman watched with silent amusement.

"What do you think?" she asked.

"It's delicious, Ms—"

"Oh, I'm terribly sorry," Eddie interrupted. "Introductions are not my forte. Richard, this is a friend of mine, Bethany Lee. She lives just a few blocks over."

"Nice to meet you," Richard said, between bites of his food. "I'm Richard."

"I must say, that's not a name you hear very often," Bethany pointed out.

"It's funny you say that," Eddie laughed, pouring himself another helping of small beer. "I thought the same thing when I first met him."

"In any case, it's very nice to meet you, Ms. Lee."

"Miss Lee, actually, but just call me Bethany."

"I'll be staying with Bethany for the remainder of my stay here in New York. I trust that after today, you have a place to go?" Eddie asked with a look of sincere concern. So it *was* New York. Richard's assumptions were confirmed.

"Well, I'm still working on that, but I hope to have it figured out by tonight. Would I be out of line if I asked why you're visiting here?" A broad smile appeared on Eddie's face as he picked up his goblet of beer in a toasting fashion.

"Well, to tell you the truth, my friend, it's a cause for celebration," Eddie continued. "I'm in this great city, getting my third book published. The hell with West Point, that's what I say. No disrespect to the academy, but I'd rather be here." With that, Eddie downed the entire contents.

Richard's ears perked up. "That's great. I had no idea you were a novelist,"

"Yes, yes, I am. Well, actually, I'm not. I mostly write poetry, but a novel is something I plan on starting sometime soon."

"And here I thought you were just a cadet. I never took you for the literary type."

"Life is full of surprises, is it not?" Eddie said, lifting his empty glass and toasting himself.

"I'd love to read something you've written sometime."

"And you shall. I've brought a few extra copies of my previous work with me, and would be delighted if you'd take them as a gift."

"Absolutely," Richard said.

Eddie's excitement never wavered as he continued to explain how happy he was to be back in New York, and how he thought that this was the book that was going to make him famous. His first two books hadn't done as well as he'd hoped, and he saw this as possible redemption.

As Richard sat and listened to Eddie speak of love lost, and regained, and how his life experiences thus far had influenced his writing, his mind started wandering to the pressing matter of getting home.

He recognized that he had no course of action. No game plan. If it weren't for the book under his mattress, he'd be dead in the water. That's when it dawned on him; he still wasn't sure where he was. It was obviously New York, but when? He was too afraid to ask.

"Come with me, Richard." Eddie's voice pierced his trend of thought, "I'll give you the books I promised. Bethany will tidy up the kitchen in our absence, won't you?" Eddie asked. It was more of a demand than a question.

"I could stay and help if you'd like?" Richard asked Bethany. Eddie laughed out-loud and handed her his empty plate as he pushed his chair back into place.

"Don't be silly, Richard, but I must say you had me going there for a moment."

"I was serious. There seems like quite a lot to do here, and we could get it done much faster if we all chip in."

"Nonsense, Bethany has no gripes about doing it herself. Besides, we all know a woman's place is in the kitchen. Am I not right?"

Richard decided to half forgive Eddie's feeble-minded views on women. After all, suffrage and woman's liberation, along with the right to vote was still a long way off.

"I can't say that I agree with you, Eddie, so let's agree to disagree." Richard reinforced his point.

I'm not sure what that means," Eddie said, "but either way, I enjoy your banter,"

After leaving Bethany to her overwhelming task, Eddie asked Richard what his plans were for the day. "Hopefully, there will be a vacancy at the hotel I had originally booked," Richard said. Eddie nodded his head in agreement, but couldn't figure out Richard's agenda, or why he was dressed the way he was.

"Since I'm staying with Bethany tonight, you'll have to find residence somewhere."

Unbeknownst to Richard, Eddie had insisted to Bethany beforehand not to utter a word about the nature of his attire, knowing that she'd been biting her tongue during the entire meal. Not only was he dressed oddly, but he also had packed nothing for his travels. As they entered his room, Eddie wondered why a man would go on a trip with nothing but the clothes on his back.

"Well, here we are. I'll get those books for you," Eddie said, rummaging through his suitcase. Richard watched Eddie as he scattered various pieces of clothing and shoes, books, and archaic medical tonics across his bed, along with a few empty whiskey bottles. He wondered how Eddie could find anything in such a menagerie of articles.

While waiting for him to finish, Richard took focus on the rest of the bedroom. It was surely a thing of elegant beauty. A crystal chandelier suspended above the king-sized opium bed reflected glinting sunlight into Richard's distorted vision, causing him to close his injured eye.

Quickly, the pain started to make its unwelcome presence known: a dull jabbing ache at first, which quickly escalated to a vice gripping migraine, feeling like he'd just gone ten rounds with Mike Tyson. He became dizzy as he looked around the room, which began rapidly spinning out of control. His stomach turned as he feared the breakfast might make an unpleasant appearance onto Eddie's bedroom floor.

"I think I found it," Eddie called out, looking up from his suitcase, noticing Richard's twisted expression. "Are you alright?"

"I think I need to sit down," Richard said, clearing a spot for himself on the bed.

"Well, is there anything I can do?" Eddie asked.

"Unless you can go to the nearest CVS, I'll just have to wait it out," he replied. It looked as if Eddie were about to respond, but he kept whatever it was to himself. Between his eye and this newfound headache, he longed for nothing more than a little Aspirin or some Advil. Hell, even some Anacin. A knock at the open bedroom door turned their attention towards Bethany, who stood in the hallway.

"Oh, hello, dear," Richard said. "Have you finished with the kitchen duty already?"

"Well, not exactly, but I will be soon. I was just coming up to speak with you about something that I didn't have a chance to mention earlier." She trembled as she spoke. "I would like to have a word with you in the hallway if you don't mind?"

"We'll talk after you finish up with the kitchen. It would look terrible on my part if Stockton were to return and find his place in shambles. Now go! Hurry it up!" Richard shook his head at Eddie's unnecessary outburst.

"Aren't you curious about what she wants?" he asked.

"Whatever it is, it can wait. Bethany is a great woman, but she tends to be rather feisty here and there, which requires me to be caring, yet firm. Don't get me wrong. I love the dear woman to death. I've been courting her off and on for years now, and I recognize where she needs discipline the most."

"But you're treating her like a pet. Don't you think that bothers her? She's hospitable enough to let you stay with her, free of charge, I'm guessing."

"Of course, free of charge!" Eddie countered. "I have no money. She wouldn't dare think of charging me." Richard had struck a nerve, so he decided it was time to let Eddie simmer down and changed the subject to a more neutral topic.

"So, Eddie, what do you recommend for fun around here?"

Eddie leaned his head against the wall as if deep in thought, checking his timepiece. "I can't believe that it's eleven o'clock already," Eddie said in a surly tone. It was apparent that he was ignoring the question. I think Mr. Stockton might be home for lunch shortly, and it's probably best if we're absent when he arrives. If I remember correctly, checkout is noon."

"It's alright if you can't find the books," Richard replied, wondering if Eddie would even acknowledge the statement. "If what you said is true, I should probably be making my way to the hotel. I don't think sleeping on the street tonight would agree with my injuries," After assessing Richard's clothing once more, Eddie decided it was time to speak his mind.

"My dear man, I try to tread lightly around other people's affairs, but I can't ignore my curiosity any longer. Please forgive my boldness, but I must ask about what you are wearing. Where exactly did you obtain it?" It was the question Richard had dreaded from the beginning. He had no answer that sounded valid.

"I found them," Richard said, studying Eddie's facial expressions like a Freudian scholar. "I found them in a bag behind my home, and I decided not to let them go to waste. Wanting to believe Richard, but still a bit skeptical, Eddie exemplified his most convincing poker face and smiled.

"I see."

"I'm serious," Richard replied. "I wouldn't make this up. The only reason I kept them was *because* they were so unusual."

"Well, in any case, you can't be seen on the streets in broad daylight wearing such a thing. I do believe I have something here that may fit you," Eddie explained, sympathizing with his friend's possible fabrication nonetheless. He began pulling trousers and vests from his luggage until ultimately coming up with what seemed like a full ensemble outfit, shoes and overcoat included.

Richard accepted the clothing, and quickly returned to his bedroom and changed out of his old wardrobe into his new, very uncomfortably fitted attire. Eddie was somewhat thinner than Richard, which made the shirt and vest span slightly around his waist area, causing him a bit of discomfort. He was far from overweight, but

Eddie was a walking feather in comparison. At least the long black overcoat seemed to fit appropriately. After retrieving his discarded coat, he accessed his smartphone from the pocket and thumbed it on. Surprisingly, it still had half a battery charge, but of course, no signal. He slipped the phone into his pants pocket and stared into the mirror, realizing how much he resembled a few of the characters from his favorite books and films. He was still young enough to coerce an attractive woman. But since the divorce, he hadn't had much interest. "It's just a matter of time before I get back out there," he'd tell himself, but months became years. It happens fast.

As he analyzed his heavy five o'clock shadow, he figured himself for a dashing Hollywood star, minus his wounded eye, which upon closer examination appeared to be getting worse. The gash had acquired a yellowish tint and was oozing a thick, foul-smelling liquid. He hadn't noticed it looking this awful the previous evening, but treatment was urgent. After rolling his old clothes into a ball, he stashed them under the bed and out of sight. While exiting his room, he decided to ask Eddie about the nature of medical care he could receive for his eye.

"Hey Eddie, could I ask if…"

"Richard! I'm so happy it fits! I thought it would, but was still a little skeptical." Richard looked down at his outfit and pulled at the creases.

"Do you really think it looks all right?"

"Of course it does. I make it a point to buy only the finest quality formal wear. However, I apologize for interrupting you. What were you saying now?"

"Well, I need to clean and dress my injury," Richard explained. "I was just going to ask if there might be something around here I can use. You can see it's not looking good."

Eddie studied the wound for a moment and made a crude face.

"Oh my, yes, I see that. I can honestly say I don't know what the Stockton's keep around for such an occasion. However, there is a general store on the way to the hotel where you may be able to find something."

"Well, I was thinking of something like a hospital or a doctor's office where I could get some real medical supplies."

"I think there's a doctor's office approximately three or four miles from here, near Bethany's cottage," Eddie explained, transfixed on Richard's gaping wound." But since I'm not from around here, I just don't know for sure." The two men sat quietly for a moment until the loud slam of a heavy door broke their silence.

"Oh, that's probably Mr. Stockton. I'll finish packing my things while you gather any belongings you have. I don't think we should take advantage of his hospitality any longer," Eddie said, throwing rolled balls of clothing into his suitcase. "And just leave your old clothes where they are, the housekeepers will eventually see to their proper disposal."

Eddie continued his task while Richard excused himself and headed back to his room to retrieve the only possession he had that mattered.

As he walked the long narrow hallway, his thoughts wandered. He was not in any rush to meet the owner again, especially in the light of day, where Mr. Stockton might recognize him as the accidental intruder. When he re-entered his temporary bedroom, he immediately noticed the faint aroma of what he identified to be formaldehyde that hadn't been present just minutes prior. With its pungent nausea-inducing odor, it began to turn Richard's stomach and increased the severity of his headache. As he glanced around the room, a feeling of dread overtook him, and he felt a sense of relief that he was leaving the mansion. He quickly lifted the mattress and retrieved the book.

After returning to his friend's room, it seemed as though he'd already left. As any suitcases or personal belongings had disappeared, along with the man himself. Tucking his book into the inner pocket of his overcoat, he proceeded down the stairs where he heard the faint sound of Eddie calling for Bethany. He headed into the kitchen, where he found Eddie leaning out the back door, continuing to call her name.

When Eddie turned and noticed Richard, he said, "Bethany must've left without telling me! At least she finished her task."

"Yeah, the place looks great," Richard said, smiling. Eddie didn't share the same enthusiasm. "So, Mr. Stockton isn't here?"

"No, the door we heard must've been Bethany. But I don't understand why she would've left like that. Do you think she may be cross with me based on my earlier demeanor towards her?"

"I honestly don't know."

Eddie scratched his head. "It's not important," he replied, waving his hand dismissively. "We should probably be heading out anyway. I must go to Bethany's cottage to see what happened. I do believe your hotel is along the way, so I'll accompany you until then."

Before leaving the living area, Richard took one last glance at the painting he'd avoided since entering the room. He cocked his head and blinked his eyes in reaction to the tranquil image: a quaint cottage that rested next to a long flowing stream.

Seven

The two men exited the mansion onto the bustling streets and into what appeared to be a festival of celebration. Folks were dressed in elaborate Jester outfits and Mardi Gras style masks, and many of the horse carriages had been brandished with extravagant decorations. A few of the festivalgoers gallantly walked high above the crowd atop towering stilts, waving and cheering as they hobbled along. There were so many distractions that the men didn't know where to look next.

"What is all this?"

"Damned if I know," Eddie replied. "I'm an out of town traveler such as you, and Bethany hadn't mentioned a word of this." After locating the path of least resistance, they began wading their way through the open gap of people that drank and cheered and cursed and puked.

As they journeyed down the street, they noticed an assortment of vendors that lined the roadways and led to the center square. Some sold goods and various wares, while others were directed more towards fun and games. And each advertised their intentions in sizeable red lettering:

See the Strong Man!

I'll guess your weight for a penny!

One vendor, in particular, had a large crowd that gathered around, holding up money and cheering. "Richard, would you like to see what all the commotion is over there?" Having no choice in the matter, Richard agreed, and both men joined the gathering sea of customers.

"Mr. Fortunato's Wonder Tonic. Cure's all known ailments big and small!" Eddie read. "How incredible is that? A cure for everything would surely be the medical marvel of the century."

"What a crock of shit," Richard mumbled to himself. He didn't want to see these people taken for a ride, but there wasn't much he could do.

"Well, I'm purchasing a bottle, and you should too. It might help with the headaches you are afflicted by."

"No, Eddie, I'd save your money. This snake oil salesman is asking five cents a bottle, which is way overpriced for something that doesn't work."

"Oh, I am certain it's not snake oil Richard. Besides, this tonic being of blue nature leads me to doubt the validity of your statement," Eddie laughed.

But Richard didn't laugh. He figured a well-deserved life lesson was in order. So without any further objections, he let Eddie fish five cents from his pocket in exchange for the watery blue substance. As they continued on their way, Eddie held up the bottle of Elixir to further examine its consistency and urged Richard to join him on the path to perfect health. But Richard refused.

"You win, dear sir," Eddie finally said, untwisting the cork to test the aroma "But I shall save you some in case you have a change of heart." After taking a giant whiff, his face wrinkled into a tight ball.

Noticing the visible reaction, Richard laughed and patted him on the back.

"Doesn't smell like roses, I suppose?" Eddie wiped the sweat from his forehead and re-corked the bottle.

"I think I'll just drink it later on. Besides, I have no affliction in need of curing at the moment." Through the ever-growing crowd, Richard caught glimpses at the multitude of buildings that took on a life of their own in the light of day. They appeared friendlier now, not quite as sinister. As they approached their destination, they passed The Skinned Calf and the giant clock, which rested at the forked intersection. Richard wondered if the bouncer would recognize him in his new outfit if he decided to venture back into the place for a drink.

They avoided the pub and made their way to the left side of the fork. The Hotel Majestic came into view, and Richard breathed a sigh of relief, until he saw the long line of patrons converging in front of the entryway.

"You've got to be kidding," he sighed. "I'm never getting in there."

"Of course you will. I don't think all of those folks are booking rooms. They just appear to be loitering."

Eddie tapped his forehead and said, "I would normally extend an invitation to stay with us, but Bethany would never allow it. Let's not give up hope yet." He led Richard through the front entrance, where a cheerful doorman wearing a colorful red, blue, and green swirled party hat greeted them.

The lobby wasn't as crowded as Richard expected. Only two people were ahead of him, and the rest were scattered around on chairs or sitting at tables playing cards and drinking. Three different marble staircases on opposite sides of the room welcomed their guests to ascend into whatever lied above. At the same time, the bright red carpeting displayed golden encrusted patterns, hugging the length of the mirrored walls on all sides, casting multiple reflections in all directions, and giving the foyer the illusion of a much larger ballroom.

"Majestic indeed," Eddie said, admiring the hotel's luxurious interior.

"Next!"

Richard approached the hotel reservation manager while Eddie admired the enormous stained-glass window. The longer he stared, the more out of place things felt. There was an odd gentleman outside, staggering around with a pint of beer in his hand. Without any warning, Richard appeared from nowhere, upset and distraught.

"I can't believe this!" he said, causing Eddie to turn quickly. "Every room seems to be booked. They said to come back in an hour."

Eddie listened but continued to be distracted by the stranger outside. He wasn't trying to be rude, but it came off that way to Richard. Eddie grabbed hold of Richard's arm with alarming force and pointed into the crowd of people.

"Look, you see that man. I know him."

Richard gazed into the sea of people.

"Which man?"

"The one wearing that ridiculous outfit," Eddie said, continuing to point fervently. "You see him wearing that puffy juvenile costume! He looks like an overweight clown!"

Richard continued to survey the area and finally spotted a man wearing large novelty-sized shoes, along with bright oversized attire that gave him the appearance of a giant bouncing ball.

"He's the man who cheated me last night. The louse with the trick deck I was talking about," he continued. "That costume isn't fooling me in the least."

"Are you absolutely certain he cheated you? He may have just been lucky."

"Nobody's that damn lucky! All the money I saved for my stay here is gone because of him," Eddie sneered. "And if he thinks I'm going to just forget about it, he would be grossly mistaken."

"Why didn't you confront him last night when you had the chance?"

"I'm not one to start a bar tussle. Besides, I'm more of an artist and poet than a brawler, but now that I've had time to think the situation over, I feel retribution is in order. Oh, don't worry, I'm not going to hurt him, I'll just give him a bit of a scare and the chance to get my money back possibly."

They stepped outside, and the sudden roar of laughter and banjo music rushed their eardrums. Intoxication and adrenaline caused many of the festivalgoers to become quite disruptive, allowing the prey to blend in with his surroundings.

"Where did he go?" Eddie demanded, walking down the steps to the loitering area. Richard understood his friend's apparent anger and tried to calm him as best he could.

"I have an hour before checking back with the hotel. I will look for him while you visit Bethany."

While thinking for a moment about the proposal, Eddie continued to scan the crowd with unwavering devotion before gathering his composure and finally relenting.

"I suppose it would seem like the obvious decision for now. Very well, I shall meet you back at the hotel lobby after my brief visit with her." Eddie tipped his top hat in Richard's direction and began to walk away, when Richard called out," Eddie! If I may ask, who is Bethany to you? I understand you've dated her off and on for many years, but is she just a friend to you now or something more?" The question reminded Eddie of joyful times spent with the woman.

"Oh my dear friend, she is undoubtedly something more," he replied and disappeared into the crowd.

Eight

Bethany sat on the sofa, admiring the elegant self-portrait that rested on the marble table directly in front of her. She had just posed for it no more than a week ago, as it was her newest prized possession and one that would capture her exquisite beauty for all time. The passion and detail the artist captured allowed a tear to roll down her rosy cheek that fell onto the long turquoise flowing gown that she kept for only *exceptional* occasions.

She was expecting company and had her most elegant dress cleaned and mended just for the event. The cottage she had recently purchased, with the help of her wealthy father, suited her needs perfectly and allowed her the luxury of independence. But the days and nights could get lonely, and she was so looking forward to the companionship that would soon be arriving.

Just as she was wiping the tears away, there was the unmistakable echo of her steel doorknocker throughout the cozy cottage. And then, excitement and anticipation fell over her.

A second knock came, and Bethany picked her gown up off the floor as to not stumble over it, and unbolted the massive lock which allowed her to feel safe at night when she was alone.

On the other side of the door, Eddie was about to knock a third time when it opened to reveal Bethany standing before him. His eyes fixated on the diamond-encrusted ruby necklace around her neck. He'd never seen it before but admired it nonetheless. He was speechless as he took in the rest of her.

How magnificent it was of her to change into such a lovely (and revealing) dress for me, he thought.

"Why, you look incredible, darling!"

Bethany looked down and blushed, turning her already rosy cheeks a darker shade of crimson.

"Thank you. I'm happy you noticed."

"Well, of course, I noticed. I'd be an ignorant man not to."

Standing before Eddie made Bethany feel a bit overwhelmed and vulnerable. Not wishing to reveal her emotions to him, she stood stern and forthcoming. She knew Eddie wasn't the kind of man who tended to dwell on trivial differences, but she *had* left him at the Stockton mansion without any word of her retreat.

"You are quite right, and if you hadn't complimented me, I might be inclined to take offense," Bethany playfully replied. "But I must be honest with you, Eddie. I was quite upset by your insensitivity earlier today."

Eddie glanced at her and nodded. "I understand that I didn't listen when you needed me to, but is that reason enough to leave unannounced? I was under the impression we were to spend the day together and enjoy each other's company like we used to."

"That was my initial intention as well, which is why I so desperately needed to discuss the unfortunate and regretful change in our plans," she said sternly.

Eddie's smile dissolved when he noticed her demeanor. "What change? I'm quite nervous about where this conversation is headed."

She lowered her head and said, "I've received word from my parents that they will be arriving today for an extended visit. I'm deeply sorry, but you cannot stay here tonight or for the rest of your stay. Do you know how terrible that would look if they arrived and saw that you were taking temporary residence with me? And you know daddy always travels with his shotgun." Eddie cringed at the thought.

"I can't say I'm not disappointed," he said, "but family comes first." He didn't say another word as he retrieved his suitcase from Bethany's marble doorstep, tipping his hat to her as he slowly walked away.

She watched as he disappeared down the road. A lump welled in her throat as she opened her mouth to speak, but only silence followed. She tried again, and finally gained enough composure to call to him, "Eddie, wait!" But it was too late. He was already gone.

After spotting a vacant bench along the cobblestone road, Eddie quickly hobbled over and placed his cumbersome luggage on the ground to relieve his knotted lower-back. He was in the same situation as Richard and felt like a scrap of rotten meat thrown out with yesterday's garbage. Reality had hit. He also had nowhere to go.

Nine

Eddie checked the time on his pocket watch that read approximately ten of three. He sat idle on the bench, attempting to absorb what just happened, and the matter of resolution he would take. It was evident that Bethany didn't want him there, but if her parents were to visit, why hadn't she'd known much sooner? Usually, they'd discuss such matters in advance. Eddie knew their relationship was anything but ideal. Most of it had been done through letters, and when they did see each other, it was usually for only a brief amount of time, usually just a day or two if they were lucky. It was becoming more difficult with Eddie having been in West Point for so long, and Bethany moving from Boston to New York. But still, Eddie was more than willing to put in the effort needed to keep them both afloat. And he often wondered if she'd been doing the same.

So at this point, he concluded that it would be better to worry about such topics later, and he decided to focus on the stragglers that roamed past him from the festival. By nature, he was a people watcher who enjoyed deciphering everyone's interests and ambitions, especially in situations like this, where most of the pedestrians were costumed and masked. It added to the allure and mystery.

After sitting for a half-hour watching and guessing, he noticed the festivalgoer wearing the puffy juvenile costume. Eddie jumped to his feet at the sight of him.

The cheating louse!

He didn't want to risk losing him a second time, so he yelled, "You there! The louse stopped and pointed at himself. "Yes, you! Come here for a moment!"

The man nodded and hobbled over, obviously burdened by the weight of his oversized outfit, and plopped down next to Eddie to catch his breath.

"What do you want?" the louse panted.

"Am I to understand you don't remember me?" Eddie asked.

"Should I? And where would I remember you from might I ask?"

"Where should I begin? I seem to recall you cheating me out of my winnings last night at the Skinned Calf. I figured you'd remember at least that much."

The louse sidetracked himself towards the vibrant blue sky as he struggled to remember the accusations. "Don't you just love how the clouds seem to form wonderful objects right before our very eyes?" the louse asked. "It's as if God approaches the canvas once in a great while and weaves something exceptional for us to reflect on when life becomes troublesome." Eddie couldn't ignore the man's whimsical insight and reluctantly turned a quick gaze to the heavens, fixating himself to the slowly moving apparitions suspended in animation.

"Yes," he said, noticing his frustration unfurl. "I will admit they're quite breathtaking," One apparition, in particular, seemed to have manifested for him alone. It began to take the form of a grand music box, which reminded him fondly of the one he purchased for Bethany on the eve of their first anniversary. His thoughts began to wander again as he momentarily snapped himself out of it. He turned towards the louse, who continued to admire the sky in a trance-like gaze.

"Excuse me, sir, but we seem to be getting off-topic. I would appreciate it if we could continue our discussion," Eddie demanded. The louse blinked and rubbed his eyes as if to refocus.

"I apologize for my rudeness. I tend to be easily distracted at the wrong times. I mean no disrespect."

Eddie nodded. "I must ask again if you remember me from last night? Surely you must recall the amount of money you won from me?"

The louse smiled as he took the last sip from the tankard he was holding, finishing his foamy brew. "I remember you," the louse smiled. What I don't understand is what you want from me? Do you want your money back? Is that it?"

"What I want is a chance to *win* it back," Eddie replied, intently studying the louse's facial expressions. "I somehow remember you being the one who dealt the cards all night, and I usually prefer a rotation of dealers to keep the odds even and fair." The louse looked again to the sky and stared blankly.

"Very well, I shall give you that chance if you so desire it." The louse stared at the sky and never once looked at Eddie as he spoke. "I do have one condition. If you lose to me again, it will be the end of this little game. I never usually give opponents a second chance to win back what is rightfully mine."

"How can you say it was rightfully yours when you had control of the deck for the entire duration?" Eddie asked. "It was a very unorthodox way of playing, in my opinion."

"And your opinion is all that it is," the louse said. After realizing the petty bickering was getting him nowhere, Eddie sat for a few moments before deciding it was best to leave. He stood while the louse finally looked down from the heavens.

"I'm not exactly sure where I'll be staying this evening," Eddie said, retrieving his luggage from the sidewalk, "but I hope to be taking residence at the Stockton's boarding mansion at 2119 Walnut Ave. Be there tonight at eight o'clock." As Eddie glanced down the road towards his route, leaving the louse alone on the bench, he wondered if Richard had yet acquired a room at the Majestic.

The louse watched as Eddie disappeared into the distance, and almost felt a tinge of guilt for having cheated him as he did. But it was this profession that afforded him the finer things in life. It was an easy way to make a living. The trick was not to get caught, and he came uncomfortably close this time. But still, it couldn't be proved. Not this time.

The louse sat for a few more moments before getting off the bench to make his way down the narrow sidewalk, admiring the elegant structures as he walked. It was a brisk day, but not overbearingly cold, which served him well, considering his oversized outfit left no room for any kind of overcoat. It was beginning to fatigue him, and he couldn't wait to rid himself of it. He was relieved to have arrived at his destination:

203 Main Street.

And not a moment too soon, because he had begun perspiring terribly underneath the formidable weight of the costume. He turned the doorknob. Locked.

The louse began knocking loudly. After no answer, he knocked again. Finally, the door opened, revealing a stunning woman, dressed in a long turquoise flowing gown and diamond-encrusted ruby necklace. His smile broadened.

"Oh, thank the heavens!" Bethany exclaimed. "I thought you were Eddie returning for further inquiries."

"Eddie? The louse asked. But my dear, I thought you ended your relationship with Eddie weeks ago?" Bethany turned away and opened the door wider for him.

"Come inside," she replied. "It's getting cold out."

The louse entered and took a seat on the floral couch next to the stone fireplace while Bethany poured them each a glass of red wine from the decanter. She handed him the crystal wine glass and sat beside him while the brief silence hung above the room.

"To answer your previous question, Charlie, I was unable to muster the courage to break it off with Eddie. It wasn't as easy as I'd previously thought it would be. But worry not, he won't be staying here, as he is under the impression that my family is arriving for a visit. It was the best I could come up under such short notice."

Charlie took a small sip of red wine and sat back on the sofa and crossed his legs. "Am I to believe that this Eddie fellow is currently under the impression that the two of you are still in a relationship?"

"Yes, but I assure you as the sun will rise, I will be ending it with him momentarily. I just haven't found the right time is all."

"Very well, I shall take your word for it." Charlie scratched his head and continued, "In the meantime, I have a surprise for you." His great enthusiasm almost dismissed the small betrayal. Bethany's eyes widened, and her breath fell short. She couldn't conceive what this spontaneous surprise could be: a trip? Or maybe another luxurious necklace? Or a diamond engagement ring, perhaps. The longer she thought about the fantasy, the more she wanted it. She pictured herself and Charlie on their wedding day, riding the horse and carriage towards a blissful sunset.

"It seems, my dear, we'll be going out tonight after all," he said, interrupting Bethany's pleasant daydream. "It turns out I have some business to attend to, which has some lucrative potential for us both." Bethany frowned, and Charlie noticed her obvious displeasure. "It will be a grand time, I promise," he reinforced to her as he removed his bulky costume. "We will drink aged brandy, engage in stimulating conversation, and rake in our winnings with the greatest of ease. And with those winnings, we shall go out tomorrow and buy anything you desire!"

Bethany's frown evaporated. The sound of lavish gifts was more than music to her ears. She smiled broadly at Charlie as she asked him the time of the evening's engagement. He took her by the hand and softly whispered the time in her ear. He then lifted her on her feet and led her up the winding staircase to the second-floor bedroom.

"I hope you're not expecting company any time soon," he smiled, laying her atop the white-laced sheets.

Ten

Richard obsessively checked the large clock located in the town square. He'd been standing outside the Majestic Hotel's main entrance scouting the area for the cheating louse for close to an hour when he saw Eddie coming towards him, still lugging his heavy suitcase and travel gear.

"They really should put wheels on those things," Richard called out. Eddie raised an eyebrow and began looking around.

"What are you talking about?"

"Your luggage, wouldn't you think someone could invent some wheels to put on the bottom so you could effortlessly pull it along?" he asked, smiling.

The scenario reminded him of the last trip he and his ex-wife took to California. The red-eye flight had been delayed several times, topped off with the airline losing his checked luggage. At the time, it felt like the end of the world, but now he couldn't help but laugh. He remembered how angry she'd been. Not just with the airline, but also with him failing to heed her warning about over-packing. Yes, he remembered Emily's voice clear as day: *If you pack too much, we'll have to check our suitcases. Those fucking airlines are always losing luggage, Richard.*

He still couldn't believe four years had passed since that trip. Time was flying by, and with each passing day, she became more of a memory. It frightened him.

She didn't die, but she might as well have. The day she told him she was leaving was the day the music died in Richard's opinion, which was reinforced by his non-stop rotation of the Don McLean tune. It was just about the only thing he listened to for three straight months, reminiscing about his former life that died the same morning.

It wasn't like he didn't see it coming. Tensions had been high between them for some time leading up to her departure. He just didn't want to accept it and chose the denial route. Most of their marriage had been great, but then little things started to creep in. His friends always said that it's the little things that cause breakups.

He recalled the last time they went to the movies together. Richard ordered the popcorn, just like he had a million times before, and ate it the same way he always had, but this time, his wife scolded him for digging his hand in too deep and eating like a pig. It ruined the rest of the movie for him.

Or the time they went to the fancy restaurant for her birthday. She sat across from him the entire evening, tweeting on her cell phone and ignoring his mundane conversation attempts. He remembered losing his temper and calling her a few choice words that ended with her storming out. Shortly afterward, he was served with divorce papers, later finding out that she'd been seeing someone for the last year of their marriage. The ink wasn't even dry on the documents when he'd heard they'd moved in together.

Richard had tried his best to hold it together in front of his students. But just as he assumed, too many of them complained about his mid-class breakdowns, and that was that. Adios and don't let the door hit you in the ass. But he understood their frustration. It was terrible for the image of the university to have a grown man break down in the middle of a history lecture, especially in front of fifty or more uncomfortable students, rambling on about his ruined life between discussions of the Gilded Age. No matter how many times he promised that it would never happen again, it always did.

He still recalled the day he walked into that early morning meeting, only to have the people he considered friends for most of his professional career cast him out on the street with his cardboard box of belongings and a swift goodbye handshake.

"Good luck to you, Mr. Linkey," one of the board members said, patting him on the back.

"Thank you, but it's Langley," Richard replied.

"Well, good luck. Either way, we'll miss you around here." But those weren't the times he liked to remember. He'd rather reminisce about the joyful moments before his marriage and career imploded like a Christian Bale meltdown.

With everything they had been through, he still loved her and was sure there was a part of her that loved him too...if only a little.

But it didn't matter now because she was gone, and she wasn't coming back. Time heals all wounds they say. Things will get better. But this wasn't the case for him. Time hadn't healed his wounds, and things hadn't gotten better. They were only getting worse. His loneliness and desperation had increased in recent months. And now, he was standing in front of a crowded hotel, homeless, and hoping for a place to sleep.

I guess this is how it's all going to end.

"Richard! You know you could've helped me!" Eddie shouted, panting as he dropped his suitcase onto the ground. Richard blinked away his daydream.

"Oh I'm sorry, I must've trailed off."

"Well, I see you found a dressing for your eye," Eddie said, noticing the white bandage taped to Richard's forehead.

"The last thing I need is for it to get infected," Richard said, lightly touching the edge of the tape. "I decided to take a walk around town while you were gone and found a small physician's office somewhere along the way. Luckily, the doc took pity on me and donated it free of charge."

"Oh, so I assume you saw Dr. Melton?"

"I honestly couldn't say," Richard said, noticing the suitcase. "I don't remember his name, just his hospitality. Eddie, why do you still have your luggage? I thought you went to Bethany's?"

"I did, but it turns out her family is visiting for some undetermined amount of time, and I can't stay there." Richard raised his eyebrows. "I might have to stay at the Majestic with you if I can get a room, or maybe make a ploy to the Stocktons' and hope they have sympathy.

"Well, we have approximately two hours until nightfall," Richard said. "I think we should try the Majestic again."

As the two men discussed their current misfortune, a pair of eyes watched them from across the courtyard. The young woman strained to hear their conversation but was unsuccessful in light of the barrage of noise around her. What she saw in Richard frightened her. Not because he was threatening, but because she had never seen anything like him before, and she didn't know how to interpret it.

She watched both men disappear through the front doors of the Majestic as she reached the foot of the outside marble stairway. She stayed close behind, following them into the main lobby, where she noticed them approach the reservation window to speak with the hotel manager.

It was difficult to hear what was said, but the discussion appeared to be taking a sour tone, as one of the strangers raised his voice and slung overzealous vulgarities at the manager. He promptly picked up his suitcase and stormed towards the front door while the other man followed. They rushed out so fast that she lost them for a moment.

As she reached the outside stairwell, she noticed the aura that surrounded the strange man had gotten further away. But it became larger and more substantial, with a change of color from an ocean blue to a deep crimson red.

She knew that if she didn't approach him soon, she might never have the opportunity again. As she walked down the steps and reached the crowd, the pulsating light dimmed as their distance widened, and the aura vanished in the crush of bodies. She rushed through the crowd, searching for him and his afterglow, but they were nowhere to be found. The woman panicked. She might have just blown her only chance.

Eleven

When Richard and Eddie arrived at Stockton's mansion, the housekeeper greeted and invited them inside. They sat comfortably in front of a roaring fireplace centered in Stockton's Renaissance room, sipping potent brandy that the housekeeper had provided. The discussion existed mostly between Eddie and Stockton, reminiscing about old times and adventures before Eddie subtly brought up the topic of staying the night.

"I cannot allow it," Stockton replied.

"I'm desperate, Tim," Eddie pleaded. "We have nowhere to go. I'll even sleep on the floor."

"I'm sorry, but it would look very unprofessional to the rest of my guests seeing you like that. Any other time would be fine. But with the festival and all, this is one of my biggest nights. The rooms are all booked."

Eddie knocked back the rest of his drink. "I understand," he said. "I guess we'll be on our way."

Stockton stirred his brandy for a moment, deep in thought. "Come to think of it, I may know of a place you could stay. But you're not going to like it."

As he explained the details to Eddie, Richard noticed that Stockton was oblivious to his identity. The bandage disguise seemed to be working correctly. The last thing he needed was to be identified and thrown into some crude nineteenth-century prison for something he didn't do. After putting that horrible scenario out of his mind, his attention drifted to the artifacts he had admired earlier that morning. The colorful high ceiling tapestries moved gently in the drafty mansion. At the same time, blue and white flames erupted from the fireplace, casting eerie shadows across the tables and up to the beautiful oil paintings. Blue flames, just like in his dream, just like in the—

Richard breathed deep and glanced at the painting above the fireplace mantle.

It had changed again.

Richard lost his grip on the snifter as it shattered onto the marble floor, dispersing splinters of crystallized shrapnel across the floor. The disturbance caused the two men to briefly abandon their conversation as the housekeeper quickly approached from the kitchen area.

"Everything is fine," Mr. Stockton said. "Go back to tending the soup."

"I'm sorry," Richard apologized. "I'll get something to clean it up."

"That won't be necessary, the housekeeper will see to it after supper." As Richard watched the liquid slowly seep along the ground in chaotic directions like a wayward snake, his head began to ache again. As far as he could tell, it wouldn't be as bad as the last migraine, but any headache was a bad headache with the lack of painkillers at his disposal. Regardless of the pain, he looked again.

The image remained of his decapitated head suspended atop a long pike, bandage included. It was like looking into a mirror.

Mr. Stockton continued his conversation with Eddie as if nothing had happened, and was oblivious to what Richard had noticed in the painting.

"Excuse me," Richard interrupted. "But may I ask what the story is with that painting?"

"I don't think I understand."

"You don't notice anything odd?" A sharp pain hit again, inhabiting his speech. Stockton and Eddie glanced up.

"I'll say," Eddie replied. "The artist could've spent more time on the river. The detail is lacking if you ask me."

Stockton frowned. "That's ridiculous. This is Samuel's finest work. His blending of color is second to none."

"What are you talking about? Eddie, there's no river. You don't see it?" He asked while wiping beads of sweat from his forehead with a handkerchief. Eddie gave Richard a strange look and began chuckling again while shaking his head.

"I believe you might've hit your head harder than you think. You're seeing things that aren't there."

"My head is just fine. I know what I'm seeing." He began to wonder if maybe the injury in the bookstore was affecting more than just his eye. He couldn't recall a time where he had headaches this severe, and now he was seeing demonic images that probably weren't there.

"My dear fellow," Stockton spoke up. "I purchased this painting for its sheer beauty and tranquility. There's nothing abnormal or horrible about it. I think that you might need to see a doctor."

"I'll get right on that. I'll just mosey on down to the Skinned Calf and seek out good ol' Dr. Bartender."

"I wouldn't advise it," Stockton said. "The whiskey alone could strip the paint off a wagon wheel." After rubbing his temples, Richard sat up in his chair and glanced directly at the painting once more.

The Irish housekeeper peeked from behind the kitchen door and rang the dinner bell. "It's about time," Stockton sighed, wearily getting to his feet and stretching.

"It's dinner time, gentleman. Get it while it's hot."

Twelve

Bethany awoke to the piercing sound of drunken debauchery caused by the roaring festival outside her window, acknowledging that it was probably no worse than the illicit activity she and Charlie had recently engaged in.

As she watched her lover sleep, a tinge of guilt crossed over her as she thought about her deception towards Eddie. He was, after all, under the impression they were still together.

As she rolled on her side, she gently shook Charlie out of his restful slumber and nervously asked him the time. He jumped to his feet when he noticed night had fallen and fumbled through the pockets of his vest that rested on the bureau, searching for his gold-plated timepiece.

"Half-past seven!" he exclaimed. "Get dressed! We're going to be late!"

Richard's headache had dissipated as he finished the last spoonful of beef stew. Managing to eat three heaping bowls worth had somehow given him a second wind. In fact, he hadn't felt that good since he'd arrived.

The three men sat before their empty plates feeling comfortably full as the housekeeper cleared the elegant tableware. Neither one had said a word since they started eating. An awkward silence hung above the room as each one waited for the other to say something. Richard was thinking about how to get home. Eddie was thinking about Bethany. And Stockton was wondering where his wife was. She wasn't there when he'd gotten home from his real estate meeting earlier that afternoon, and none of the housekeepers had seen her. He figured she'd been cavorting around the town festival, but it was getting late, and she never usually missed supper.

As the festival began to thin out, Mrs. Stockton stood by the bedroom window above the town square. Her hair was disheveled, and she wore nothing but a smile as she lit her hand-rolled cigarette.

"Why don't you come back to bed?" a voice said from across the room. She inhaled a filterless cloud of tar and nicotine.

"Haven't you had enough?" she asked.

"I don't know the meaning of the word."

"You're sweet, but I really must be getting back home. I don't want to be gone too long."

"Would you like to walk around town with me for a while? I'm curious to see what all the excitement is about." Mrs. Stockton walked over and sat on the edge of the bed.

"You know there's nothing else I'd like more," she said as she began to get dressed. "But I can't be seen in public with you. I apologize, but you will have to go alone. Besides, we're having a party tonight, and I must attend."

"Yes, but it isn't starting until later. As your husband's business partner, I know his schedule better than he does. And we both know how Timothy gets at these gatherings. He'll be so drunk by nine o'clock he won't even notice you're missing."

"You have a point. I think we may have a little more time," she said, crawling back into bed. "Will you be making an appearance tonight?"

"I'm afraid not," Grant replied, popping a sliced apple into his mouth. "I have certain matters of urgency that I must adhere to this evening, but I will stop by tomorrow to meet with Timothy about the Springvale Hotel venture."

"Very well," Mrs. Stockton said, removing the remaining apple from his grasp and placing his hand on her left breast. "Well, what are you waiting for?"

Richard sat silently and listened to Stockton as he explained the details to Eddie.

"I'll be sure my valet sees you both safely to the Sixth Ward this evening. I wouldn't recommend you traveling on foot."

"I appreciate that," Eddie replied. "I also want to thank you for allowing me to stay for the party. I apologize for inviting that louse without your knowledge, but I wasn't sure where I'd be tonight."

Richard was unsure of what the Sixth Ward was. Stockton didn't elaborate much on it, but his reference was unflattering.

He began thinking about the people he might never see again, and the places he would never go. Even though they were divorced, he would never have the chance to make amends with Emily: something he'd always planned on doing.

"Would either of you be interested in seeing my latest purchase before my guests arrive?" Stockton asked. As Eddie downed his remaining brandy, he squinted and nodded his head silently. And since Richard had no choice, he raised his glass and agreed.

The men made their way into a small out-cove in the living room where a large steel doorway presented itself. Stockton retrieved a black painted metal key that rested on a wooden shelf next to the entryway and turned the lock with a harsh echo. The three men followed Stockton's oil lamp down a narrow staircase. As they reached the bottom, his eyesight struggled to adjust to the darkness as Stockton proceeded to light the numerous lamps that adorned the dark stonewall, instantly casting shadows onto the room's murky interior.

"Well, what do you think?" Stockton gleefully asked. The room remained silent. "I apologize. You probably don't know what it is."

"I know what it is," Richard replied, focusing on the enormous crescent-shaped blade that suspended itself from the ceiling, high above a sizeable decrepit slab of concrete.

"Excellent sir, I'm happy to hear we share some of the same interests. And Eddie, are you familiar with this type of device?" he asked, watching Eddie as he examined the instrument of death.

"I can't say that I am." They listened to Stockton explain the intricate details of the pendulum. He demonstrated how the chain-crank lowered the blade towards its impending destination, and how the Pendulum swung from one wall to the other in brutal fashion, past what appeared to be a row of iron maidens along the right-side wall, waiting to slice and separate any target that blocked its intended path. But the sway was hypnotic, and Richard felt the device absorb and entrance him. It was evil. It was beautiful.

Eddie continued to listen as Stockton explained the history of the instrument from the fourteenth century onward. "Of course, I have no intended use for the device," he assured them. "I present it merely for exhibition purposes." Richard trusted Stockton about as much as he would trust Dr. Bartender to perform open-heart surgery.

Something was not right about the man, and he suddenly felt uneasy in his presence.

"Does something like this have a name?" Eddie asked.

"The auction house explained that it's called a pendulum," Stockton replied as he extended his finger, just as the blade made a downward pass. Richard anticipated an air-born finger in a few moments, realizing the precision had to be perfect. The blade arrived and lightly grazed the tip of his index finger, drawing only small droplets of blood. "Seems unoriginal to me," Stockton proceeded after noticing Richard and Eddie's gasps. "But if it has any other name, they failed to mention it."

Eddie thought about Bethany while Stockton continued his demonstration. He wondered how she and her family were enjoying themselves and hoped that he could briefly spend time with her before needing to leave town. She'd surely grant him at least that much he assumed, even with her family around.

Thirteen

A polished wooden carriage slowly halted in front of the Stockton mansion. "We're here," called the valet, jumping from his high bar and opening the passenger door for Bethany and Charlie. As she gazed out the window at the familiar layout of Stockton's doorway and steps, she began to understand where they were.

"It can't be," she said. "I must be dreaming."

Bethany sat silently in the darkened carriage while the valet continued to hold his hand out. "What has gotten into you?" Charlie asked. "Don't keep the man waiting."

She took a deep breath to ease her rapid heartbeat and carefully stepped down the folding steps onto the dimly lit street. She glanced around, hoping she'd been mistaken. She wasn't. Her legs produced a rubber effect, and her cheeks flushed.

"What is wrong with you, darling? You look like you've seen a blasted ghost." She held her forehead and grabbed onto his arm, almost pulling him down.

"I just need to sit for a moment."

"Let us go inside," Charlie suggested. "I'm sure there will be plenty of places to sit."

"No!" Bethany shouted, arousing stares from passing strangers. "I want to leave!" She said intentionally louder, prompting more stares from the pedestrians. Some of them wandered into the Stockton mansion, while others proceeded in different directions.

"You see, dear, it's a party," he said, lowering his voice to almost a whisper. "Now, would you please regain your composure so we can enter the place with some damned dignity?"

The guests filtered into the living room of the mansion and enjoyed the amenities of Stockton's hospitality. Most were still drunk from the festival, filling their plates from the buffet table while puffing some cigars that were free for the taking. The brandy flowed while their laughter increased to heightened decibels, just as Richard, Eddie, and Stockton re-entered the room from their downstairs excursion. Stockton grinned and admired the striking crowd. "Would you look here? I'm going to make a fortune off this festival!"

Forcing a smile, Richard asked, "I thought you were already worth a fortune?"

Stockton pondered the question for a moment. "You don't know anything about money, do you?" he finally replied, smacking Richard on his shoulder. Eddie checked his timepiece that now read approximately forty minutes past eight o'clock. As he began weaving his way through the crowded area, he wondered if the louse would show up at all, when from a dark corner of the room, he noticed Bethany alone. A blissful confusion fell on him, and he immediately weaved his way over to her, filling his empty brandy glass along the way. He wondered if maybe her family had decided not to come after all.

He took a seat on the empty chair next to her, greeting her with a smile. She didn't notice him and was more preoccupied with her thoughts as she gazed out the elaborate stained glassed window, admiring the kaleidoscope of colors.

"Hello, Bethany." She jumped in her seat at the sound of Eddie's voice. "Are you all right?" he asked, noticing her flush appearance. "I didn't mean to startle you."

She had told herself he wouldn't be there. Reassured herself before stepping foot into the mansion. She quickly glanced around the room and noticed Charlie sitting at one of the big tables, holding a cigar in one hand and a fan of playing cards in the other. From the look on his face, he must've been doing well.

"Yes, Eddie, I'm fine," she finally replied. "I'm just feeling a bit under the weather."

"Maybe you shouldn't be here if you're not well." Eddie leaned in. "And come to think of it, why *are* you here?" he asked, seeing a perfect opportunity to present the question. She solemnly raised her head and attempted to look him in the eyes.

"Eddie, I think I need to level with you. My family—" From behind, someone gripped his shoulder.

"I don't believe we've met before," Stockton grinned, eyeing Bethany like a bag of found money. "Aren't you going to introduce me to your lady friend?"

"No disrespect, but we were kind of in the middle of a—"

Stockton paid no mind to his friend's feeble remarks and held his hand out to Bethany. "I'm Timothy Stockton," he continued, planting a kiss on the top of her delicate wrist, "owner and proprietor of the mansion. But you can call me Timothy, or just Tim if it so pleases you." Bethany nodded and mustered a grin.

"And you are?"

"Bethany Lee."

"Well, I apologize for the interruption Miss Lee, and if there's anything you need, anything at all, you just let me know." With a tip of his hat and a shit-eating grin, Stockton disappeared into the throng of people.

"I'm sorry for my friend's rudeness," Eddie said, anxiously awaiting Bethany's explanation. "Please continue."

From across the room, Charlie noticed Bethany conversing with his opponent, and they appeared to be getting a bit too comfortable with each other. He stood in his seat and waved Eddie over to the card table, anxious to get him away from her.

They didn't notice him as Bethany explained how she lied about her family coming, and that she hadn't been happy for a long time. "I met someone else," she continued. "Someone more suited for me." I'm sorry you had to find out this way, but I would, however, like to remain friendly."

Eddie didn't say much. This was the last thing he expected to hear. Other than the long-distance issue, he genuinely felt things were going well between them. "Who is he?" Eddie quietly asked.

"It's not important. It's not anyone you know."

He hated that response. It didn't answer his question, and it took every ounce of self-restraint to keep from slapping her clear across her sweet face.

It was sweet, indeed. But it had changed in the last few minutes. It had grown dark. The longer Eddie studied her rosy cheeks, her pouty lips, and her tear-filled blue eyes, he began to notice imperfections he'd never seen before. They weren't physical imperfections, but imperfections of her soul, and he found himself loathing her. His confusion boiled as he felt the urge to love her in light of his hatred. He stood from his seat, and without saying a word, walked away.

For the second time that day, Bethany watched him leave her. Only this time, she knew it would be forever. She kept her eyes fixed on him as he joined the crowd in the party area and took a seat next to the man Eddie had introduced her to that morning at breakfast. Pausing for a moment to remember his name. Richard?

It all seemed so long ago to her. And seated directly across from him was Charlie. It made her incredibly nervous. Her heart began to squeeze, and sweat beads formed across her forehead. She felt faint, lightheaded.

Richard didn't notice Eddie seated next to him, as he was too busy conversing with the louse to notice his friend's troubled state of mind. The louse, however, did notice.

"Dear man, you look as if you've just lost your best friend," he bellowed, laughing at his own wittiness. Eddie was not amused and knew the louse was making light of the situation.

"Are you okay?" Richard interrupted, noticing Eddie's grim demeanor. "You don't look so good." Eddie reached in his pocket and pulled out a diamond necklace with matching earrings: a gift he had looked forward to giving Bethany during his visit.

"I'm okay for the time being," Eddie muttered, returning the jewelry to his pocket. "If it's all the same, I'd like to start the card game now if that suits you?"

"That would be fine," the louse replied, wondering why Eddie was talking to his beloved Bethany. "Can I ask how you know Beth—"

The louse was interrupted when he noticed Stockton from across the room sitting next to Bethany, laughing and conversing. He slammed down his drink and stood to get a better look.

"Excuse me for one moment," he spoke up, quickly leaving the table.

"What was that all about?" Richard asked.

"I don't know," Eddie replied, "and I don't care. I just want to get this over with."

Richard watched the louse make pleasantries with both Stockton and Bethany, appearing to have a false cheery disposition towards him. Eddie was too busy staring at the diamond necklace and earrings to notice. Although physically present, his mind and emotions were gutted.

After their conversation, Stockton stood and moved to another area of the room. The louse made his way back to the table.

"Some people, I tell you," he groaned as he turned to check on Bethany. After seeing her alone, he quickly took his seat and adjusted his top hat and collar. "Now, where were we?"

"We were just about to begin playing," Eddie reminded him, his patience running thin. "Can we get on with it, please? The louse picked up the deck of cards and began dealing. "No," Eddie spoke up. "I will deal."

The louse reluctantly handed him the cards and allowed him to deal. And after his first loss, Eddie insisted on dealing again, and again. After two straight losses, his pockets were wearing out, and by eleven o'clock, he was practically broke. The crowd had thinned out, leaving only a few stragglers left in the party room, which included Eddie, Richard, Stockton, a few other way-wards, and Bethany, who sat quietly in the corner. The fireplace had died out, and the room had a coldness surrounding it. Most of the guests didn't mind due to extreme inebriation, which was now apparent with a number of them, including Stockton, who had gotten aggressive with a number of the female guests before their better halves had put a stop to it. It might've been the brandy or the excitement, but he'd somehow forgotten that his wife was still absent.

The wooden ladder the workers had used to fix the mansion's roof that spring was Mrs. Stockton's best option at gaining access inside without being spotted. She was already late, and to enter through the front door would be the kiss of death. Placing the ladder gently upon the window ledge, Mrs. Stockton climbed her way to the second floor, and carefully, silently, raised the glass pane and slipped in unnoticed.

Once inside, she quickly surveyed the vacant hallway for any on-lookers, before pushing the ladder back down and slamming the window.

Downstairs, Stockton, oblivious to his wife's liaisons, was having a great time. Eddie was not. He was down to nothing. His cash was gone, and he'd lost all his valuable belongings to the louse, including his prized timepiece. Thinking back on how he'd originally acquired it brought a slight smile to his face. It was a present given to him by his stepfather on the morning he departed for West Point. He remembered shining it every morning in the cadet barracks, making sure the gold glistened sharply, taking more pride in it than he did his rifle. And now it was gone—along with his lover—along with a lot of things.

The thought of losing it was too much to bear. He quickly thought of a way to re-acquire it as the louse collected his winnings and bid everyone farewell.

"Wait!" Eddie called to him, placing the diamond necklace and earrings on the table. "Double or nothing, winner takes all.

Richard leaned over to Eddie. "Are you sure you want to do this? It's everything you have."

"Yes, I'm sure. What do you say?"

The louse leaned back in his chair. "Before we go any further," he replied, "I would prefer to know the name of my adversary. You have yet to tell me." In that moment of false confidence, Eddie figured it couldn't hurt.

"Eddie, my name is Eddie."

"I'm Charlie."

"I didn't ask," Eddie proceeded. "So do we have a deal? Winner takes all?" Charlie rested his arm on the table and sipped his brandy while eying Eddie. "Well, what are you waiting for? Deal the cards."

Fourteen

The snow had begun to accumulate on the desolate streets and sidewalks by the time Bethany's carriage halted in front of her cottage. After bidding their valet farewell, the couple entered the cozy, yet frigid interior, as silence and tension hung in the air. Bethany, still furious with Charlie, relaxed on the sofa and watched him light the strategically placed oil lamps that hung from the walls and rested on various marble and oak tables. He spoke as he went about his chore, asking her why she was so upset with him. But she felt he already knew the reason, and continuing the conversation would only lead to more pointless arguing. She preferred the silent treatment for the time being. Besides, there was *something* else that had captured her attention, something she couldn't explain.

Charlie received the hint from his lover and retired up the stairs for the night, leaving her alone in the living room. She continued her curiosity with the self-portrait that she'd been admiring earlier that day. It had changed somehow. She wondered how Charlie hadn't also noticed it. Either way, she couldn't allow this ugly version of herself to be seen by anyone. After jumping to her feet, she moved quickly towards the portrait and grabbed it from off the table, hoping to dispel the image as nothing more than a pure illusion. But the grotesque features remained. Darkened caverns engulfed by hellfire stared back at her, while faceless demons with erect penises violated her naked image.

The thought even occurred briefly that this was some sick joke executed somehow by Eddie to get even with her, but she quickly dismissed the notion, realizing that she'd been in his presence all evening.

Her head hurt from thinking. She threw the table drawer open, flung the portrait in, and slammed the door shut, successfully sheltering the rest of the world from its imagery. As she sat slowly back on the sofa, one thing was clear: she would soon pay a visit to Samuel Damone, the man who etched her likeness to canvass.

As promised, Stockton readied the carriage for Richard and Eddie's departure, giving his valet the necessary instructions as both men boarded. With a jerk of the reigns, the two horses began their journey down the deep snow-covered street. It was beautifully haunting, especially for Eddie, who was more than aware of their destination. The silence echoed throughout the desolate nineteenth-century roads, except for the clopping of horseshoes against cobblestone.

This was new and unfamiliar territory for Richard, especially since they now headed away from the town square that he'd gotten somewhat accustomed to in the last day and a half. The curiosity was eating at him, as he was entirely in the dark as to where they were headed.

The once magnificent mansions and wondrous streetlights quickly gave way to decrepit shacks and dark alleyways where the forgotten homeless lined up along the cold, depressing walkways, huddling around burning barrels to keep the hypothermia at bay. The ghastly sights made Richard pull his coat tighter as if to protect himself. He wasn't sure if it was his imagination, but it seemed to be getting colder and darker.

He also sensed the hostility rising in Eddie, and the tension caused substantial discomfort. He didn't want to say anything that would deepen the fresh wounds and understood he'd have to choose his words carefully.

"Do you know where we're going?" he asked. Eddie remained silent, watching the snowfall. "Are you okay? You haven't said a word in twenty minutes."

"I'm just thinking," Eddie replied, continuing his one-dimensional gaze out the window. "It's Bethany."

"What about her?" Eddie seemed reluctant to respond, but he told Richard everything that transpired in the mansion between them. And after explaining the entire situation, he appeared drained, with a sense of finality creeping in. Richard's kindhearted condolences did little to relieve the pain.

"And to answer your earlier question," Eddie continued. "We're headed to the land of rotted hopes and broken dreams. In other words, we're going to the Sixth Ward." Richard never heard of it.

"I've heard of the Sixth Ward," he lied, "but I'm not too familiar with it."

"Don't worry, my friend," Eddie said, leaning down to tie his soggy shoelace. "You're about to become very familiar with it."

Richard decided it was probably best not to ask what that meant. After glancing towards the outside homeless, he'd rather not know.

Fifteen

After seeing both Eddie and Richard safely on their way, Stockton returned to the comfort and sanctity of his mansion and flopped on one of the many red velvet embroidered sofas. Everyone had retired for the evening, and he was alone in the shambled room. It looked as if a typhoon had rolled through and destroyed everything in its wake, leaving chairs overturned, broken glass on the floor, and dirty plates on the tables. But Stockton was too tired and drunk to care. It was something he would have his housekeepers address in the morning, or afternoon, depending on when he would awake to nurse the impending hangover.

It didn't matter to him either way. Every bedroom was rented, and his guests had a wonderful time. Not to mention the large sum of money he'd be pulling in over the weekend. He smiled contently, and then, from the corner of his eye, he noticed something stirring from across the room, causing enough concern for him to rise to his feet and stare with reassurance. The painting over the fireplace mantle had morphed into a liquid consistency, as if he could touch it and cause the very surface to ripple out.

The brandy is finally tweaking my senses, he reasoned with himself, figuring his eyes were just playing alcohol-induced tricks on him. Shaking his head in bewilderment, he decided that this was his cue to retire for the night. He made his way to the stairs, walking quickly and quietly across the lonely room. He kept his gaze locked on the banister railing, not breaking contact for even an instant but keeping a watchful eye on the painting with his peripheral vision. A violent ripple lashed out, and Stockton quickly twisted his body to see the image of a blonde-haired woman, wearing a lavish blood-stained crimson dress. She appeared in agony as the picture animated itself into a frightening form, revealing vibrant streaks of crimson that poured from her golden crown and down her pale sullen face until it engulfed her entire body. Electricity coursed through his limbs when he recognized the woman as his wife.

"Who's doing that?" Stockton called loudly, as he tripped over a wayward chair in a futile attempt to run frantically for the staircase, subsequently causing him to lose his balance. He saw the edge of the hardwood table getting closer, but even extending his hands to brace his fall wasn't enough. He cracked his forehead on the side, right before he landed on the cold marble floor.

The scenery hadn't improved outside the carriage window. Not only had the situation worsened, but it had become downright terrifying. Richard tried his best to ignore his bleak whereabouts by making small talk with the valet while Eddie nodded off to sleep, blissfully ignorant to his surroundings.

At approximately twelve-thirty-five AM, the carriage slowed to a stop in the middle of a neglected intersection.

The Poe Predicament

"We've arrived," the valet called out, turning to the men.

"There must be some kind of mistake," Richard said. "I think you took a wrong turn."

"No, he didn't," Eddie spoke up. "This is surely our stop." While gathering his luggage, he ignored Richard's protests and proceeded to exit the carriage.

"Eddie! You can't reasonably expect us to stay here tonight?"

"Sir, would you kindly exit the coach?" the valet instructed. After taking one last glance out the window, Richard reluctantly opened the door and joined his friend on the broken cobblestone sidewalk, realizing that a night of decent sleep was shot to hell. As the valet whipped the reigns, he bid his passengers farewell. Richard didn't return the gesture.

The icy wind and bitter cold sliced through his clothing as the falling snow accumulated on his wavy auburn hair.

In a moment of desperation, he lightly closed his eyes and wished himself home in his warm bed, watching one of his favorite television programs or reading a familiar book. When he opened his eyes, his surroundings remained the same, and Richard begun to feel the strains of his situation.

"Where the hell are we, Eddie?"

"You don't want to know. Come on, let's go get settled into our boarding house."

Richard quickly glanced around at the five-pointed intersection, which spindled out from the center like a wagon wheel, for something that might resemble a livable space. But what he saw only frightened him further. Rows of women and children lay on the street, barely clothed, shivering, and sharing scraps of rotten meat with the gutter dogs while they huddled around enflamed barrels in a vain attempt to keep warm. Most of the structures had broken windows. Some even appeared to have been partially burned to the ground at some previous point. Piles of garbage littered the sidewalks and streets causing the overwhelming stench to filter out in every direction, turning Richard and Eddie's stomach on end as they made their way through the misery towards one of the many abandoned buildings.

It was hard to see in such darkness, as most of the gas lampposts were as black as the cold night sky. The newly fallen snow, however, cast a bright, welcoming luster over the entire intersection. It mentally warmed Eddie and allowed him and Richard the strength to carry on. He was furious with his so-called friend, Stockton. Furious for being practically homeless and for being turned away by someone he'd considered trustworthy. It broke him.

He instinctively followed the remnants of rotten fruit and vegetables that lined a path in front of the two men in a trail-like formation, leading them on. The instructions Stockton had given him were simple enough. He was to give the motel clerk the note he had written and signed for Eddie, which would supposedly grant free access to one of the many rooms.

This particular motel was another of Stockton's many real estate ventures. He had bought it cheap in the hopes of turning it around and building it into an attractive place to stay for the traveler passing through town. It did not turn out as planned, and he decided to focus his attention on more lucrative investments, leaving the place practically dormant.

From the second floor of her temporary residence, a woman rested next to a roaring fireplace as she gazed out her bedroom window at the peaceful snow falling onto the brightly-lit intersection. A blinding light had woken her from a deep sleep, but she didn't mind. Truthfully, she couldn't believe her luck. Here was the second chance she desired. Richard's luminous aura disappeared into the front door of the ram-shackled motel across the street, causing her room to darken as the outside light faded. Her face remained blank as she sat on the edge of her bed, in thought.

By the time the valet arrived back at the Stockton mansion, the snow had accumulated to five inches, causing the last couple blocks of his journey to become debilitating as the horses slowed to a lead-footed crawl. He breathed a sigh of relief as he hitched the Thoroughbred and Mustang to their designated posts, patting them on their sides as a sort of "thank you" for making it through.

As he entered the mansion he noticed far across the room the shadow of a man crawling slowly across the floor toward the staircase. Red liquid streamed down his face and glistened in the torchlight.

"Sir," the valet said as he ran to Stockton's aide. "What happened here? Were you attacked?"

"I don't think so," he replied. "I remember tripping and falling. I must've hit my head."

"That doesn't look good. Remain seated for a moment while I retrieve a towel for you."

"Wait!" Stockton yelled, grabbing his valet's arm. "It was that damned painting. I remember now!" He pointed to the landscape on the wall.

"What about it?" the valet asked.

All that remained was an ordinary painting with a peaceful stream running aside a rustic cottage. "Nothing, help me up."

After tending to his wounds, Stockton thanked the valet and wished him goodnight as he walked into his frigid bedroom, eager to curl up to the warmth of his wife. He then remembered through his foggy senses that he hadn't seen her all day.

On most nights, either he or Mrs. Stockton would light the fireplace on cold evenings long before bedtime, but it had not been lit. Amidst all the commotion with the party and his unfortunate fall, he failed to attend to it. But she always remembered, even if he didn't. And now it was so cold that he could see his breath form smoky shapes in front of his eyes.

As he struck a match and lit the brittle logs, he thought about what he saw in the painting and what it could've meant. It frightened him to conjure the images back into his mind, and he shuttered at the thought. As he shook them away, a second chill ran up his spine, and he made haste to the bed for reassurance that his wife was safe and sound.

"Darling, are you alright?" he asked, laying a hand gently on her arm. She rustled, but did not respond. He left her alone and rolled on his side to watch the fireplace dance to a tune he had in his head.

Stockton's room was cold but not as cold as Richard and Eddie's. With the absence of any fireplace and the night growing later, the temperature hovered around the ten-degree mark. Richard now understood what Eddie meant by his earlier warnings. This place was shit. Half of the wall was missing in the lobby, and there was no attendant around to pass the note along. So the men found the only empty room in the boarding house and made it their home for the night.

Richard took the filthy mattress next to the bedroom's door-less entryway. He figured if someone were to approach, being next to the entrance might alert him to the intruder. Eddie took refuge along the back wall to keep an eye on the doorway, keeping his luggage hidden out of sight against the corner. With his lowered sense of security, Richard clutched the book under his coat, holding it securely in his grasp. He watched through the glassless windowpane as snow continued its steady fall, and the arctic winds howled through the cavernous opening. After each blast, he closed his eyes and squeezed his book, thinking something, *anything* might occur. But he knew it wouldn't. He'd spent part of the day wracking his brain for an answer, and the other part worrying about where he would sleep. As far as he could gather, he was entirely out of options, and there was nobody he could turn to here.

The room's silence indicated Eddie was asleep. No movement came from his corner of the room, and the only noise was that of the outside wind. Slowly, he untucked the book and carefully brought it into view, studying its flawless appearance and flipped through the pages.

"What do you have there?" Eddie's voice echoed out from the darkness, causing Richard to drop the book onto the grimy floor.

"Oh," Richard said, quickly picking it up. "It's just a collection of poems I've been reading."

"Well, that sounds interesting. You'll have to let me read some tomorrow."

"Sure thing," Richard replied, gazing at the front cover. "Just be careful with it. At this point, it's pretty much the only thing I own."

"You don't have to worry about that. I treat every book as if it were mine."

"Of course you do," Richard replied, smiling.

"Well, goodnight," Eddie called out, turning on his side.

"Goodnight." Richard continued to stare at the cover. It was the first time that day he could be alone with his thoughts. He stared at the book until close to fifteen minutes had passed. He couldn't hold it in any longer.

"Eddie," he whispered. "Are you awake?" Eddie stirred and sat upon his cold slab of concrete.

"I am now. What is it?" Richard hesitated. He kept thinking about what a fool he would sound like telling such an unbelievable story. Fuck it.

"Eddie," he proceeded. "You've only known me for a day, but would you say we're friends?"

"I suppose so. Why?"

"Well, I need to tell you something about this book. It might sound completely ridiculous, but I ask that you at least keep an open mind." Richard quickly and carefully thought about what to say. He had every word picked out, and just when he was about to spill the beans, he froze up.

"Richard, just tell me."

"Yes. I mean, no. I don't know. Look…just forget it. I don't think I can. Maybe another time, goodnight," Richard said to his puzzled companion. As exhausted as Eddie was, and not wanting to press the issue, he turned on his side and drifted off. Richard lay awake for another two hours before finally falling asleep.

The nightmares that plagued him the previous night eluded him that evening and sleep, however brief it might've been, was restful and refreshing.

Stockton, however, was not so lucky. The night was long and cold and he was in a state of unconscious hell. He experienced vivid nightmares of torture, his extremities set ablaze by an army of devils, leaving him in a consistent state of agony. But unable to scream, unable to move. He remained that way until the sun rose. When morning broke through the scattered storm clouds, the snow had stopped, but the angels' frozen tears left a blanket of crystal across the land.

Sixteen

Richard awoke the next morning, not in his bed as he'd hoped, but to the chilling sight of Eddie hovering over him. He didn't say a word, causing Richard's uneasiness to increase. Then he noticed Eddie holding a book in his grasp.

"Eddie? What are you doing?"

"If you wanted to read this, you didn't have to steal it from me," he replied, holding the book up, shaking it so erratically that Richard had a hard time identifying it. "Well?" he continued. "What do you have to say for yourself?"

"I have nothing to say for myself," Richard replied, realizing what the book was. "I have nothing to say because that's *my* book your waving around in the air like a lunatic. You asked me last night what I was reading, well there it is, a book of poems, just like I told you."

"Of course I know it's a book of poems," Eddie snapped. "What I don't know is how you managed to sneak it out of my travel luggage without me noticing."

"I could say the same for you. When I went to bed last night, it was tucked on the inside of my coat. But you somehow have it now."

"It was lying there on the floor when I awoke, along with this," Eddie said, holding up Richard's cell phone. "Just what is this thing anyway? I've been trying for the last hour to do something with it, but I can't figure it out. It looks like some kind of elaborate paperweight if you ask me."

"Shit," Richard mumbled under his breath. "Well, I'm an inventor, like Thomas Edison."

"Who's Thomas Edison?"

"Never mind," Richard mumbled again. "Forget Thomas Edison. Why are you so concerned with this book anyway? It's not like it's a first edition of *Dante's Inferno* or anything."

"Because it's the only copy I own that I didn't lose to that louse! And now it appears you've confiscated it from me."

"Eddie, I swear I didn't. You saw me reading it last night with your own eyes." Eddie sat down on the cold floor and flipped through the book. For a few long minutes, he was silent.

He finally spoke up. "Well, what did you think?"

"What did I think about what?"

"The book of poems…did you like them?" Eddie softly inquired with a look of curiosity across his face.

"Yeah, of course I liked them. Look, why don't you just recheck your bag? This can't be yours."

Eddie listened to the advice. He tossed Richard's phone back and checked his luggage. After rummaging through for the better part of five minutes, he finally came upon something.

"I think I've found it!" he exclaimed, turning quickly to Richard and lowering his voice to a more modest level. He frowned. "I apologize for my accusations. It was buried between some rolled up clothing."

"I told you I didn't take it."

"Right you are, and I'm sorry," he responded. Richard accepted the apology as he got up from the filthy floor and brushed himself off. In the broad daylight, he was better able to see the cobwebs and spiders that inhabited the room. As he watched a cockroach scurry across the floor to take refuge in one of the corners, he was relieved he hadn't been aware of them the night before.

"I feel like a complete fool right now," Eddie said, putting his clothing back in the suitcase. "I'm glad there are no hard feelings."

"None at all, it was just a little miscommunication." Richard gazed out the window to the bustling five-pointed intersection. It really *was* a shithole. He'd honestly never seen such poverty in his lifetime. But then again, this wasn't his lifetime. And then, Eddie asked him a question he never thought he'd hear.

"So would you like me to sign it for you?"

Richard turned away from the window. "Come again?"

"Your book," Eddie replied with a smile. "After all, I did write it. I'm quite happy there are people out there buying it, even if I haven't seen a penny yet. So just out of curiosity, where did you purchase it?"

Richard thought silently for a moment, not quite sure how to respond. "I bought it in a Manhattan bookstore," he replied, watching Eddie's eyes widen.

"Really, may I ask if there were many copies in this bookstore?"

Richard raised the book and turned it over. "Look, Eddie, I hate to break it to you. But you didn't write this."

"Of course I did," he firmly responded. "I would surely know what I did and didn't write."

"Okay then, what's the author's name?"

"That's easy, A Bostonian. Me."

"All right, but what is the author's actual name?"

"You know my name, Richard," he said and laughed. "I already told you, A Bostonian wrote it. Well, I'm that Bostonian. What more proof do you need?"

Richard was beginning to enjoy this little game of cat and mouse. It was probably the most fun he had since he'd been there.

"Eddie, the author's actual name is Edgar Allan Poe, and I highly doubt you're him," he replied while flipping through the pages of the pristine book.

Eddie's face twisted at his friend's response like he'd heard something that shocked him. "How could you possibly know that?" Eddie asked, completely stunned.

"Because his signature was on the inside cover, *was* being the keyword. It disappeared once I...never mind."

"Well, I've never signed a single copy of anything, and signatures don't usually get up and walk away." His eyes didn't move to Richard. Not once. His fixation remained on the book.

"You're right. They don't. But you almost had me convinced." Richard sighed, joining his friend on the windowsill.

He watched the children on the street playing what appeared to be a game of snowball tag. Actually, it was more like snowball freeze tag, considering whenever a child was struck, they froze in place.

He'd always assumed it was a much newer game and was surprised they even had freeze tag in the nineteenth century. As he watched them run and play and freeze, he noticed how much fun they seemed to be having. He couldn't imagine any modern-day kid being so happy and carefree living under such conditions. Their clothes were tattered and worn, their faces darkened with dirt and soot. But they seemed happy, if only for the moment.

He noticed a few snowmen scattered around the courtyard dressed in clothing of the period. Instead of coal, the children had strategically placed stones and small rocks to resemble a smiling face, with each snowman having their own unique hat. Two resembled checkered multi-colored berets, while another looked more like your traditional stovepipe hat. It reminded himself of his childhood and how quickly time had passed. Would he be better off staying in nineteenth-century New York? It wasn't like he was missing very much back home. Still, deep down, he knew he didn't belong.

Turning from the window, he noticed Eddie holding up a white paper document with some printing scrolled across it.

"What's that?" Richard asked.

"These are my discharge papers from West Point. Not that it's important, but I am always motivated to prove a point, and you wanted proof of my name. Well, here's your proof." He handed the document to Richard, who snatched it from him with an innocent curiosity.

Everything looked official. As he examined it for authenticity purposes, he didn't say a word. However, he became visibly flush as he approached the lower portion of the document.

This is to certify that the United States Military Academy of West Point, New York, is hereby discharging Cadet <u>Edgar A. Poe</u> from the military service of this institution on this day <u>January 28th, 1831,</u> on the grounds of gross negligence with court-martialed status.

Eddie continued to watch Richard's expressions while he snatched the document from his hand. "See, I told you I was telling the truth. Oh, and forget about that rubbish you read towards the end about me being court-martialed, and all the gross negligence nonsense," he said, shaking his head. "Nothing happened to me that I didn't willingly allow." Richard promptly left his spot on the windowsill and began circling Eddie like a vulture, intricately studying his facial features. "Can I ask what in God's name you're doing?" Eddie asked, backing away from Richard.

"But, you look nothing like him."

"I look nothing like who?"

"You look nothing like...you," Richard replied, dissecting Eddie's features.

Eddie's face was clean-shaven, his hair seemingly cut down to approximately an eighth of an inch for military purposes. The man was young, and as far as Richard could tell, probably not even of drinking age. He figured around nineteen or twenty years of age.

He then began to imagine Eddie about ten years older, with long black hair and a mustache. He couldn't believe it.

"My goodness, you look awful, Richard. Here, sit down on the mattress," Eddie insisted. Richard took a seat and held his forehead in a futile attempt to stop the spinning sensation. "Do you feel any better? I honestly don't understand what's gotten into you."

Richard looked up and mustered a slight grin. "If I explained it, you wouldn't believe me," he said between breaths. "I think I need something to drink. I'm getting dehydrated. Can I please have some of the elixir that you bought at the festival yesterday?"

"Oh, I'm sorry, but I also lost that in the card game. Right about now, that louse is probably sipping on it and gloating over his win. I hope he chokes on it!"

When the louse awoke earlier that morning, he decided to pop the top and take a sizable swig as he walked down Bethany's winding staircase to the first floor. What he didn't know was that the elixir was nothing more than mere peanut extract mixed with ground-up berries. His initial reaction was quite disappointing when the claims presented on the bottle didn't come to fruition, as no extreme mental focus or muscle growth occurred.

But a few things were apparent as he examined himself in the parlor mirror, his breathing had become constricted, and his heart raced. Since he disliked nuts his whole life, he was completely unaware that he had a serious peanut allergy that could potentially wreak havoc on his system. Within the hour, the louse had collapsed against the wall, his face blown up like an overripe watermelon, gagging and choking over and over—just as Eddie had hoped.

When Bethany found him, his face was completely unrecognizable, his breathing shallow, but he was alive. Luckily for her, the closest doctor was only two blocks away, and if not for her swift action the louse might not have pulled through, regardless of Dr. Melton's misdiagnosis. "I believe this condition is derived from poor bathing habits," the doctor said, who was apparently guessing. After all, the physician was fresh out of medical school by no more than three months, which was also less time than it took him to become certified to practice medicine. But according to him, a one-month course to fulfill his dream of becoming a doctor was more than enough and he felt he was now knowledgeable enough to treat the needy.

Despite his misdiagnosis, he did one thing correct that saved the louse's life, giving him an herbal concoction that he claimed would open up the esophagus and allow for more natural breathing. Again, he was guessing, but it worked. Within a half-hour, the louse was sitting up on the sofa, breathing more comfortably and looking better. After receiving his five-cent payment, the doctor gave the louse some half-baked orders and made his way down the un-shoveled sidewalks to his office.

It seemed to him that the festival might bring in a great deal of business due to drunken injuries and poor judgment. But the snow seemed to keep many people from attending, leaving the town square barren compared to the previous day.

Dr. Melton no sooner had his key in the front door lock when someone frantically began calling his name from behind. It was Stockton's valet pulling up to the front of the office building in a hurry, still calling the doctor's name. The horses halted and he quickly jumped from the carriage.

"What seems to be the matter?" the doctor asked as he turned to face his pursuer.

"It's Timothy, doc! He sustained an injury last night, and he's worse than I first believed. He's sitting in his living room, staring at the wall and talking crazy."

"Oh, I see. Could you refresh my memory? Timothy...?"

"Stockton. Tim Stockton. Please, we should hurry!"

Cha-ching! The doc thought to himself, realizing the day may not be a complete bust after all. Stockton was loaded. Everyone knew that.

"Well, let's not keep the young man waiting," Dr. Melton insisted as he climbed aboard the carriage.

Seventeen

"Wow, Edgar Allan Poe," Richard mumbled, as he awaited Eddie's return from a bathroom scavenger hunt. He hoped it would be soon, considering his bladder was about to burst. The sun beamed through the open window, giving the room a certain warmth that had been absent through the night and early morning hours. But he hardly noticed it. He was still in shock from learning his friend's true identity. He wondered if all of this wasn't just some strange cosmic accident. Maybe there was a reason for what had happened. He felt like a kid on Christmas morning. To rub elbows with the original master of horror was something that was not only implausible but also impossible. Poe had been dead for well over a hundred and fifty years, yet, here he was.

An obnoxious beeping rang out and prompted him to jump to his feet. He initially thought it was an odd-sounding smoke alarm when he remembered it was his smart phone's alarm clock, set for his Thursday morning shrink session.

"Looks like I'll be missing that one today, doc."

After hitting the shut-up button on the phone, he noticed the battery indicator hadn't moved at all. It was strange, considering his phone was usually down for a dirt nap after about six hours off the charger.

After exiting the alarm clock, he opened his apps window and began searching through his games. He fired up Tetris, figuring it was probably the best way to kill time, but was careful, however, not to get caught. It seemed Eddie was already suspicious of the device, and he didn't need him walking in and seeing a video game that wouldn't be invented until the next century.

Eddie studied the crisp twenty-dollar bill that he clenched in his hand as he walked down the long hallway of the boarding house. He ignored the beggars and diseased degenerates that grabbed his sleeves and shouted obscenities while he set his sights on reaching the staircase as quickly as possible. Most of them were relatively harmless, but some became aggressive when they saw him holding the crumpled money.

Realizing it was a moronic decision to examine currency in such a place, he promptly tucked it back in his pocket and out of sight, but that didn't stop the harassment. The obscenities continued as they proceeded to pull at his clothing and grab at his feet while he walked, almost tripping him. Eddie had just about enough when another degenerate grabbed his ankle and wouldn't let go.

"If another one of you miscreants touches me, I will be forced to pull my pistol with intent to use!" he shouted, swiftly kicking the legless beggar's hand off his ankle. He reached inside his vest in a gesture of ill will, hoping to frighten his depraved pursuers.

They promptly backed off, thinking he had a weapon, allowing him to reach the crumbled staircase quickly. And just in time too, as the musty odors caused by the rotting flesh and stagnant urine had begun to turn Eddie's empty stomach, producing a dry heaving reaction that started in the pit of his gut and rose to the back of his throat.

As he reached the bottom of the stairs, he grabbed the railing and tossed his suitcase on the floor while taking a seat on one of the steps until the heaves passed. There was no bathroom in the building just as Eddie had predicted, but he figured it was a good excuse that allowed him a graceful exit. The odors on the ground floor lobby were substantially better than what he'd just experienced, but the foul aroma seemed to cling to his clothing, causing the pungent scent to linger. He took a deep breath and forced some saliva down his sandpapered throat—the result of the previous evening's liquor consumption. Figuring this was a safe zone, Eddie carefully reached in his pocket, pulling out the twenty-dollar bill.

He examined it thoroughly and noticed it was unlike any other currency he'd ever seen. The man on the front of the bill was the current President of the United States. That made sense, but nothing else did. After flipping the note around from front to back, his eye finally caught a glimpse of a year printed on the bottom: *2016*

Upon reading the year, Eddie began to wonder who his friend upstairs really was, and what he'd been hiding. It was probably the worst counterfeit job he'd ever seen, but if it *was* legitimate, Richard had a lot of explaining to do. Not to mention the contraption on the floor next to Richard.

After slipping the money back into his pocket, Eddie felt a small sting of regret but ignored it the best he could. *It's not stealing. It's just borrowing,* he re-verified to himself.

He peeled himself off the staircase, retrieved his suitcase, and headed for the front door of his residential nightmare. Just as he was about to exit, he stopped halfway between the open doorways. He turned and looked up the staircase, fighting an inner battle of guilt.

It's not stealing if I plan on paying him back. Besides, I may be doing him a favor considering the reaction he got the other night at the pub.

Feeling better after his self-assuring inner speech, Eddie turned his attention from the staircase to the outside doorway and exited the motel while focused on the main reason he was in New York: getting his book published.

By the time Richard reached the fifth level of Tetris, he understood that Eddie should've returned long ago. He had no way of knowing the exact time, but he estimated somewhere around forty minutes had passed. As he powered off the game, he noticed Eddie's suitcase missing from across the room. He hadn't seen him carrying it and wondered why he would've taken something like that to the bathroom. He decided to stay a few more minutes and amuse himself by watching the outside bustle of children joyfully jump through the slushy puddles, figuring it was better than staring at the paint-peeled walls.

He sat on the window sill and watched the unfortunates wander the intersection in search of things they would never attain like peace, comfort, and stability. And then he saw Eddie, quickly trucking across the town square. Richard adjusted his eyes, ready for the mistaken identity to reveal itself. But there was no mistaking that Eddie had jumped ship. Richard hadn't felt this betrayed since his wife left him.

"Oh my God, Edgar Allan Poe just ditched me!" he said. "I can't believe this."

"You can't believe what?" asked a soft voice from behind. Startled, Richard turned quickly, almost falling off the ledge to see an unfamiliar woman standing at the room's entrance. He felt his cheeks run red from embarrassment.

"I'm sorry. You surprised me."

"You'll soon see I'm full of surprises," she replied with a sensual grin. As she stood before him, he couldn't help but admire her striking beauty and porcelain complexion. The golden tips of her auburn colored tresses wrapped loosely around her shoulders, past the bright emerald earrings, flowing gracefully down her chiseled back in loose ringlets. The glamorous black and white dress she wore hugged her body tight, enticing even the purest of men to her stately figure. She pursed her ruby lips together, looking at the dilapidated conditions. "We need to talk, Richard," she said in a kind and welcoming tone as she walked further into the room.

It had already been close to an hour since Dr. Melton left Bethany's cottage. Charlie silently recovered on the couch while Bethany rifled through the drawer that she stashed her self-portrait the night before, prepared to have a word with Samuel to inform him that his so-called work of art was an abomination. After pulling it from storage, she quickly noticed its normal appearance and felt immediate relief.

She concluded that the recent stress she'd been under had caused her to imagine the whole thing and proudly redisplayed the portrait on the tabletop.

"It looks great, darling. Why did you have it in the drawer?"

"I didn't want the doctor gawking at it, so I threw it in there before he got here," she replied, hoping he'd believe the lie. She placed the portrait back down and took a deep breath before turning to face Charlie.

"Look, I'm going to be straight with you." She paused and took a seat on the couch next to him. "First, I wanted to apologize for my behavior last night. There was a reason, however, that I was acting so irregularly. One of the guests at last night's party was Eddie."

Charlie struggled to sit up. "You mean…"

"Yes, that Eddie," Bethany quickly responded. "And since he was still under the impression we were involved, you can imagine the kind of predicament I found myself in. I did, however, officially end it with him last night."

"I see," he said, watching her play with the ruffles of her dress. "So which of those men was Eddie? If he was there last night, I must've been in his presence on more than one occasion."

Bethany released her ruffles and stood up. "It's not important that you know."

"Was that the same Eddie I was playing cards with?" he asked. Bethany wondered if she should lie, but she didn't. She told him the truth, figuring it wouldn't matter. Charlie didn't seem to care one way or another, but he did appear to revel more in his victory than he previously had. If there was one thing Charlie didn't lack, it was ego.

Richard remained seated by the window while he watched the towering beauty approach him. She slowly crept across the room's brittle floorboards, making sure not to step on anything questionable, until she reached Richard. She sat by the window next to him and gazed outside at the crowded streets below. But Richard only watched *her*.

"You know, when I first came here, I was appalled when I saw that everyone was living in such shitty conditions." Her profanity caught Richard off-guard. It was the first cuss word he'd heard since arriving in the nineteenth century. "Look right there," she proceeded, pointing at the crowd of people that lined up for food below. "They do this every morning. They stand in line for hours, hoping to get a meal. And do you know what breakfast is?" Richard looked at her, then back down at the people.

"No idea," he replied.

"They stand there in that long line for cabbage water! Yuck! It's so sad."

"Yes, it certainly is," he responded, continuing his compliance.

"But the interesting thing is that they don't appear to be unhappy. I think it's because they don't know any better," the woman whispered, putting a delicate hand on her chest. "They have no other way of life to compare it to."

"Or maybe it's a blessing," Richard spoke up. "They say ignorance is bliss."

"You may be right," she sighed. "I never thought of it like that. Do you know what I think? I think we're going to get along just fine."

Who was this woman? He needed to know. "So, where did your friend get to?" she asked. "I saw you two enter the boarding house last night but I don't see him anywhere." Richard stood and placed his hands firmly in his pockets.

"Before I answer any other questions, I have a few of my own."

"Ask away," she replied, pausing for a moment. "Is it because I know your name?"

"That's a good start," he answered, surprised that she volunteered the topic.

"Look, why don't you gather up your belongings so we can get out of here?" The mystery woman walked over to him and laid a hand on his shoulder. She smiled but remained silent. Richard did his best to pretend she wasn't resting on him by staring down at his mud-covered shoes. As he stood in the middle of the room, he instantly caught the potent floral aroma of her perfume.

"I'm a friend," she said. With that, she walked over to the open doorway. "Are you coming?"

Eighteen

As Richard and the mystery woman stepped out into the snow-covered streets of the Sixth Ward, the white glare of the freshly fallen snow partially blinded the two travelers. The sun gleamed brightly off the thin layer of crystallized ice that had formed over the top of the snow, causing a prism of colors to refract off the surface. Richard had never seen anything like it before, not even in the massive snowstorms that accompanied his New York winters. It resembled something he may have read in a fairy tale series or seen in a Spielberg movie.

"Excuse me," Richard spoke up as they approached the main intersection. "I have to ask what is with the snow?"

The mystery woman looked around. "What about it?" she asked.

"The collage of colors, it's amazing. But I've never seen anything like it."

"That's right. I keep forgetting you're not from around here," she replied, bending down to scoop up a handful. "It's clean. There's no pollution here, so the snow is as pure and uncontaminated as you could imagine." Richard studied the pile cupped in her hand. She was right. It resembled nothing of the dull white and gray snowfalls he was accustomed to.

"I never would've thought."

"Don't overthink, you might implode," she replied, throwing the handful of snow in Richard's direction, hitting him directly on the top of his head.

"That hurt," he scolded, just to play along.

"Oh, stop being a big baby. That didn't hurt."

"You're right. It didn't." He smiled and picked up a large handful of snow from a nearby carriage and prepared his aim.

"I wouldn't do that if I were you," she said, walking over to him, knocking the snow out of his grasp with a quick swipe. "You boys are all the same. Don't you know you shouldn't start something you can't finish?"

"I had every intention of finishing until you interfered."

"Intentions are hollow. And expectations will disappoint you. As I said, don't start something you can't finish."

"Oh, I always finish, believe me."

"All right, that's enough double-entendres for one day."

Richard brushed the remaining snow off his hands and looked around. "So, here we are standing in the middle of a large intersection, joking around like we've known each other for years, so I think it's only fair that you tell me your name, especially since you already know mine...or is that top secret information?"

The mystery woman pulled her long coat tighter as a burst of arctic wind blasted past them. She hesitated at the question, pausing to ponder her decision on whether to reveal it to him. Richard quickly noticed her apprehension.

"How about I guess?" he suggested, immediately thinking of some old nineteenth-century female names. "I'm leaning towards Ethel." The woman gave him a smug look. "I'm taking that as a no. Esther?"

"For God's sake, no. You're completely off. I'll just tell you. It's Alice. My name is Alice. There, are you happy?"

"I like that name, Alice."

"Thank you, Mr. Langley," she said, sitting on one of the small snow forts constructed earlier by a group of imaginative children. The breakfast line grew larger, stretching out to where Richard and Alice rested. They looked cold and dejected, frail and malnourished. It was the first time Richard had a good chance to look at the massive intersection in the light of day from ground level.

Across the way, a blacksmith worked diligently on the morning's tasks while a cluster of horses surrounded his work area awaiting their turn, much the same as the people in line. As Richard watched them gobble down their cabbage soup, he was suddenly aware of his hunger, but still not enough to resort to cabbage soup.

As uncomfortable as his growing appetite had become, his dehydration from last night's alcohol consumption had placed a crippling thirst within him. He found himself fantasizing about a tall glass of cold spring water, and how it would feel rolling down his coarse throat.

"Excuse me, Alice, but is there any place to get a drink around here?" She looked around the courtyard and quickly pointed in the direction of a gathered crowd.

"Right there, they serve simple beer all day, every day." Richard cringed as he saw the rows of barrels filled with booze.

"No, I don't want alcohol. I need water."

"Well, good luck drinking the water. You're free to consume as much as you want, but you'll most likely contract cholera. I'm not very good at cleaning up puke, so I wouldn't recommend it."

"Cholera, right, I forgot about cholera. What about—"

"Damned Irish!" an oddball man interrupted, quickly approaching Richard and Alice.

"Excuse me?" Richard asked.

"I said, the damned Irish! Coming over here by the boatload, day after day, stealing all of our jobs, eating all of our food, and poisoning us with their Catholic belief system! It makes me sick if you ask me!" Never mind the fact that Richard himself was Irish, he took no offense to the statement as he remembered reading about this in history books, and even touched on it briefly as a professor. But the realization that he was actually living history hit him, and his moment of clarity came.

"Wait a minute. Are we sitting in the middle of Five Points?" he blurted out.

"Five Points, yes, we are. Where the hell did you think you were, Ireland?" the stranger asked. Alice buried her head in her hands, attempting to conceal her laughter. "Are you an immigrant?" the man bluntly asked while taking giant bites of an apple.

"Not that it's any of your business, but—"

"Well, I'm making it my business." The man spoke with a stern yet elegant tone.

"I was going to say, not that it's any of your business, but you don't notice an accent, do you? I was born and raised in Philadelphia."

"Good! I don't like the Irish!" the man said, tossing the apple core onto the snow and wiping his mouth with a white-laced handkerchief he'd retrieved from his breast pocket.

"You'll have to forgive Samuel," Alice spoke up. "He comes off a bit brash at times, but he means no harm, really." The man seemed out of place. He sported an elegant gray overcoat with shiny gold buttons down the front in a vertical fashion. His pants matched the coat, and his shoes gleamed like mirrors.

"I'm guessing you two know each other?" Richard asked.

Alice nodded. "You guessed correctly. But if Samuel had it his way, he would know me a little more than he does. Isn't that right, Samuel?" she asked, turning in his direction.

"I don't know what you're talking about." He blushed before turning back to Richard. "So, whoever you are, why is your head all bandaged up? It looks like you owed the wrong people some money."

"It's a long story," Richard replied, lightly touching the blood-stained bandage. "I'm sure you wouldn't want to hear it."

"I do want to hear it! If I didn't want to hear it, I wouldn't have bothered asking."

"Oh, would you calm down, Samuel," Alice demanded. "He tripped and injured himself on the corner of a bookshelf while trying to make a hasty exit. There, are you happy?" Richard quickly turned to Alice. He didn't say a word. He just looked at her.

"Well, that wasn't as exciting as I thought it would be," Samuel said with a sigh. "But then again, you do seem like rather a dull fellow."

"Thanks for the compliment."

"It wasn't supposed to be a compliment," he replied, frowning at Richard.

"So have they been getting worse?" Alice asked.

"Has what been getting worse?

"The nightmares, you seem to be more on edge than usual." After looking to the sky, Samuel ran his fingers through his hair and glanced back at Alice.

"Worse than ever," he said. "They are most definitely getting worse, and I don't know what to do."

"Wait," Richard interrupted. "Could you describe these nightmares?"

"I could, if it was any of your business," Samuel snarled.

"You don't understand. I also experience nightmares."

"So anyway," Samuel said, turning to Alice and dismissing Richard completely now that he knew he couldn't continue his row about him being born in Ireland. "What time is your performance tonight?"

"I'll answer your question if you answer Richard's first," Alice instructed.

"Oh, fine! I just don't like to think about them. Hellfire, demonic imagery, pitchforks, mutilation, black demons of some kind. There, are you happy now?" Richard hung his head.

"That wasn't so tough now, was it?" Alice asked. "My performance is at eight, but I didn't think you were coming?"

"I'll be there. I managed to change my appointment at the last minute." He smiled, pulling two tickets from his coat pocket that read:

BOWERY THEATRE
SHAKESPEARE PLAY
ADMIT ONE
FEBRUARY 12TH 1831
$2

Alice flashed a phony smile. "Wonderful," she responded. Richard could tell she wasn't happy with the news. He was still mesmerized by the year printed on the tickets. At this point, he had accepted his situation, no matter how irrational it seemed. Alice knew things she shouldn't. But this intrigued him, offered a glimmer of hope. Right now, she was his only prospect.

Unfortunately, Samuel didn't see it this way. He was a man of few convictions and few morals, but he was a very gifted painter. His client list was vast and catered to the wealthy such as Stockton and Bethany, just two of his many satisfied customers. Most people agreed that it was a shame all of his talents couldn't afford him a better personality.

"What are you doing on this side of town?" Alice spoke up. "I thought you hated it here?"

"Why else would I be here? To see *you*, of course, and to give you the good news of my attendance," he replied, waving the tickets in the air. In his mind, he felt like he'd been making progress with Alice, even if it was slower than he had initially hoped. When he first caught a glimpse of her beauty during the early December snow, he was instantly cast in her spell, and from that point on, attempted to win her heart through his artwork and poetry. And now, someone was trying to interfere with his agenda. According to him, Richard was nothing more than a bug that needed to be squashed under his boot heel.

Alice didn't have the feelings for Samuel that he'd hoped, but he was unaware of it. When he looked in the mirror, he saw a handsome billowing man of twenty-five years, instead of the reality staring back at him, which was that of a chain-smoking forty-eight-year-old out of shape specimen with an affinity for hard liquor.

"So, what matter of activities are we participating in today?" Samuel asked, hoping to be included in whatever the answer might be.

"Richard and I have pressing business to attend to, so if—"

"Is that so? And what is this pressing business if I may ask?"

"Nothing for you to lose sleep over," she quickly replied. "So, Samuel, we should be going." She cleared her throat and turned to Samuel. "But it looks as though I'll be seeing you tonight at the theatre. Okay?" With a stern look, he took heed to Alice's words, realizing he'd been beaten.

While glaring to the line at his left, he asked, "So is this green soup any good?"

"The people here seem to like it," Alice replied and began to walk away.

"Maybe I'll try some!" he shouted as their distance increased. "Just to see how the other half lives!" He gathered himself at the end of the long line, where a helping of cabbage soup awaited. Strangers gawked at him, not accustomed to seeing a man of his status awaiting handouts. He watched Alice and Richard from across the center of Five Points, analyzing their every move. A rage stirred within him that combined a dangerous mix of jealousy and betrayal.

From where he stood, it appeared as though Alice and Richard had stopped in front of a blacksmith's shop, seemingly resting on a large bale of hay. It was worse than he thought. Alice was slipping through his fingers.

By the time Samuel reached the front of the line, Alice and Richard had disappeared from view. Looking down at his bowl of green-colored water, he lost every bit of hunger that previously gnawed at his insides. His mind was too preoccupied to think about eating that garbage. In a burst of frustration, he flung the bowl onto the ground, spilling the contents and turning the virgin snow a pale shade of green.

"What's the big idea? I would've eaten that!" a voice abruptly called out. Samuel turned and caught a glimpse of his valet, sitting with a bowl that was devoid of any content.

"I apologize. I didn't see you there."

"Don't feel bad, no one ever does," he said, chuckling. "You seem upset again, what's wrong?"

"It's nothing, forget it."

"I recognize this behavior," the valet replied. Taking a deep breath, Samuel turned around. "You can't go on tormenting yourself. This woman is slowly eating you up inside."

"I can't help it. She's all I ever think about." As the two men spoke, the once crowded hub of Five Points began to thin out as people retreated to start their daily routines. The breakfast line had disappeared, and crowded areas where people congregated became barren. All that remained were the resilient children playing in the snow and the permanent fixture of the homeless that lined the sidewalks. It invoked a sense of eeriness and desolation for any person unfortunate enough to remain. Neither man had ever seen the town clear out so fast.

Most of them disappeared when the clouds grew darker, shrouding the sunlight. The winds whipped and the sky groaned overhead, but neither one noticed the thin hooded apparition that watched them diligently from a short distance away.

As the heavens crackled with unsettled energy, the sun completely extinguished itself, casting a shadow over the entire square, prompting even the children to take refuge. "Maybe we should leave," the valet suggested, noticing the sudden change in weather. Samuel wasn't paying much attention. He'd become transfixed on the towering hooded dark figure. A long black cloak flowed to the ground, engulfing the rest of its form. No facial features or extremities were visible, just the impending sense of despair that he began to feel. It overpowered him swiftly and without remorse, paralyzing him with fear.

As the wind blew harder, each gust rustled the apparition's cloak, causing it to dance an unearthly waltz. But the figure remained still.

"Yes, I think you're right," Samuel replied, locking his gaze upon the dark entity. "Let's get out of here."

As the two men began their quick departure to their awaiting carriage, the once motionless figure began to glide a few inches above the Earth towards their direction with unnatural grace and elegance. Samuel grabbed the valet's forearm and pointed in frozen terror.

"Jimmy, do you see it?" he asked in a trembling voice. "What the hell is that?" The valet looked in the direction that Samuel motioned, but saw nothing other than a single stray dog wading through a thick pile of snow.

"I think it's a Dalmatian."

"I'm talking about that *thing* coming towards us," he whispered, hoping whatever it was wouldn't hear him. "It's just like in my dreams." Jimmy looked again but saw nothing.

"I don't know what you're talking about, Sam. There's nothing there. Look, maybe we should go see Dr. McCabe. You haven't been yourself lately." Samuel released Jimmy's arm from his grip and took a few steps backward. "What has gotten into you?" Samuel remained speechless as the figure continued its approach. The pungent odor of rotting flesh wafted around Samuel as he fought back the urge to vomit, inducing a flurry of dry heaves. As the apparition slowed to a complete stop approximately six inches from his face, its hot breath erupted from its faceless void.

"Help Jimmy!" he pleaded, looking in his valet's direction.

"No one can help you," the apparition said. "You can only help yourself." Its voice resembling an otherworldly echo that mirrored the sound of broken glass. "Listen closely. Your object of affection, the one you call Alice, is threatening to unravel everything we've worked for. It is through her companion, a man named Richard, and his friend, Eddie, that this will occur. They all must be stopped. You know what you need to do."

"I don't think I understand. I'm only—"

"You don't need to understand," the figure continued. "You just need to stop them. Dispose of Eddie and Richard, and only then will Alice be yours. That is your reward."

The figure stood perfectly still and waited for a response.

"I don't know if I'm capable of something like that," Samuel spoke up.

"That is of no concern to me, but if you fail, Eddie and Richard's fate will be your own. Do you understand?"

"What fate?" he asked. The moment the words left his lips, a blinding flash ripped through. The apparition was gone as quickly as it had arrived, leaving him alone in the courtyard with Jimmy, who repeatedly called his name. Finally, Samuel snapped out of it.

"Yes, I hear you," he called out.

"It looked as if you had drifted away for a moment. Why don't we go see that doctor?"

"No doctors. I have work to do."

Nineteen

"Where are we going?" Richard asked as he and Alice continued down a long unpaved roadway.

"I'm not sure. I kind of figured we'd keep walking until we find somewhere interesting."

Richard didn't care for the answer. They could feasibly walk for days until something happened. "Well, what if we don't find anything interesting?"

Alice smiled. "Then we just keep walking until we do."

"That doesn't sound like much of a plan."

"I prefer just to see where the world takes me," she replied. "Besides, where else do you have to go?"

They continued down the narrow street until it widened into grand structures. With the dilapidated buildings behind them, they continued on. Richard slowed as they approached a familiar location. He studied the front of Stockton's mansion, wondering if Eddie was inside. Alice turned when she noticed her companion had lagged behind. "Are you coming?"

"I know the people that live here. I stayed a few nights ago, but I think I'm no longer welcome."

She paused and looked up at the house. "You never told me what happened to that friend you were with last night."

"Does it matter?" he asked, looking towards her.

"I think it does. So who was he?"

"He was somebody I *thought* was my friend. But he abandoned me the first chance he got. Is that a good enough explanation?

"It's a start," Alice replied. "But I want more information. What's his name?" Richard sighed. "His name is..." A door flew open behind them, and Dr. Melton darted out. He looked disheveled and distressed.

"Don't go in there!" the doctor shouted, running down the short flight of marble steps and showing no apparent consideration for Richard as he pushed him out of the way. "He's gone crazy, I tell you!"

"Who has?" Alice asked.

"Who do you think? It's Timothy! He's completely lost his mind!"

Stockton's valet appeared in the doorway, calling for the doctor. "Where do you think you're going?"

"Anywhere but here!" he shouted back. "He's possessed by the devil himself!"

"I need your help! Come back!" the valet shouted, but it was too late. The doctor was already walking briskly down the sidewalk, ignoring the valet's pleas.

From a side alleyway, two blocks down the street, Samuel spied on Alice and Richard silently while the doctor disappeared into the distance. He planned to approach them, but the sudden interruption sidelined his agenda. What he'd concocted was simple enough. He was to pretend a chance run-in with them, after which he would play tag-along until the time was right to strike.

He watched his opportunity disappear into the front door of the Stockton mansion. His chance was gone, for now. He decided to knock on the door as he slowly approached the front marble steps.

And after walking up the stairs, he held the heavy solid gold knocker in his hand, ready to slam it down when a voice from behind startled him.

"Excuse me, sir?" Samuel spun around to see a young man standing at the bottom of the stairs. "I'm Grant, Mr. Stockton's business partner. I'm assuming you're here to see him."

"Oh, I'm sorry. Where are my manners? I'm Samuel," he said nervously, extending a handshake.

"Yes," Grant replied. "I think I know you. I was just admiring your work the other day."

"Well, I always appreciate a compliment."

"Timothy is pleased with his latest purchase," Grant smiled. "You're a fine artist, indeed. I'm also an art collector and would be interested as a buyer if the price is right, of course."

"I'm confident you could afford it," he answered, hoping to end the conversation. "Well, it looks like we both have business here, so don't let me hold you up any longer," Grant replied. Samuel turned from Grant and looked at the grand doorway for a moment before slamming the knocker against the large oak structure.

As the two men waited, the abrasive sound of a struggle echoed from inside the house, and a loud crash came, accompanied by a piercing scream.

"My God, did you hear that?" Samuel asked.

"Yes I did, excuse me." Grant quickly pushed past the artist and threw the door open to see Stockton pinned on the ground by Richard. He noticed an unidentified man and the valet lying on the floor, unconscious next to each other, while Alice knelt in a corner screaming hysterically. Grant hurried to the bloodied valet.

"What happened here?"

"Forget about him!" Richard yelled. "Get over here and help me!"

As he tried to subdue Stockton, the young man's strength became too much for Richard, and he pushed him off with ease. Stockton quickly got to his feet and grabbed a nearby vase from one of the marble tables, and began to swing it frantically in all directions.

"What do you want me to do?" Grant asked. "I've never seen him like this before!" Stockton paused for a moment to eye his confronters. Richard and Grant stood on guard and waited for his attack. Samuel hung back a safe distance, hoping Stockton would take care of Richard for him. It would certainly make it a lot easier to claim the prize he was promised.

Bethany and Charlie stepped outside from the recluse cottage. The snow was deeper than they'd expected, and with Charlie feeling better, they decided to risk going to the festival.

As they began their short journey, they noticed Dr. Melton frantically attempting to enter his office down the block. After dropping his keys several times, he finally looked over at the couple, calming down a few degrees. He smiled as they approached.

"Oh, well, it looks as if my advice has worked," he said and nodded. "You sure seem like you're doing better young man."

"Yes, he is," Bethany replied. "And thank you for all your help earlier."

"Just doing my job," he said with a shaky tone.

"Are you all right, doctor?" Charlie asked, taking note of Dr. Melton's vibrating hands. "You seem nervous."

"Oh, yes, I'm quite all right. I just left a house-call over at Tim Stockton's place, and things got a bit out of hand, that's all."

"We were there last night, weren't we darling?"

"Yes," Bethany replied, quickly dismissing Charlie. "May I ask what happened?"

"Oh, nothing for you to worry about. I'm sure that the man Timothy attacked will be quite fine." The doctor looked in the air. "Yes, I'm certain he wasn't dead."

"Oh no," she said, turning to Charlie. "What if it's Eddie?"

"Yes! That was his name," Dr. Melton said. "At least that's what I think they were calling him."

Charlie spoke up. "Would you please forget about this Eddie fellow, your relationship with him has ended. I took him for everything he had, twice, and the man just came back for more. He has no idea when to quit. Now would you please just leave well enough alone?"

Bethany thought for a moment. "So what if I do?"

"I beg your pardon?"

"I said, so what if I do still have feelings for him?" she asked. "I mean, just because we are no longer together doesn't mean I can just completely forget about him."

"You can't be serious!"

"Maybe I am," she said, turning to the doctor. "Are you sure this man's name was Eddie?"

"Yes, I'm quite certain. As I said, that's what the other men were calling him."

"Thank you," Bethany announced her gratitude towards the doctor and quickly addressed Charlie. "You can stay here if you want, but I'm notifying the police. And then I'm going over there to see what happened.

"My God, I'm not staying here, not when there's a lively festival going on just up the street," he said, watching Bethany hail down a passing carriage. "Darling, what are you doing?"

"What do you think? You can go to your festival, but you already know where I'm going."

"Just hold on!" he shouted, swiftly walking over to the carriage and pulling the folded stairs down to ground level.

"I am aware it's not my place to get involved," Dr. Melton said. "But you might want to reconsider your decision. According to my eye witness account, this Timothy fellow has completely flipped his lid. I strongly advise against going over there."

"I appreciate your concern, doctor," Bethany replied, "but I think we'll take our chances."

"We will?" Charlie asked. "Now wait just a minute. Maybe we should listen to what he's saying. If Stockton *has* gone crazy, maybe it's best if we just stay out of it."

Bethany dismissed Charlie and quickly ordered the valet to take them to the Stockton mansion. After jolting him back, the carriage promptly accelerated down the cobblestone road as he cursed under his breath.

Stockton held his ground. "Are you just going to stand over there watching, or are you going to help us?" Richard asked Samuel.

Richard hadn't thought much of the artist when they'd met earlier, and now his feelings were reinforced. The last thing Samuel wanted was to help his target, but he also didn't want to appear un-heroic in the presence of his love interest, so he slowly made his way over to Richard and Grant. Eddie and the valet remained motionless on the floor.

"What can I possibly do?" Samuel asked. Richard looked around the room at Stockton's vast collection of medieval weaponry and spotted several devices that could assist him.

Stockton looked at the men and smiled wide, showing his pearly browns. "It's alright, I'm fine now," he said, turning away and putting the vase back on the table. Carefully, he lifted a medieval dagger off the display rack and concealed it behind his back. He then turned to face Richard and Samuel and Grant.

"My God, Timothy, what happened to you?" Grant inquired. "You had us scared out of our skin."

"Something I must have eaten. But really, I'm much better now," he said with another odd grin. Samuel began to walk away after the realization that Stockton wouldn't be finishing the job.

"Where do you think you're going?" Richard asked. A groan sounded across the room, and he turned to see Eddie struggling to his feet.

"See, he's fine, nothing to worry about now," Samuel said, staring blankly at Richard.

"He's right, you should listen to Samuel," Stockton announced, walking over to Samuel. He put a hand on his left shoulder and muttered quietly, "We will finish this."

Samuel instinctively knew what he meant and nodded. He recognized the same dark entity that hovered behind Stockton as the one that visited him earlier at Five Points. The thing kept itself close to Stockton as if to protect him and guarantee the disposal of Eddie and Richard. "We are in this together," Stockton assured him, glancing at the painting on the wall that Samuel had finished for him just a week prior.

Richard appeared apprehensive. He tried to ignore the painting on the wall and focus his energy on a resolution, but the longer he avoided its hypnotic glow, the more drawn he became. He began to feel the same murderous urges that Stockton and Samuel experienced. Eddie had done him wrong, but never would he purposely want to cause harm to the man. The painting continued its transient brainwash on Richard, and he slowly became unaware of his surroundings. It spoke to him through airy breaths. "Kill. Kill Eddie. Kill yourself."

Just when he was about to cease fighting the tranquil voice and give in to temptation, a wayward hand gripped him by the arm and broke the trance. Richard found himself in Samuel's grasp and peering into Stockton's hollow soul. Stockton smiled and raised the glistening dagger blade in the air. Richard closed his eyes tight and awaited his fate. He could hear the faint screams in the background as his ears rang. A jolt, then he crashed to the ground.

Is it over? He wondered. *Am I dying?*

He slowly opened his eyes and looked down to where the dagger should have been, but his chest and gut remained unharmed. No blood. No pain. He did notice Alice on top of him, however. "Stay down," she whispered. "He missed you, but someone else wasn't as lucky." Richard looked up from the ground to see a very distraught Stockton still holding the bloody dagger that protruded from Samuel's wrecked chest.

As he looked to the front door of the mansion, where the dark translucent figure stood and watched, he attempted a step. But his legs didn't answer, and he collapsed head-first onto the hard surface. Everything around him then grew dim and faded away. Stockton remained still, holding his devilish gaze upon Richard and Alice.

As Samuel crawled towards the front door, he left a trail of blood that stretched across the once pristine marble floor. The echo of his agonizing pain is all that was heard. As his screams became louder, he acquired a piercing ring inside his eardrum that grew louder with each second.

Eddie's blurred vision had dissipated, and his senses improved. Unable to helplessly watch the sickening display any longer, he staggered to help the stranger, almost slipping on pools of blood as he stumbled across the large room.

Gore spurted with every pulse tick as the dagger remained embedded in Samuel, painting crimson red brush strokes across the white door. While he struggled to his feet, he grasped the doorknob for support as he witnessed his muscles collapse and unconsciousness set in. He then slumped to the ground, silent and still.

As Eddie approached Samuel, he understood the dagger needed to be removed quickly, or the man wouldn't live. As he grasped the ivory handle and began to tug slowly, the door unexpectedly swung open just as he pulled the dagger from the body. A flood of daylight entered the darkened room that revealed Bethany, along with Charlie and one of New York's finest, standing in the doorway.

Eddie remained on the floor, bloodied knife in hand. As he looked up, his eyes fixated quickly on Bethany, then on the officer and the louse? "Wait! He's not dead. I was trying to save him!" Eddie yelled.

"He looks dead to me," the officer replied. As Eddie glanced down at Samuel, it became clear that the cop was right. The man's eyes remained open, yet no breath existed. Training his eyes back to the police, he became aware that he was kneeling over a dead body, holding an incriminating murder weapon.

"Put your hands in the air!" yelled the officer, drawing his pistol on Eddie and aiming it directly between his eyes. Startled, Eddie swiftly threw his hands up. "Drop the weapon now!" he yelled once again, this time cocking the hammer with a loud click. The dagger dropped to the floor and landed directly at Bethany's feet. She gasped and gripped Charlie for support when she recognized the corpse on the floor as the man who had painted her portrait. And now, she knew that asking him about its bizarre transformation was out of the question.

"You're under arrest! Put your hands behind your back!"

"But I didn't do anything!" Eddie pleaded. "This isn't what it looks like. I swear."

"This is your last chance! Put your hands behind your back, or I *will* shoot!"

"No!" Bethany screamed. "Don't hurt him!" She instantaneously stood between the officer's gun and Eddie.

"Ma'am, you need to move out of the way."

"Darling, what in the hell are you doing?" Charlie asked, grabbing her wrist and pulling her out of harm's way. Surprised, Eddie looked at both Charlie and Bethany.

"Wait, did you just call her darling?"

"Indeed I did," Charlie announced, grabbing Bethany around the waist.

Eddie sighed. "Please tell me it isn't so." As he rose to his feet, he slowly felt his breathing increase.

"That's far enough! Put your hands behind your back! Or would you like me to do it for you?" Deep down, Eddie felt something inside snap and he lunged at the louse. But before he could carry out his malice intentions, the swift arm of the law interfered, knocking him to the ground with a forceful blow to the face. Down he went, hitting his head on the doorframe and landing directly on top of Samuel's lifeless body. Bethany screamed as the officer rammed a bony knee into his back and subdued him tightly with archaic steel handcuffs, restricting his circulation.

"You're going to hang for this," the officer said with a raspy voice. As Eddie relented, he peered up to see Richard, Alice, Grant, and Stockton staring down at him.

As angry as Richard was with Eddie, he wasn't about to let him go to prison for something Stockton did.

"Excuse me, officer," Richard spoke up.

"It'll have to wait," the officer grumbled.

"No, this can't wait." Richard quickly recapped the entire scenario, explaining what really happened.

Grant, having much to lose, understood that if Stockton went to jail, their whole business partnership would be over. It could also mean scandal and bankruptcy. He wasn't about to take that chance.

"If I may intervene for a moment, that's not how I saw it," Grant said. "This man broke in through an upstairs window, and Timothy caught him in the act. The two men you see on the floor were doing their best to protect him from this man's attack," he added, pointing at Eddie.

The officer glanced at Stockton. "Is any of this true?"

"Of course it is. As my business partner has already confirmed, these deceased men were friends of mine and were simply defending me from these two thieves."

"This is ridiculous!" Richard shouted. "Stockton is the one who went crazy and killed these men. We were just trying to subdue him and keep him from causing any more harm."

"Well, one of you is lying, and so far, it's two against one," the officer said, pulling Eddie to his feet.

"No, it's not," Alice interrupted, walking from the shadows, drying her tear-soaked eyes with a white-laced handkerchief. She looked at herself in an oval-shaped pocket mirror and sighed. "I apologize for my appearance as I tend to be overly emotional at times."

"Wait a minute. Who are you?" the officer asked.

"My name's Alice. I was here the whole time and can attest to what Richard is saying. Mr. Stockton, for whatever reason, went mad and began attacking everyone around him. He retrieved the dagger from a table over there and proceeded to—"

"This is insulting to stand here and listen to this utter nonsense," Stockton interrupted. "Can't you see I'm being framed, Jonathan?" After Stockton blurted the officer's name, Richard knew they were fucked.

"If I may interrupt for a moment," Officer Jonathan said. "You mentioned something about two thieves, Timothy. What did you mean by that?"

"Well, I found this man in my house a couple of nights ago," Stockton explained, walking over to Richard and gripping him by the collar. "He was skulking around in my upstairs guestrooms. It scared me half to death if I may say so. And because it was so dark and he's disguised with that bandage, I somehow didn't recognize him until now. But yes, it's definitely him."

"Well, out with it," the officer replied, turning to Richard. "Is that how it went down?" The beads of sweat across his forehead trickled down his cheeks. The one thing he'd hoped wouldn't happen had suddenly come to fruition.

"Well, technically it is, but there's a straightforward explanation for why I was in his guestroom."

Stockton laughed. "This should be good."

"I woke up in there," Richard replied.

"That's your explanation?" the officer asked. "I'm afraid you will have to do better than that." Anything Richard said would be his word against Stockton's since there was no proof for either case. He thought quickly.

"Yes, that's right. You see, my reservation was made with Stockton approximately two days prior. I can see how he might have forgotten, though, as he and his wife were just returning from a dinner party, and I could see that his senses were considerably duller than usual due to his alcohol consumption. So as you can see, it was just a simple mix up."

"That is a ludicrous statement. I was out of town for a week and wouldn't have been able to speak with him, or anyone else for that matter until I returned from my trip— which I might add, was earlier that same day I found him creeping around my upstairs."

"I can't believe I'm hearing this," Bethany chimed in. "Mr. Stockton and Eddie are friends and have been for a long time. Why are you doing this to him?" she asked, looking directly into Stockton's blank, emotionless eyes. He said nothing. Instead, he pretended to adjust the time on his pocket watch as if she weren't even in the room.

"All right, Timothy, I think I've heard enough," the officer said while walking over to Richard. "Sir, I need you to turn around and put your hands behind your back." Richard's heart raced. He knew that if he went to prison, he would never get home. Stuck in a cycle like a hyperactive hamster on a wheel.

As much as he wanted to run, Richard knew he was innocent, and as far as he was concerned, justice would prevail. So he played along and did as the officer said. After hearing three loud clicks, and feeling the steel wrap tightly around his flesh, he was secured and handcuffed for the first time in his life. And although he didn't consider this a legitimate arrest, he still felt dehumanized.

"I'm sorry you had to go through all this, Timothy. I will send a message to the coroner and have him see to the bodies. You needn't worry about anything."

"Thank you, Jonathan. I greatly appreciate your kindness. I just hope to never go through anything like this again," Stockton smirked.

"You fucking liar," Eddie grunted, feeling the rage fester in his body.

"That's enough," demanded the officer. "Or I'll slap you with another charge—language unbecoming of a gentleman."

"Is that a real charge?" Richard asked Alice.

"I'm afraid so."

"Alright, enough talk. Let's go down to the station." The officer gripped Eddie and Richard under their arms and hauled them out the door. Stockton watched as the men were loaded into the back of a horse-drawn prison cell. He tried his best to hide the joy, but a small grin broke across his face.

Alice lowered her voice. "You won't get away with this. I promise you that."

"Promise me anything you want, my dear," Stockton replied in the same low tone. "But if you don't get off my property within ten seconds, I'll physically throw you off myself."

"That's bullshit. I know you won't."

"Oh my, what language from such a lovely young woman," Stockton said, concentrating on the familiar jewelry that hung elegantly from her ears. "Just one more thing before you leave. Those emerald earrings you are wearing belong to my wife. So you should consider yourself lucky to be thrown out of here, instead of taking a ride with your friends. I don't tolerate thieves."

"They're mine. Stop making unscrupulous accusations."

"Wrong, I know they aren't yours," Stockton continued, "because I purchased them while on vacation in India. As I see it, you have two options. The first would be to give them to me and walk out of here, no questions asked. The second, well, let's just say you wouldn't like the second option very much.

"Well, maybe she misplaced her pair because I bought these a long time ago. So how about you go fuck yourself. The only way you'll get these earrings is to strip me naked and tie me down."

"That sounds like a pleasant offer," he replied, taking a step towards her.

"I'll see myself out." She quickly retrieved her handbag from a suede-lined wooden chair and took one last look at the lifeless bodies that lie on the floor. She didn't say another word while storming outside past Charlie and Bethany.

Stockton glared at the couple one last time and slammed the door.

"It looks like the show is over darling," Charlie said, putting his hand on Bethany's waist, attempting to lure her down the front steps. "How about we leave before anything else happens?" Bethany watched Alice, who was already a half block down the street. Inside, Stockton remained silent as he walked across the room, past Grant, towards his Renaissance throne located to the right of the fireplace. He sat down slowly, contently, and gazed into the painting.

Twenty

Richard and Eddie were booked at the station, and each put in a separate solitary cell. Thankfully, they were side by side, so they at least had company. The rats didn't count, nor did the cockroaches or spiders that seemed to appear without warning. The place was a lot bigger than Richard had thought. For some reason, he imagined an old Wild West type of prison with approximately two or three cells per jail. This was nothing like that. The sheer size of the prison had overwhelmed him when they entered the general population area. It reminded him of a wagon wheel, with a central hub, and each row of cells spoked out in multiple directions.

Prison guards stood along the rafters, desensitized to the echoing screams and moans of inmates in the distance. The howls tore through the rafters as Richard listened to their agony, locked away behind a cage of crazy.

Both men cringed at the crippling odor that reminded them of rancid meat simmering on a hot summer day. It caused Richard's stomach to turn the instant he entered. Because a phone call was out of the question, his first request was a tall glass of water and something to eat, hoping it would cure the nausea, to which he was promptly informed he would get something when they felt like giving it to him. At least they remained in their street clothes for the time being, and neither man had to hand over any possessions. He was grateful for that because his book of poems was something he refused to part with.

It was still the most important thing he had in the world, and he'd be damned to let any of these prison guards get their grimy hands on it. He clutched it tightly in the cell, wishing for home more than ever.

They were imprisoned on level two, row six. When the bars clanged shut behind Richard, and the sound of the key locking the cell rang out, he stood entirely still for well over ten minutes, recoiling from the hollowed screams that surrounded him. And for a moment, he considered the possibility that this was all just a very vivid nightmare.

Richard and Eddie were separated when they'd first arrived, and neither one thought they'd see the other anytime soon, except maybe in the mess hall, or the courtyard. Richard wondered if they even had courtyards in 1831 prisons. He'd been in his cell for well over an hour when the sound of bars clanging rung out. Eddie then appeared, shuffling into the vacant cell next to his. Richard was glad to see him. Through all the disruption that had occurred, he'd almost forgotten who Eddie really was. But as he felt the book's solid binding beneath his coat, it came rushing back. All of the animosity he'd felt towards Eddie in the mansion and in the presence of the painting dissolved, and he was thankful because it went against his nature.

He was grateful to see Eddie, but even the fact that he was practically sharing a cell with Edgar Allan Poe was hardly a consolation or a—

Richard had a harsh realization. Poe never spent time in prison. It would've been documented, and Richard would have read about it in the history books.

He wracked his brain, trying to remember hearing anything about it. There was no memory of it because, as Richard remembered, Poe never went to prison. But here he was, sitting next to him in a jail cell. Richard then knew that history might've already been severely altered. And not only altered, but Poe might not be remembered as the brilliant writer that he was, just a torrid murderer.

Richard, in this grim reality, could do nothing to help his friend's innocence while locked up. He needed to get out of there as soon as possible.

Richard poked his face between the bars into his friend's cell. "Pssst! Eddie, are you awake?" They'd spoken briefly when Eddie first joined him as a neighbor. But there were too many unanswered questions. Eddie stirred on the tattered cot but didn't respond.

Richard wasn't upset with him for having passed out. After all, it had taken them the better part of the day to reach the prison, not to mention the lengthy booking procedure. He imagined it to be somewhere roughly around eight o'clock at night, as it stood. As Richard's mind wandered, he found himself missing his modern-day conveniences again as he watched the candles burn down on a table next to his cot. Not that it would do him much good in jail, but even modern-day prisoners had access to the internet and television. He found himself paging through his book of poems, searching for the absent signature. Moving it closer to the candlelight, he wasn't surprised that it remained missing.

After deciding to pick up where he left off before falling asleep that fateful night, he glanced through the book, trying to find a familiar page number. Page 32 looked about right. He began to read the clean print, taking short breaks to look over in Eddie's direction periodically. He remained silent and still, except for the occasional snore. It was apparent that Eddie was a beaten man.

He went back to his reading, and was on his second poem when he was snapped out of his concentration by a deep voice that bellowed,

"Lights out!" Richard sat up quickly and almost dropped his book from the initial shock.

"Are you deaf, asshole?" said the voice coming from outside his cell. "Did you not hear me call lights out?"

Richard turned to the metal bars and saw a tall man in the darkness, holding a nightstick and staring directly at him. He wore blue military-type attire that could've been easily mistaken for a Union Civil War uniform.

"I'm sorry," Richard replied. "I didn't know that—"

"Oh, you're sorry? Well, let me tell you something, new fish. You can take your sorry and stick it where the sun don't shine, boy!" The guard raised his nightstick and slammed it hard into the metal bars. Richard jumped to his feet and quickly searched for anything that resembled a light switch.

"What the hell are you doing? It looks like you're not only deaf but stupid! The candles are right next to you. Now, blow them out before I have to come in there and extinguish them with your face."

Richard felt stupid, having momentarily forgotten the complete lack of electricity thing, but he did as instructed and extinguished the three dancing flames. As the candles smoked out, he stood for a moment in the dark, watching the guard, wondering if he could see him.

"It's about time, new fish. From now on, you do what I say when I say it. Understood?"

"Yes. I understand," Richard quickly replied.

"You better. I'll be keeping an eye on you." As the guard slowly walked away, Richard was able to breathe again. Visibly shaken, he walked over to a small round metal table in the corner of his eight-by-ten cell and carefully placed the book on top. He couldn't remember the last time he'd felt so defeated.

***

Stockton remained in the same chair he'd been sitting in all day. He'd been there when the coroner's cleanup crew arrived. He was there as they hauled the bodies off. And he was there when Grant left for the day. Stockton had not moved in hours. Instead, he sat and stared intently at the painting on the wall. It spoke to him. It spoke in ways most people would find objectionable. It had fed him lies, offering fame and power. And somehow, what he once found to be terrifying, he now found comforting.

The dark cloaked figure in the painting assured him that everything was going according to plan, and the circle was practically complete. It reinforced to Stockton how proud it was of him, and how Samuel and the valet were necessary casualties in the grand scheme. It explained how Samuel had now joined them, and was under their protection, his soul cleansed and purified. And through Samuel's artwork, it allowed them access to Earth's realm. The figure even materialized from out of the painting to stand by Stockton's side for a brief time.

He didn't hear Grant say goodbye, nor did he hear the Coroner addressing him or Mrs. Stockton pleading for an answer to her pressing questions. He was outside of himself, in much the same way Samuel had been, practically unaware of his own actions and controlled by something not of this world.

Alice tried her best to concentrate on her performance as Desdemona in Othello. However, the distractions from earlier that day were eating at her. She was forgetting her lines, and it felt like her acting style was wooden, at best. The fact that the theater was packed with five hundred prying pairs of eyes didn't help the situation. She sensed them drilling into her head as she stumbled over each line.

Luckily for her, she didn't see most of the audience members due to the blanket of darkness that shrouded them. The real distraction was the brilliantly lit balconies, where she could see the dignitaries and socialites mocking her performance. Yes, she was sure that's what they were doing as they ate and drank and laughed. The only thing keeping her afloat was her brief improve group training at the local theater back home. And every time she improvised a line, she glanced up at the rafters to review the balcony's reactions, which remained mostly unchanged.

There was something that had changed, however. Behind one of the elegantly dressed socialites stood a figure in black, wearing a hood that obstructed any visible facial features. Unfortunately for her, it was a familiar sight—a sight that she'd seen more than once before and had dreaded every time in the past. This time was no different, as the glaring apparition had proved itself more distracting than anything else in the theater. Next to it, the faint outline of a familiar man hovered. His facial features appeared malformed and twisted, almost unrecognizable.

It was Samuel. She was sure of it. His transparent body floated beside the dark entity, his black eye sockets maliciously locked on Alice. A slice of terror flowed up her spine, and icy cold chills ran through her arms as she became aware of the unsettling truth. Although Samuel had been deceased since earlier that day, he attended her performance after all—just like he had promised.

Alice felt sick as the third act came to an end, and the curtain began to drop. She stole one last glance to the upper balcony, expecting to see the dark figure and Samuel staring at her. But the only things visible were the dignitaries applauding the performance. She squinted to get a clear view but as she focused, the elegant maroon and gold curtain obstructed her perspective as it fell before her eyes, and all that could be heard were thunderous applause from a satisfied crowd. She assumed the claps and cheers weren't for her, but she pretended to accept them as she as the rest of the cast emerged from behind the curtain to take their bow.

She felt like a failure, defeated, as she entered her dressing room, feeling as though she had let the audience down. But as she opened the door, she noticed a large bouquet of twelve long-stemmed red roses on the makeup table. Next to them stood the play's director clapping as she walked in.

"That was wonderful, Alice. Just wonderful!" he said, continuing his applause. She said nothing but forced a fake smile to appease the gentleman.

"Well, thank you," she replied. The director walked over to her and lightly held her delicate hand.

"Here, my dear, you've earned it," he smiled and placed a wad of rolled money in her palm. "Consider this an advance for future performances."

He nodded and left the room, leaving her alone with her money and roses and confusion. As she took a seat in front of the large mirror, she carefully tallied the cash. While approaching the ninety-dollar mark, her heart began to beat rapidly. Ninety-*eight, ninety-nine...one-hundred-dollars.*

Maybe she wasn't as bad as she'd thought. She placed the money in her handbag and caught a glimpse of herself in the mirror. Her shimmered hair fell neatly over her shoulders, and the dark crimson dress she wore accentuated her natural ruby lips and curvaceous figure. The dangling emerald earrings didn't match the rest of her attire, but it didn't matter because she never removed them for personal reasons.

After she stood and retrieved the roses from the table, she noticed a familiar reflection in the mirror close behind her. Horrified, she dropped the roses onto the floor, but she couldn't scream, and she couldn't move. A shrill inaudible voice echoed off the walls of her room. Alice took a deep breath and turned sharply to confront the figure, but it was gone.

Twenty-One

The next morning, Richard woke to the pleasant aroma of rank vomit. While trying to remember where he was, he sat up in his cot and looked around the cell, wiping the sleep from his eyes. At least it had been the best night of sleep he'd had since arriving. Eddie was sitting in his cell, eating what appeared to be some kind of scrapple from a large metal plate.

"Look who's awake," Eddie said over a mouthful of food. "It appears you might have missed breakfast."

"I don't even care. I just need something to drink. Ever have a serious case of cottonmouth?" he asked, reaching up and touching his tongue.

"I'm not quite sure I follow what you mean. But if you're thirsty," Eddie said, pointing to a tall metal glass on the small round table, "that glass of water over there might be just the thing you need to cure this so-called 'cotton mouth' of yours." When Richard noticed the book of poems sitting next to the water, he breathed a sigh of relief.

"You have no idea how dehydrated I am," he replied, jumping off the cot and rushing to the water as if he were approaching a finish line. The water had a cloudy brown appearance. He almost put it back on the table, but his thirst won the battle.

He downed it in one swift gulp, and when he finished, the awful metallic and stagnant aftertaste caused him to shutter impulsively. Eddie noticed his face and managed a smile.

"Not as good as you would have hoped, I assume."

"No, it's pretty awful." Richard shuttered once more and placed the empty glass on the table. After staring at it a moment more, he had a brief realization.

"Is this made of lead?"

"What else would it be?"

Richard paused. "Of course it is. Right now, we have to concentrate on getting out of here. Neither of us belongs here. You know that, and I know that, but we need to convince everyone else of that."

"That's impossible," Eddie replied. "We are both doomed men. You will probably spend multiple years here, and I will...well, let's just say I will probably not live to see the spring sun." Eddie hung his head at the sound of his own words. "And that is one of the reasons why I want to come clean about something."

"Look, Eddie..."

"I feel terrible about what I did, but you *do* have to realize that I consider you a friend. So let me just start by saying that I would like to apologize for running off like I did yesterday. It was wrong of me. Secondly, I took this from you before I left." Eddie pulled a twenty-dollar bill from his black vest. "You were still sleeping and it had fallen halfway out of your pocket, just visible enough for me to see it."

"And you just decide to steal everything you happen to see?" Richard asked. In light of this new information, he felt betrayed even more than he had before. It was, after all, indirectly Eddie's fault that he was sitting in a prison cell.

"I know, but it sounds worse than it is. I was simply borrowing the money to help with my new book's publishing costs. Having raised one-hundred and seventy dollars before leaving West Point was helpful, but not adequate."

"Wait a minute. Do you mean to tell me you had that much money on you? I thought you lost everything to the louse."

"I did lose everything. That money was given to me by several cadets during my last week at the school. Each donated seventy-five-cents to my publishing venture, which I have the money set aside for. And to answer your question, I don't have it on me. It's tucked inside my suitcase in Stockton's parlor." Eddie trailed off toward the end of the sentence after hearing his own words. "But in any case, I do have something for you, Richard. It's not much, but hopefully, it will ease your will to accept my apology. Just take a look at the inside cover of your book."

Richard carefully lifted the book off the table and opened the front cover to reveal a brilliantly written signature, identical in location and style to the original. It surprised him so much that he almost dropped it on the floor.

"I noticed it was sitting on your table this morning," Eddie continued, "so I requested a pen and ink from one of the guards. He complied, as you can see, but I've given up any kind of visiting rights or courtyard activities for one month, according to him. But I think it was worth it. I also want you to have this back." Eddie studied the money one last time before handing it to his friend through the bars. Richard tried his best to stay mad, but he couldn't. Eddie's kind gesture had softened his heart and his will.

"Thanks, Eddie...for everything. No hard feelings, okay?"

"Never," he said softly as he moved to the center of his cell and took a seat on an uncomfortable wooden chair.

Neither man said a word for minutes. Eddie stared at the floor, and Richard continued to admire the newly inscribed signature.

Richard broke their silence. "I have a question. Why call yourself Eddie if your name is Edgar?"

He thought for a moment. "Well, it's really quite simple. I prefer the name. One of my childhood peers began calling me Eddie, and it stuck. I only use my legal Christian name for my published books and signing of legal documents." Eddie remained silent for a moment, hesitant to reveal what was on his mind but ultimately proceeded. "Now I have a question for you, Richard. I know I may not deserve an explanation, but that twenty-dollar bill is not quite—"

"Yes, I know what you're going to ask," Richard said, pulling the tender from his pocket. "I figured you probably noticed that."

"Well, it's a bit difficult not to notice something like that, especially when there's a printed date of 2016 on the bottom. What is even more confusing to me is that I observed a portrait of Andrew Jackson, which would be correct considering he's our current president, but nothing else is consistent."

Richard took a deep breath and looked at the bill, then at Eddie. "Well, it's going to be difficult to explain. Let me say that much."

"That's all right because I'm tired of guessing. I've been studying that money since it's been in my possession, and I can't come to any conclusion. It's quite baffling to me."

"I can imagine it would be," Richard whispered while examining the note.

"But it's not just the money. The clothes you were wearing when I met you, and that odd contraption that you possess. None of it makes any sense," Eddie said calmly, rising to his feet.

"You mean this contraption?" Richard managed a smile and pulled his smartphone from his pocket. Eddie quickly walked over to get a closer look at it. He'd never seen anything like it and stumbled backward a few steps when Richard flashed the LED screen to life. His wallpaper was an old picture of his wife and him that was taken during happier times on a trip to the Boston area. It had been on his phone since before she left, and he still couldn't bring himself to remove it.

He held the phone up for Eddie, revealing the glowing image, and realizing how tired he was of hiding his secret.

"No," Eddie yelped. "Get that black magic away from me!"

"Don't be so dramatic," Richard said and laughed. It was amusing to wield the kind of power that caused people to tremble before him. "Look, Eddie, there's nothing magical about this thing. It's just an ordinary phone, see?" Eddie took another step backward and studied the picture."

"How did you and that woman get inside there?" he asked.

"That would be too complicated to explain, but I can assure you there's absolutely no magic involved," Richard said, putting the phone back in his pocket. "It's nothing more than a piece of technology. Too advanced, I'm afraid, for you to understand. But don't feel bad, because I don't even understand how it works. I just know that it does."

"How do I know what your saying is true?"

"Well, you're just going to have to trust me. Believe me when I say I'm just as confused as you are. I don't even know what I'm doing here!" he yelled, feeling the frustration mount just as an unfamiliar voice broke through.

"Hey! Keep it down in there!" the guard shouted. "Unless you want to spend the next two days in the crypts." Richard didn't know what the crypts were, but he was sure he didn't want to find out.

"What do you mean you don't know what you're doing here? You were framed Richard, just as I was."

"No, I didn't mean here in prison. I meant here in 1831. I'm not exactly from...this century. I'm not even from the next one either. I fell asleep one night with your...I mean, *a* book on my lap, and I somehow woke up in one of Stockton's guestrooms. I'm completely alone and confused."

"You mean that really happened? I thought you made it up!"

Richard took a deep breath and shook his head. "All right, here goes nothing."

***

It took Richard two hours to explain everything, starting in the bookstore, and ending with him sitting in a prison cell. He didn't tell him everything, leaving out specific details about the book and the signature and the destiny of Edgar Allan Poe as a writer. He allowed Eddie to retain the notion that he was just an ordinary man, struggling to make his way in the world, leaving out any personal information.

He remained eerily silent for most of the explanation and listened with enthusiasm, occasionally nodding. When Richard finished, he studied Eddie's expressions, attempting to get a grasp on what he might be thinking.

"That is probably the most outrageous story I've ever heard," Eddie finally said. "But, I believe you. Under normal circumstances, I would tell you that you probably belong in an insane asylum, but I've seen the proof. I can't deny it."

"Believe me, everything is true."

"So, what is 2016 like?" Eddie asked anxiously. "That thing you call a phone, what is it used for exactly?"

"Well, I'm actually from 2021, but the phone is—"

"Hey, fish!" Richard turned to notice a hulking guard waiting on the other side of the cell. Alice stood with him. "Looks like someone took pity on you," the guard called out. "Congratulations! You've made bail! And you, Mr. Edgar A. Poe. The judge is waiting to see you. You've got thirty seconds to get yourself together!" The guard unlocked Richard and Eddie's cell doors and opened them wide. Eddie quickly jumped up and proceeded to slip his black lace-less shoes into place while Richard retrieved his book, exiting into cellblock six's central area. Eddie soon joined them after being handcuffed, and they proceeded down the long corridor accompanied by the guard.

The groans of other inmates continued to bounce off the walls of the facility. Richard was glad to be leaving, but he felt bad for Eddie, who might be spending quite a while there. "Try and keep your spirits up, Eddie, and don't let them break you down. We'll get you out of here as soon as possible," he assured him.

"I hope so."

"We have to."

As the quartet approached the main entrance, the guard turned and slapped his goliath hand on Richard's shoulder. "The warden will process your release, fish. And don't you be wandering too far away now, you hear? The judge is going to want to see you too. Real soon," he said and smirked.

Richard was processed while Alice anxiously awaited their exit. They were both accompanied to the front gate before having it slam behind, leaving them by the side of a sprawling dirt road. There was nothing on either side except for vast fields of dried up grass, which seemed to go on for miles.

He'd only been behind bars for one night, but it felt much longer. Time seemed to stand still in that place. Within one day, the snow had already begun to melt as the sun looked down, leaving large puddles of mud as a reminder of the storm. The temperature seemed to be lingering around the sixty-degree mark, and he even heard some birds chirping, welcoming him back. Richard studied the overwhelming stretch of road.

"Alice, how are we supposed to get out of here?"

"Hmm, I'm not sure."

"What do you mean?" he asked. "How did you get here?"

"I hitched a ride on a carriage that was traveling this way. The gentleman was very generous for letting me come along, and told me he'd even wait for us."

"Well, apparently, he decided not to."

She laughed. "You wanted freedom, Richard. It looks like you've got it."

"Maybe we shouldn't walk on the road," he suggested. "I would hate to see your shoes ruined by the mud.

"The grass might be just as bad. Take your pick." He admired Alice as she glowed in the sun. Even standing next to a crummy dirt road, she looked gorgeous.

"Thank you for getting me out of there," he said, extending his hand as a gesture of appreciation.

She rolled her eyes. "Put your hand away. We're not closing a business deal here. And you're very welcome. I couldn't just let an innocent man rot away in a place like that." She began walking along the left side of the road, carefully examining the dead grass to avoid the puddles.

"But what are we going to do about Eddie? Why did you bail me out and not him?"

"We'll talk about that later."

"We should probably talk about it now."

"I told you, we'll talk about it later," she called back to him. "Are you coming, or are you just going to stand there?"

"Yes, I just think that maybe there's an easier way out of here than this."

"Trust me, there isn't. I know you're not used to walking anywhere with your fancy automobiles and such, but we'll just have to suck it up and deal with it for now." Richard ran to catch up with Alice. "I don't know what you're talking about," he said quietly. "What's an automobile?"

"Wow, you're a worse liar than I thought," she said, eyeing him. "Look, Richard, you don't have to play games with me. I told you already I know all about you. You're just fortunate that I was lucky enough to get the money for your bail. Otherwise, you'd still be sitting back there in shit-block six, mister."

"Well, I appreciate it, but we still need to do something about Eddie."

"I sympathize with your friend's predicament, but I'm afraid we have more pressing matters to address right now."

"I can't just leave him in there. You don't understand how important this is."

"All right fine," she said reluctantly. "Well, I've spent almost everything getting you out. If we're planning to spring Eddie, we're going to need a lot more money."

Richard stopped walking. "I have an idea."

Twenty-Two

"Guilty!" The judge's mallet slammed against the large wooden slab with finality. "You will hang from the neck until you are dead for the murder of Samuel Demone and Robert Baker!" he called out. "The sentence will commence on the twenty-fifth of March, in this year of our Lord, 1831. You are to be remanded to this facility until the execution is carried out—and may God have mercy on your soul."

Eddie wanted to direct several obscenities toward the judge, but he couldn't talk. The courtroom became smaller as his vision pinpricked, and his breathing lessoned. He lost consciousness as the guards gripped him under the arms, handcuffing him into place. One of the guards escorted him a grand total of two paces before he collapsed to the concrete floor.

Richard and Alice had walked nearly five hours before they reached the town square. He'd never been so happy to see the Hotel Majestic and the Skinned Calf come into view. The square that once bustled with an overflow of festivalgoers, drinking their swill and spending their hard-earned cash, was eerily desolate and practically devoid of any people, save for a lone straggler on the Calf's open porch sipping a flask, and a young couple that walked hand and hand from the entrance of Sid's Blacksmith and Barley shop.

Due to the location of the sun, Richard figured it was somewhere in the late afternoon, an assumption that was verified by the giant clock next to the Calf, which read half-past three. In the time it took them to travel back, not a single carriage that passed had offered to help. They tried to offer money and even pleaded, but no one cared or listened. It was a humbling experience, but it allowed them to get to know each other.

Alice remained tight-lipped as to how she knew as much about Richard as she did, but he continued to chip away at her for information, and her resistance had begun to wear thin. Richard was more open than she was and explained his days as a professor, his failed marriage, and his love for literature. He also clarified his elaborate plan to bust Eddie from the clink, which was actually far from elaborate and consisted solely of breaking into Stockton's house for the necessary funds. But the question of how they were to proceed was still undecided. One thing was for sure, he was much more comfortable with Alice after their five-hour bonding session than he grasped. It reminded him of how he felt the first time he'd met Emily. But the last thing he needed now was allowing some silly schoolboy crush to cloud his judgment. Even as he attempted to keep it as unobvious as possible, Alice caught him catching glances of her from the corner of her eye but decided to save him the embarrassment.

They walked further into town and approached several saloons. "So would you like to grab a quick drink?" she asked, looking up at the

Skinned Calf's sizeable wooden sign. "I think I could use one after that long hike."

"I thought we were going to Stockton's?"

"Oh, come on, Richard. We can't just walk into his place and rob him."

"We aren't robbing him. Like I explained, we're simply reclaiming Eddie's suitcase from the living room area."

"Fine, but we're still going to need a plan, right? So let's go in here, get a drink, and we'll discuss it over a warm buzz."

Richard hesitated when Alice began walking toward the porch area. "I don't think I'm allowed back in there."

Alice stopped and looked at him. "What do you mean?"

"It's kind of a long story. I was thrown out a few nights ago for something stupid, so we should probably find somewhere else to go."

"Don't worry about it," she insisted. "I know these guys well and as long as you're with me, you'll be fine." She walked briskly up the steps and greeted the man on the porch by name. It was apparent that everyone knew her. Richard watched her disappear through the doorway and into the darkness. Reluctantly, he followed her.

They decided on a table next to the grand piano in the far left corner of the room. The tavern was mostly empty, but they were still careful not to let anyone overhear them. Richard quickly assessed the area. No bouncers. Good.

As he sat back and looked around the room, he began to admire the structural integrity of the bar and the handcrafted woodworking.

"There's nothing like this where I come from," he said. Alice nodded and poured herself a second shot. "Don't you think you should take it easy?"

"I don't think you need to worry about it."

"I think I do, especially if we're going to work together. And I'm also going to need some questions answered."

Alice opened a silver case and retrieved a hand-rolled cigarette. She struck a match and lit it, inhaling deeply. "Fine, what kind of questions do you have?"

"Well, like I already asked, how do you know so much about me?"

Alice pondered the question for a moment before quickly downing the shot she'd been eying. "I've been here quite a long time," she replied. "I'm guessing it must be at least six months by now. And do you want to know what I've been doing here?"

"I honestly don't know."

"The answer is simple. I've been looking for you."

Richard glanced up from the table and leaned closer. "You were looking for me? For six months? But I've only been here a few days."

"Yes, but I didn't know that," she said with a laugh. "I almost gave up too, but all that matters is that I've found you. When I saw you the other day, I wasn't entirely sure if you were the one I was searching for, but your aura was brighter than anything I'd ever seen. It turns out I was right."

"So, where were you before you got here?"

"Much like you, I'm from our mutual timeline. In case you're unaware of it, we're part of an elite group of people that are called upon to intervene when history becomes threatened by change or catastrophic events. Well, it's actually more like a *random* group of people, but either way, you're here for a reason, and so am I."

Richard stared at her a moment, then slowly shook his head. "Ordinarily, I would laugh at such crap, but my rational thinking has gone completely down the shitter." Richard sighed, holding his head to curb the onset of a slight headache, due mostly from hunger and dehydration.

"Your head, isn't it?" Alice asked, noticing Richard's comfort level change.

"Yeah, I just wish I had some Tylenol."

"Oh, wait a minute. You might be in luck." Alice proceeded to rummage through her elegant handbag and pulled out a small white bottle.

"Take some of this," she said, handing it under the table. "Just don't let anyone see you."

He looked at the label and squinted. "Anacin?"

"It takes my headaches away without fail, every time," she said, surveying the rest of the bar for prying eyes. While Richard struggled to get the cap off, he noticed some disturbing print on the side of the bottle.

"Alice, there's an expiration date of April 27th, 1982, on here. I can't take these."

"Would you please lower your voice," she whispered. "I bought them in January of 1980. It was only two months before I ended up here, they're fine."

"So, are you saying these are new?"

"Of course, go ahead and take them. They'll wipe that headache out in no time."

"Alice," Richard continued. "Are you telling me you're from 1980?"

"Yes, and I'm still pissed I never got to that Ramones show at CBGB. I had the tickets bought and everything. It was two days away. But then, of course, I ended up here."

"Really? Well, I never got to see them either. I wish I could've."

"Let's make a deal," Alice said. "If we ever get out of here, let's go see them together! I don't care where."

"Hey, Ho, Let's Go," Richard replied, smiling a little. He popped two pills in his mouth and handing the bottle back. "It's a deal."

Alice smiled back. "Good, now we have a real goal to shoot for. Anyway, let's get back on track. I understand this is all a lot to take in at once but right now we have to focus on helping your friend out of prison and getting you home. I'm here to help you complete whatever task you're here to do, and I can't leave until I've seen it through. There's only one problem. I don't specifically know what that task is."

Richard frowned. "What do you mean you don't know what it is? I thought you had this all figured out?"

"Well, it has to be something serious, or neither of us would be here. One thing I do know is that we need to intervene somehow to keep history the way it's supposed to be. Certain forces are threatening the past, and I also think that Stockton guy is somehow related. There's something oppressive inside that house. I felt it the second I walked in."

Alice continued to speak, and while Richard listened carefully he also noticed something from across the room. It stood by the open doorway and peered at him. The faceless apparition ate away at his spirit.

"Alice," he whispered. "I think I see one of those things you're talking about." He was careful not to speak too loudly, hoping it would not hear him. "Don't turn around. Just keep looking at me and talking as if nothing is wrong."

Alice nodded and proceeded to sit as still as she could. "Is it coming closer?" she whispered while playing nervously with a loose strand of hair.

"No, it's just standing in one spot, but it's looking at us."

"What should we do?"

"You're asking me? I know nothing about those things. You're the expert here."

"I'm no expert," she quickly responded. Richard noticed beads of sweat forming on her forehead. She was ultimately no different than him, just a regular person thrust into an overwhelming situation without answers. As Richard pretended not to notice the dark figure, something else caught his eye. Entering through the open doorway of the pub was Stockton.

He walked to the bar and leaned onto it with one hand, holding a large brown woven sack in the other. The spirit seemed to linger behind him, gliding over to where he was standing. It appeared as though Stockton hadn't noticed them yet. It would only be a matter of time if they hung around.

"We have to get out of here now," he quietly said.

"Shit! Is that thing coming over here?"

"No, but Stockton just walked in." He cringed at the sight of him. Nothing in recent memory brought quite as much resentment to Richard as the wretched excuse for a man that stood at the bar. "Is there a back way out of here?"

"Yeah, I think there's an unloading area in the back, but we'll have to push the piano out of the way to get to it."

"Then that's what we'll have to do," Richard said.

"Are you crazy? That thing weighs a ton."

"Stockton will see us if we leave by the front door. Just leave it to me," he reassured, figuring this might be an excellent opportunity to impress her with his ingenuity.

Stockton hadn't yet noticed either of them sitting in the corner. His only concern was acquiring a stiff drink. Eugene knew him well, as did everyone else in town. Most people liked him, but others simply saw him as an eccentric millionaire without much merit otherwise. As Eugene greeted him and asked what he wanted, Stockton noticed two patrons to the left of the bar, struggling to move a piano.

"What in the world are those two idiots doing?" he asked, unable to see their faces clearly. Eugene leaned over the bar to steal a glance and saw Richard attempting to move the piano. It reminded him of a humorous vaudeville act.

"Good God, I have no idea!" Eugene laughed. "They look ridiculous." Stockton watched the entertaining antics as long as possible before breaking a small grin across his face. "I could be wrong, but it looks as if they're trying to steal the piano," he said, then laughed. It felt good. He needed a good laugh today, especially after what he had witnessed earlier that morning. It wasn't enough that he provided his wife and business partner with extravagant wealth and fortune. They wanted something more—each other.

He'd left in a hurry early that morning and told his wife he wouldn't be home from his business venture until nightfall, but the trip had become interrupted when his new replacement valet failed to keep the horses at a pace that suited his liking. After using his antique hatchet to bludgeon the man's scalp, Stockton decided to drag the body to a nearby meadow and hide his victim under a small bridge. Before leaving, he used his machete to lop the valet's head off to ensure the body was unidentifiable. Afterward, he placed it in the same woven sack as a souvenir and slung it over his shoulder. It was the first time he'd ever killed anyone but he knew it wouldn't be the last. As far as he was concerned, he was just warming up.

With his trip cut short, he arrived home to witness his wife and business partner together in his bed next to one of his prized Renaissance paintings. A painting that he'd purchased for fifteen thousand dollars at the local auction house for his wife's twenty-fourth birthday.

All he could think about now was the look on their faces as he walked through the door and the hollow apologies that followed. But it did them no good.

Twenty-Three

"Do you think he saw us?" Richard asked Alice as they slipped out the back door. Having successfully moved the piano enough for them to shimmy out the doorway, they found themselves in a nearly deserted alleyway, save for a few stray dogs and cats and a vagrant that slept against a pile of thick blankets.

"Are you kidding me?" she said. "Of course he saw us! Unless he's completely blind or an absolute idiot, it was the most obvious getaway of all time."

"All right, I admit it was sloppy but even if he did see us, the question is, did he identify us? We had our backs turned to him for most of the time and I did my best at hiding my face. He probably doesn't even know it was us."

"I hope you're right," Alice replied, looking down the long stretch of alleyway. The tall, forgotten stacks of trash laid scattered about and the homeless desperately scavenged for a scrap of rotten meat or spoiled fruit.

The red-brick walls on either side seemed to go on for miles with almost no end in sight, and Richard could feel each approaching vagrant stare him down, wondering how much money he had and debating if it was a good day for a robbery.

Luckily, it wasn't that kind of day and both travelers made it out of the alleyway and onto the main dirt road where the welcomed sight of busy carriages passed. As the sun began to set, the town square had started to fill up with the wealthy socialites, all looking for a night on the town.

Richard breathed a sigh of relief. "Well, at least we made it without getting jumped."

"You mean you were actually scared back there?" Alice asked, laughing. "I think you need a few hard months in this place to toughen you up."

"I don't want to stick around that long. Besides, I wasn't scared. I was more concerned about your safety than my own."

"Don't bullshit me," she said, whacking him on the shoulder. "It's fine, though. Like I said, if you spend enough time here, you'll get used to that sort of thing."

This was the side of Alice that Richard liked. He found it irresistible. Not only was she one of the most gorgeous women he'd ever seen, but she could probably kick his ass in a fight.

He smiled at the thought.

"So, what's your big plan now, ace?" Alice asked, watching the sun wink-out behind the Majestic Hotel.

"It's starting to get dark, and the way I see it, we have a platinum opportunity right now while Stockton's getting his drink on at the Calf. Without him home, this might be easier than we expected."

Alice stopped and stared at him. "You want to go there now?"

Richard shrugged. "He's not at home. It's a perfect chance."

"Possibly, but we never went over our plan. I just don't want it to be sloppy—or worse." She began twirling her hair again around her sleek fingers while staring down at her feet like a naughty schoolgirl just caught in the act.

Snapping himself out of it, he tried to remember the last thing she said.

"I'm sorry, what was that?"

"I said I don't want to get caught!"

"Oh, of course not, but nobody's getting caught as long as we're smart about it."

"Great, now I feel so much better," she said. "So, tell me this plan of yours."

The sun had disappeared by the time they reached Stockton's mansion. With a blanket of darkness shrouding the landscape, they both hoped it would make their job a bit easier. They stood at the bottom of the marble stairs and glared at the large front door, keeping their eyes and ears open.

Their plan was simple. They had to gain entry undetected, and if Eddie's suitcase remained in the Renaissance room where he'd said it was, they would quickly snatch it and make a clean exit.

Richard knew this depended on a number of factors. Was the front door unlocked? Was Stockton's wife home? Were the housekeepers and servants present?

Alice watched Richard check up and down the streets for any sign of Stockton. "You know, that suitcase isn't going to retrieve itself," she said. "Don't tell me you're getting cold feet? The longer we stand out here, the greater our chances of him coming back and catching us."

"Thanks for reminding me," he said, continuing his obsessive lookout. Alice assumed some initiative and started her way up the marble steps. "Are you coming?"

He never wanted to step foot back in that house again, yet he followed her up the steps to the oversized door where the gleaming gold handle awaited. He reached out and pressed down on the top latch and leaned gently on the door.

"It's locked," he said.

"No shit."

"You know, for someone who's supposed to be a lady, you sure do swear like Richard Pryor on a New Year's Eve coke binge."

"Are you serious? You should've heard me before I arrived here. Every other word was either fuck-this or shit-that, but people aren't used to foul-language around here, so I learned to adapt. And by the way, I happen to love Richard Pryor."

"Me too," he replied. "And, we share the same name." He paused and gazed up the building to the room.

"So what do we do now?" he asked. "We obviously can't get in this way."

"You're asking me? This is supposed to be *your* plan. I thought you were in the driver's seat."

He quickly looked to the exterior, peering between the narrow passages that separated Stockton's mansion from the buildings on either side.

"Follow me," he instructed, making his way back down the marble steps and proceeding to the right-side walkway of the home.

"Good thinking, they might have a backdoor," she said.

As they slowly crept around the side of the house, Richard recalled the times he and his childhood friends went out on mischief night. Sneaking around the neighbor's properties while pool hopping, soaping windows, smashing Jack o' Lantern's, egging passing cars, and stealing expensive hood ornaments.

It was a yearly tradition that he never missed. By the time Richard reached his eighteenth birthday, he'd accumulated hundreds of ornaments which he'd kept in a large knapsack tucked safely away in his bedroom closet. It remained untouched for approximately eight consecutive Halloweens. That was, until his mother noticed a silver Jaguar ornament on his closet floor, hanging out the opening of a shoddily hidden sack during a routine spring cleaning. She immediately ordered him to throw every single one away, including a Bentley ornament that could've probably paid his college tuition for at least the first two semesters. She even threatened to turn him into the police if he didn't comply. *Oh, the sins of youth!*

The fond memories put a smile on his face and rejuvenated his confidence in their goal.

The dry winter grass led them to the Stockton's backyard, which nestled itself around oversized Azalea bushes and a private fenced-in garden that probably flourished in the spring and summer months. Nothing was there now except a sizeable desolate flatbed of wet mulch.

A well-crafted granite sundial rested in the middle of the backyard that registered nothing in the pitch black of night except for the white pigeon shit that splattered its outer edges. Leading behind from the sundial was a red-bricked walkway that winded past two stone benches and headed in the direction of a wood-paneled black door with a golden lion's head knocker and silver handle.

"Alice, do you see that?" Richard spoke up, pointing into the darkness.

"Do I see what? I can't see shit back here."

"Right there," he said, proceeding towards it. "Do you think it's open?"

"Be careful. Make sure there's nobody inside."

"You must think I'm an idiot." He peered through the back window into the house and noticed a series of candles engulfing the darkness, flickering off the walls and casting shadowy imps on the kitchen ceiling. After witnessing the disturbing figure in the Skinned Calf, Richard wasn't sure if it was just his imagination or if something might be in there watching him.

"Is it open?" Alice called out.

"Hold on a minute," he replied while squinting. "I don't know yet."

"Well, what are you waiting for?

Richard ignored the scathing comment and turned the knob while slightly pressing his body weight against the center of the wooden entryway. "We need another way in," he announced, hopping off the steps onto the lawn.

"It figures." Alice pursed her lips and blew some blonde strands of hair off her face. It had drooped across her eyes all day but was now starting to aggravate her. Not to mention the cold temperatures setting in, causing tiny ice crystals to refract off the dried grass at her feet. She figured it must've plummeted about thirty degrees in the last hour and a half, reintroducing itself to her in the form of a smoky mist that materialized with every exhale.

She rested down on one of the moss-covered benches and watched Richard frantically attempt every locked window along the side of the house. His luck changed in the form of an old wooden ladder poking out of a large hedge. He pulled it from the brush and even though it was rotted and wilted, it would have to do.

"Alice, come here," he called out, turning to see his traveling companion curled in a tight ball, sleeping on the bench. She looked content, and he ultimately decided not to disturb her until his mission was complete.

As quietly as possible, he sat the ladder under one of the upstairs windows and quickly noticed it didn't quite meet the bottom of the pane. But this was no time to hesitate. He took one last look at his sleeping beauty and began his silent assent, nervously aware of every creak and crack the ladder announced.

After making it to the top, he paused for a quick prayer, something he hadn't done in years. While looking down from the very top, he prayed for a safe entry and that the ladder wouldn't give out and collapse under his feet. After inhaling a cold gasp of air, he glanced one more time at Alice and gave her the thumbs up just in case she awoke and was watching. He took one more deep breath, gathered his strength, and just as he was about to throw open the window, a distorted object slowly crept past the wavy glass in front of him.

Instinctively, he grasped the sides of the rickety ladder and quickly ducked under the windowpane, hoping whoever or whatever it was wouldn't spot him. He waited another minute and then carefully raised his head above the pane and peered inside. Whatever was in there had disappeared. Slowly, he pushed up on the base of the window.

The world looked blurry as Alice opened her weary eyes. The right side of her face was numb from the cold bench where her head had rested. While struggling to adjust her focus, she noticed Richard's outline at the top of a ladder as he attempted to enter the mansion.

Her head ached when she sat up and wiped the sleep from her eyes. As she stood and regained focus, she squinted at the dull sight of a man carrying a woven sack in the distance, hastily approaching the front of Stockton's house. He was staggering and uneven. As he hobbled down the sidewalk, he stopped, just long enough to fumble for a key.

Alice jumped up from the bench to warn Richard but lost her footing. She then collapsed from the blinding pain in her head as if being pushed down by an unidentifiable force. She managed to call out a half-second too late, just as Richard climbed inside and out of sight. It was no coincidence.

Twenty-Four

As Richard fell onto the center of the hallway floor, a raspy, high-pitched voice echoed from off the walls and pimpled his skin. "Excuse me!" it rang out.

Jesus Christ!

This time he wasn't praying. "If you're planning on staying another night," the female voice continued, "you will have to make the necessary arrangements with Mr. Blanch. He's handling all of the payments while Timothy is out of town." Richard hurried behind one of the hallway doors and watched from three rooms away while the distraught housekeeper scolded what appeared to be an uninformed guest. "No exceptions!" she blurted out to him.

After tucking her purse under her arm, Alice managed to get to her feet. It was apparent Richard needed her help, so she followed after him up the ladder and was ready to climb inside when she noticed him down the hallway and hiding behind an opened door.

"Richard, Stockton is home," she stage whispered through the open window. "He's home," she repeated a bit louder. But he appeared oblivious, continuing to focus on the housekeeper. "Damn!" Alice squealed as the housekeeper quickly turned to walk in their direction.

"Shit!" they said in unison.

While the distinct sound of footsteps became closer, Alice swiftly ducked out of sight and Richard acted quickly, pulling the door closed and settling inside a darkened guestroom. The woman hesitated. "Is someone there?" she asked, seeing the door magically shut before her eyes. "Hello?"

Richard quickly assessed the low-lit room. Visibility would have been impractical if not for the roaring fireplace on the left side of the wall. The knob of the bedroom door turned and the woman entered, holding a burning candle. The hot wax dripped over her hand, but she didn't wince.

Alice watched helplessly by the window while awaiting the fate of her companion. She could see the candlelight from the room but could not make out what was happening.

The bed was elevated just enough that he could lay flat underneath it. Those days at Planet Fitness helped for once. As the housekeeper walked further into the room, Richard's view of her became obstructed as he held his breath and watched her feet from under the bed. He heard her roaming around the room and rattling the handle of the closet. A different voice called from in the bed. "Who are you?" a woman said. "What are you doing in my room?"

The housekeeper quickly twisted her body around. "Oh my, I'm very sorry. I was unaware there were guests in this room!" she turned quickly and made an awkward exit. The housekeeper closed the door behind her, hoping not a word of this would make it back to Mr.

Stockton. She valued her job, and she didn't want to be made an example of.

Alice's heart continued to pound as she watched the housekeeper fix her apron and touch up her dark curly red locks in a pocket mirror. The bedroom door remained closed, and Alice wondered if Richard was still inside.

The maid clicked her mirror shut and sharply looked over in Alice's direction, prompting her to duck out of sight again. She was certain the maid had spotted her this time as she could hear the distinct sound of footsteps approaching the window.

She was about to conjure up a bullshit story consisting of her being a guest that forgot her key or a sloppy drunk who mistakenly wandered onto the wrong property. But the window above her unexpectedly slammed shut, and the distorted view of the housekeeper skulked away.

She was grateful for remaining unseen, but her only way in was now blocked off by a giant wavy glassed behemoth of nineteenth-century design. It was a far cry from the convenient folding, easy-glide windows she had installed in her condo approximately four months before ending up here, but judging from the minuscule frame of the woman who'd just slammed it shut without much effort, she figured it was doable.

While she loathed the archaic design of the window, it took a moment for the rustling in the yard below to register. It sounded like a wild animal or a stray dog, but when she glanced down, she noticed Stockton walking along the side of the house, still carrying the woven sack and heading to the backyard. Alice felt her legs turn to rubber and the blood drain from her head. She braced the top of the ladder for support while Stockton staggered over to the stone bench where she had napped.

His presence was disheartening, but what concerned her more was losing her balance and falling to the feet of a deranged madman. She had no intention of becoming a cosmopolitan corpse. Luckily for her, Stockton appeared way too distracted by his woven sack to notice her. She hoped he wouldn't look up, trapping her.

The five-minutes Richard waited under the bed seemed like five hours. After listening carefully, he heard the woman's breathing deepen as she fell back to sleep.

He quietly crawled out, holding his breath. After getting to his feet, he crept across the hardwood floor, watching the bedroom door draw closer. The distinct sound of snapping came from the fireplace just as he clumsily caught his shoe on the woman's slung-about suitcase, causing him to lose balance and tumble headfirst into the doorframe. The woman screeched and quickly sat up in bed.

"I apologize, just a big misunderstanding," he assured her. He was out the door and halfway down the hall before he finally heard the woman's outburst cease.

Stockton was not moving. Neither was Alice. He examined whatever was inside the woven sack by holding it in the air and moving it from side to side, but fortunately for her, it was too dark to make out what it was. With Stockton occupied, she figured this was the perfect time to make her move.

Grasping the bottom of the frame, she put forth every ounce of strength and the window flew to the ceiling, hitting the top of the frame with a dull thud. While cringing, Alice glanced in Stockton's direction, hoping he hadn't heard the disturbance. Her spirit sank when he abruptly stood up and swiftly threw the object into his bag.

He stood immobile in the darkness for a moment, a blackened shape with a face obscured by night. She decided to remain stock still until he showed signs of movement, even if it took all night. A muffled crash from the first floor distracted Stockton. He picked up the sack and proceeded to the kitchen door where he disappeared from view. Alice held her breath and listened for a key to turn and a door to open. When it did, she exhaled, feeling some apprehension dissipate from her body.

She poked her head through the window and looked both ways down the hall like she was about to cross a busy road. Luckily, the hallway was anything but lively. First one leg, then another, she slid through the window and quickly rushed over to the bedroom.

"Are you in there?" she whispered against the closed door. "Stockton's home, we should get out of here." No response. "All right, I'm coming in." She slowly opened the creaky door and entered the room, scanning its corners for any signs of her companion.

"Richard?"

"How many times do I have to ask you to stay out of my room!" the frazzled houseguest announced, startling Alice.

"Oh, I was just looking for—"

"This is the third time I've been interrupted tonight, and if you don't—"

"You have a good night, now," Alice interrupted, shutting the door while the woman carried on. As Alice walked down the hallway, she listened to the old lady's verbal rant, and a smile broke across her face.

With himself hidden behind the suit of armor, Richard recognized just how big a problem he had. With Stockton sitting in the kitchen area and the Irish housekeeper dusting various collectibles just mere feet from where he was hiding, it was just a matter of time before he'd be spotted.

It all happened quickly. Minutes earlier, he reached the bottom of the staircase and surveyed the area where Eddie's suitcase should've been. But it was gone, and the last thing Richard needed was an overzealous scavenger hunt. He was weighing his options and searching behind the various artifacts when he accidentally knocked the suit of armor to the ground. He quickly set it back in place just as Stockton muddled in the back door and wandered right into Richard's zone. He acted fast and hid behind its tall frame, and that's where he's been ever since.

All he could do was wait and hope. Hope for a clean escape, and especially hope that Alice hadn't been discovered sleeping on the bench.

The housekeeper wandered into the kitchen area just long enough for him to attempt a hasty exit. Just as he was about to try his luck, the ill-fated painting above the fireplace caught his eye. Gone once again were the tranquil images, replaced by the familiar dark figure that followed closely behind Stockton at the Skinned Calf.

He could feel his senses dull and his headache return, along with the overwhelming urge to abandon his cause. It was as if the entity were speaking directly to him, spewing lies that almost had him convinced to drop everything and walk away. He acknowledged Alice's earlier warning about the oppressive nature of the house and his own experience with it. But now, he was feeling its true force, even more overpowering than before. He recalled how Alice forced him to the ground as Stockton plunged the knife into the wrong target, unintentionally breaking him from the trance—but not this time. He would have to resist on his own.

"Let him rot in that prison cell." Richard could hear the entity's telepathic commands. "What has he ever done for you except steal your money?"

As the beast continued its barrage of lies, the housekeeper retreated to the kitchen where she held an inaudible conversation with Stockton. He continued his mental battle, shaking the oppression from his mind and sensing the painting's power wane as he turned away from its odd display. He wasn't going to let the opportunity slip past him twice. While looking about the first floor, he noticed several open walkways that lead to numerous areas of the mansion. Finding the suitcase would be an arduous task, but he had to start somewhere.

The unexplored territory beckoned Richard, calling him gently. Quickly, he bent down and began untying his shoes behind the suit of armor just as he saw Stockton in the kitchen.

He untied faster, attempting to detangle the knot that stood between him and partial freedom. Stockton extinguished the candles, causing a blanket of darkness to obscure any voyeuristic activities on Richard's behalf. He continued to fumble with the laces until they finally untangled and allowed him to remove his shoes. With his newfound silence, he crept across the hard marble floor, listening to Stockton's footfalls approach. He felt that if he glanced over his shoulder he might have turned into a pillar of salt or something equally horrendous, so he kept his eyes straight ahead on the room. He entered through the blackness of a doorway into uncharted waters.

Alice descended the familiar staircase, confident she would find Richard either in the living area retrieving the suitcase. Or if lousy luck had its way, apprehended by an enraged nut case. She hoped for the first option.

Upon reaching the bottom of the stairs, she noticed an eerie candle glow making its way through the large dark room. An orange glimmer beamed off a man's distorted face. Following closely behind was the shadow of a mysterious entity, barely visible in the shroud of night. Alice and Richard both watched from their own designated hiding spots, unaware of each other, as the man took a seat in front of the roaring fireplace.

The picture began to ripple once again and transform into the hellish image. As the transformation occurred, Stockton rose to his feet and held out his arms as if welcoming a guest. Alice used every ounce of restraint to keep her screams withheld, keeping her hands cupped tightly over her mouth just in case. Heavy smoke traveled from the painting and descended to the floor. It materialized at Stockton's feet, rising almost to the high ceiling.

Much like the other figures, it was faceless and frightening. But the thing stood approximately five feet taller and was imbued with a crimson essence. It carried a large golden urn in its bony left hand and a large pike in its right.

Twenty-Five

Bethany lounged around her cozy fireplace, reading some Shakespeare and Dante while taking a break from her piano playing. Her mind had not been right since witnessing Eddie and Richard's arrest the day before. The scenarios repeatedly played out in her head until it hurt to think. She hadn't seen Charlie since last night when she asked him to leave for being an "insensitive louse." She called him the one word he detested most, inducing an aggressive rage, striking her.

A line was crossed as far as she was concerned, and there was no going back. Verbal abuse was one thing, but physical violence was something she refused to tolerate. Charlie never came across as the type of man who'd be capable of such behavior, but here it was, as evident as the large welt across her cheek.

All-day she'd been thinking of going to the police to protest the arrest of the two men. Something had stopped her each time. But now, the more she weighed her options, it seemed like the only right thing to do.

Bethany had the influence to potentially clear both of them. She only needed to run crying to the police and then follow up with her politically connected father, and it was a done deal.

Yes, I'll go in the morning.

No wait, I'll go tonight.

Closing her book on Ichabod's adventures, she assumed her fingers were well-rested enough to practice a few more minutes before venturing out. Deciding on Beethoven's Moonlight Sonata, a song she felt matched her current mood, she sat, laid her fingers on the keys, and struck the first note, only to be broken out of her currently relaxed state when the portrait across the room caught her eye. Again, it presented a disturbing image of her. She hung naked from a rope, upside down from a rotting apple tree. Demons and dark entities violated her with fiery pitchforks and phallic metal objects. A sharp chill ran up her neck as she quickly turned away, closing her eyes tightly.

She didn't know what to do next. Samuel was dead and could offer no explanation for this. As she sat on the piano bench paralyzed with fear, she could feel the portrait's subtle influence. It began to speak to her in much the same way it had with Stockton and Richard. The only difference being, Richard's strong will to resist its temptation.

It warned her of the interference she had contemplated. The voice instructed her to forget her motives, explaining that if she involved either her father or the police, she would suffer the consequences.

The pressure in her head mounted into a full-blown migraine, prompting her to hurl obscenities at the possessed portrait. She jumped from her bench, sending it to the ground with a collision of wood against marble. She quickly got to her feet and darted swiftly across the room. Her eyes played no tricks as she approached. The disgusting images remained and even more detailed with closer inspection. Out of anger, she grasped the portrait with both hands and tossed it onto the floor.

The ordeal mounted her anxiety, but the pressure in her head dissipated. Still, she had no intention of heeding the warning. Her plan to free Eddie remained in place. Just as her breathing began to slow to a steady rhythm, an obnoxious pounding at her front door came in piercing intervals, inducing a second stream of fear. Bethany couldn't imagine who'd have the audacity to pound on her door at ten o'clock at night, but the unwelcomed visitor's intent could only be malicious.

She dry-swallowed and asked, "Who is it?" No answer. The banging resumed, and her fear turned to anger. "I believe I asked you a question!" she continued, grabbing a cast iron candlestick holder from off the piano. An eerie silence hung in the air as she slowly crept to the door. The knocking persisted, ignoring her request. Even as she shot the deadbolt and unfastened the lock, it continued. She turned the knob slightly to the right, hearing the familiar click. Nothing stood between her and the evader on the other side of the large oak slab.

Exterior gaslights brightened the neatly pruned trees and cobblestone streets as she threw the door open, but no one was there. The initial shock caused her to drop her weapon to the marble floor. Her heart pounded rapidly, and her eyesight tunneled. Gathering herself, she stepped into the cold silent night and thoroughly examined the streets.

The area was quiet. Not a dog barked or a beggar begged. It was terror to her ears. The only audible sound was that of the heavy wind whipping her long burgundy gown wildly in the breeze.

A single snowflake fell from the gray sky and landed on the tip of her nose, leaving a tingle of dew, while the faintest sound of haunted laughter sounded in the distance. As the seconds passed, it grew louder and fuller, echoing throughout the empty streets, mocking her gullibility.

Desperately, she backed up through her doorway to escape the resonating echo that was swiftly approaching and causing a dark chill to run up her spine and through her veins. The circling laughter billowed from behind, blowing her hair forward onto her face and partially thrusting her out of the doorway. Instinctively, she turned and immediately caught a glimpse of the most inhuman image she'd ever witnessed…

A translucent black-robed apparition loomed no more than five inches in front of her.

As her legs buckled, she grabbed the doorframe in a feeble attempt to remain conscious. The world around her slowly faded as she crashed to the ground, blacking out, and the last thing Bethany saw was a large golden urn dangling before her.

Richard had decided to take the opportunity and have a look around the dining area while Stockton entertained his ghostly houseguest.

He checked all four corners of the room, opening all the cabinet drawers and lurking under the three wooden tables, crawling around on all fours like a wounded soldier.

After the room was picked apart with no suitcase to be found, he glanced out the doorway to see what Stockton and his pet ghost were doing. But the room was unoccupied, the only inhabitants being the orange and yellow flames of the persistent fireplace. In a far corner of the room's living area, the shadowy outline of a woman's figure appeared next to the grand staircase.

He bent down as far as he could without his knees creaking and quietly snuck across the room's threshold, clutching his shoes close to his chest. Upon reaching the large sofa in the center of the room, he managed a better view of the motionless silhouette.

It looked like Alice, but he wasn't certain enough to ask, so she did it for him. "Richard, is that you?" Her voice emerged in a loud whisper.

"Alice? You have to get out of here. Stockton is home."

"I know, you big dummy. Why do you think I'm here?"

"What are you talking about?"

Alice sighed. "I saw Stockton arrive home while I was outside so I snuck in through the window to warn you."

"All right, just wait right there. I'm coming over."

"Where else would I go?" She mocked him with a slight chuckle.

"I'm glad you think this is funny because I sure don't." Richard darted across the remainder of the room and settled into the dark corner next to Alice.

"You need to lighten up," she replied, putting an arm around his shoulder. "I'm scared, too, but it's important to keep a sense of humor."

"So, how long were you standing over here for?"

"Long enough," she replied.

"Did you see where Stockton went?"

Alice sensed his nervousness and released his shoulder. Instantly, he felt the sting of disappointment with her touch removed, hoping for its comforting return. "Yes, he walked right past me and up the staircase. Thank God I noticed a chair to hide behind."

Richard didn't know what to say. He wanted to grab her and tell her how beautiful he thought she was and how much he wanted to touch her perfect skin. Instead, he said, "Good job."

Good job? What a jackass I am, Richard thought to himself.

After sitting up, he took her hand and stared into her eyes. He was about to tell her how he felt when again, he faltered and blurted out, "You need to get out of here."

Damn it.

He said quickly, "I want to look around a bit longer but I want you out of harm's way. Just go out the front door and wait for me in our original meeting place behind the mansion. I'll try to be as quick as possible."

"Quick as possible isn't a quality I usually look for in a man," she said, smiling. The unsettling sound of footsteps cut through the hollowed room, blocking any further response from Richard. They listened while it approached, growing louder with each methodically placed step. Alice grasped Richard's arm tightly and gently twisted it out of fear, inflicting his first Indian-burn in over thirty years.

"Someone's coming down the staircase," Alice whispered, releasing her grip from Richard and rising to her feet. "Quickly, follow me."

"Where are you going?" he whispered, watching her creep over to a large steel doorway.

"This way, hurry," she demanded. While peering to the second floor, he noticed the shadow of a man approaching the mid-section of the stairwell. After realizing he had only moments, he jumped to his feet and joined Alice, who struggled fervently to pry the door open in the dark out-cove.

"Help me get this open, he'll see us here," Alice panted, wiping the sweat from her cheeks.

"Are you crazy? Let's just hide behind the chair."

"There's no time, and it's not big enough for the two of us. I barely fit behind it myself."

"Fine," Richard whispered, pulling the heavy door with every ounce of strength he could muster. "It won't budge."

"Shit, I think this is a single-sided door."

"What does that mean?"

"It's probably bolted from the other side is what it means. There might be an alternate entryway."

"So, what does that mean?" Richard asked as he pulled on the steel handle.

Alice released her grasp and ceased the futile attempts to gain access. "I think it means we're fucked," she replied. At that moment, Richard began to recall the night of Stockton's dinner party.

"No, we're not fucked. Not yet at least." The footsteps had almost reached the bottom. With no time to waste, he felt along the cold stone wall for a wooden shelf.

"This is no time to search for a trap door," Alice said.

"No, there should be a key here." Running his hands along the dark jagged surface, he accumulated cobwebs and insects onto his fingers, but no shelves.

"Hurry up!" Alice whispered.

Richard almost gave up and accepted their fate when his finger caught the sharp edge of a splintered piece of wood. He continued to blindly feel around the flattened shelf space when he discovered the sensation of cold steel in the shape of a key.

"I think I have it." He found his grasp and picked it up. "I got it."

"Give it to me," Alice demanded, retrieving it from his nervous grip. She hurried to the keyhole while he watched her fumble with the lock, waiting for the inevitable click of redemption. Even in the drafty mansion, Alice could feel the hot sweat form on her body and the tingle of anticipation seep through her pores as she searched.

"Shit! Richard, I can't find the hole."

"Better you than me."

Just as hope disappeared, the key found its home, sliding in with ease. "Never mind, get in there." She motioned him as she pulled it open. Richard and Alice quietly made a swift exit through the doorway and closed it behind them, just as the anonymous figure reached the bottom of the stairs, stopping directly in front of the door to curiously survey the area.

The half-inch crack in the doorway allowed Alice to view the silhouette of a woven sack in the hands of their pursuer. "Guess who it is?" she asked Richard, who was already halfway down the dimly lit staircase warming his hands over a glowing wall-torch. He breathed a sigh of disgust.

"Okay, so what do we do?"

"I don't know," she said, peering through the open door crack. "I guess we just wait until he's out of sight and then make a break for it. Or we could try our luck and see where these stairs lead."

"That's probably not the best idea," Richard said. "I've been down there before and I think it's a dead end."

"Oh, shit."

"What's wrong now?"

"We may not have a choice. He's right on the other side of the door searching around for something." She held the key up and waved it in the air. "Looking for this, asshole?"

Richard sighed. "He probably doesn't know the door is unlocked. Let's get out of here before he realizes it."

Alice threw the key in her handbag and followed Richard down the winding staircase. Spiraling further down, it appeared to go on endlessly with only the torches that lined the wall to guide them. As the ground floor drew near, so did the darkness. The soothing radiance that accompanied their way thinned out until not a single flicker remained and a hexing dark veil surrounded the bottom room. By the time she reached her final step, Alice was so dizzy she felt like she'd just consumed five of her usual Sunday afternoon Martinis.

"Alice, where are you?"

"Ouch, I'm right next to you. Next time try not screaming in my ear."

"Sorry, I can't see a thing. Do you have any matches?" he asked.

"Not anymore. I'm not allowed to play with fire." She laughed. "Bad things happen."

"I'm sure," Richard replied. "Wait here. I'm going back up to get the nearest torch."

"What if Stockton comes down? You'll run right into him."

"That's why I'll be quick."

"Like I said before, not a quality I find appealing in a man."

Richard didn't answer.

"It was just a joke," she said, exasperated, but Richard was already out of earshot and halfway up the spiraling staircase taking two steps at a time. He kept the fear of running into Stockton tucked away in the back of his mind as the spiders and cobwebs and centipedes became visible along the wall. Hope had appeared, and he wasn't slowing down. He hadn't moved like this since his college track days as he hurdled the steps like a gazelle. The glow became brighter until a torch loomed in front of his face, beckoning him.

He grasped its base and tried pulling it off the holder but it wouldn't move.

"Damn it!" he announced. As soon as the words left his lips, the faint echo of footsteps sounded above him and a shrill scream rang out from the bottom floor.

Panicked, he quickly ran back down the stairs, taking the steps three at a time until he reached the bottom where Alice stood, holding a flaming torch in her right hand and a look of horror across her face.

"What happened?" Richard asked. With the room now brightened, his question was answered when he caught the terrifying glimpse of a man and woman helplessly shackled to an elongated concrete table that rested directly beneath a hanging pendulum. Richard immediately recognized them as Mrs. Stockton and Grant.

"I'm sorry," Alice spoke up. "It turns out I had matches in my handbag after all." He kept his gaze fixed on the horrific scene.

"Don't worry about it," he muttered.

Mrs. Stockton had been stripped of her clothes, a cloth gag across her mouth, double-knotted behind her head. Grant had landed the same fate, except he had a terry cloth around his waist. They were both shackled with metal chains that clasped around their ankles and wrists that extended to the top and bottom of the concrete table. They were conscious but barely responsive.

"We can't just leave them here," Alice said, tugging at one of the secured chains.

"Don't you recognize him? He's partially responsible for having me arrested."

Alice continued to tug at the chains. "Yes, I remember, and you can bitch him out later, but come help me for now."

"Fine," he said, walking to the other side of the table. He lifted one of Mrs. Stockton's handcuffs and examined it before dropping her hand. He looked around the room and noticed a steel wall lever in the corner attached to three separate ropes that extended directly to the ceiling where the pendulum waited.

"I don't think there's anything we can do for them," he said, walking over to the staircase and peering up. "But right now, we need to worry about getting out of here. We can go to the police and tell them Eddie was framed. Here's the proof right here in front of us."

A clang rang out from above, followed by the distant sound of footsteps. Neither Richard nor Alice moved from their frozen positions while they listened. As the echo grew closer, Richard broke from his trance and spun around to Alice. "We have to hide quickly." She was unresponsive. "Alice, did you hear me? We have to hide."

"Yes, I heard you, but where?" She quickly moved the torch around the dim room and spotted a row of iron maidens lined against the right wall. "Right there," she whispered. "We can hide inside these."

She ran to the wall and quickly placed the torch back in its holder while Richard sped across the room and pulled open one of the creaky torture devices. Multiple rows of thin metal spikes greeted him, waiting.

"Get in," he said, holding it open for her.

"Be careful," Alice instructed, climbing inside her solitary cell. "Don't close it all the way."

"I understand that, thanks." He gently closed her lid and said, "Tell me when to stop."

"That's far enough," she replied.

Richard left Alice, moving to an empty torture device, and eased his way into the precarious space. Since it was so dark, he slowly pulled the door closed while rusted hinges creaked and spikes closed in on him, missing his flesh by less than an inch.

They each watched the stairwell through their tiny eyeholes, waiting and hoping they wouldn't be discovered. After a moment, a pair of legs came into view, followed by the rest of Stockton. He looked hollowed and malnourished, his features gaunt in appearance, almost unrecognizable. As he shuffled across the room to the large table, he carried the familiar red-stained sack over his shoulder. Mrs. Stockton stirred as he approached, while Grant pulled at his chains, rattling them with intensity.

"Settle down," Stockton seethed. "It will all be over before you know it."

Twenty-Six

The room hung silent. "Bethany! Wake up!" The man said, slapping her cheeks. His attempts appeared to work and she slowly opened her eyes, catching the blurry outline of a man hovering above her. "What happened?" he asked, lightly brushing snow off her face.

"Who's there?" she gently asked, squinting. The man's facial details and prison guard uniform slowly came into focus. "Edward?" she asked, touching his rough face. "You n-need to s-shave."

"I agree," he replied. "But it doesn't appear to be a priority in prison." Bethany sat up in the open doorway of her cottage, brushing the snow off her dress, which had blown through the open area and accumulated on her extremities and living room floor.

"W-w-what are you doing h-here?" she asked, vibrating from the intense cold.

"Let me get you inside so we can close this door. You don't want a case of frostbite, now do you?" Eddie lifted her on her feet and with one arm over his shoulder, they walked across the snow-covered carpet to the main sofa where he gently eased her onto the soft fabric.

She wiped the melted snow from her eyes and face as Eddie closed the front door and rekindled the fireplace.

"I, t-thought you were in j-jail?" Bethany asked.

"I was, but they must have underestimated my West Point military training. Let me just say that I was probably half-way here before they noticed I was missing," he proudly announced. "Not to mention an indignant prison guard who now knows what it feels like to wake up wearing my inmate garb, accompanied by a nasty bump on his head."

"You knocked out a guard?"

"...and took his uniform. But I'm an innocent man, and I refuse to rot away in a damned cell, just waiting to be executed," he said as he took a seat next to his former lover.

"I was planning on getting you and the other gentleman out of there, but *something* stopped me."

"Who did?"

"It wasn't a person, it was a thing," she said, recalling the unfortunate image. "I've never seen anything like it before."

"Bethany, am I missing something here?"

She hesitated a moment while Eddie waited, his eyes watching her patiently. "That's why I was in the doorway," she said. "I was about to go to the police and tell them you were innocent, but I was attacked. I don't know what it was, but I don't wish to think of it any longer. I fear I may be losing my mind."

"We all are, my dear." Eddie's eyes cut to the door then back to Bethany. "Look, I can't stay here long. This will be the first place they'll look for me since they're aware of our affiliation. I apologize that I must cut my visit short, but I just wanted to come and say goodbye. You'll never hear from me again, as I will most likely be in hiding for the rest of my worthless life."

"But—"

"No, listen, you need to hear this. I wish I could give my best regards to you and the louse, but I would rather be honest with you than sour my farewell with obvious lies. The reason for this is because I can see the kind of person he really is. Maybe you're blind to his foulness, but someday, I trust you won't be. I do hope you take care of yourself and see him for what he is."

"Charlie is gone," Bethany replied softly.

Eddie's eyes widened. "What do you mean?"

"I *mean*, he left and is not coming back. I told him I never wanted to see him again after...after he struck me," Bethany said, touching the pronounced bruise on her cheek.

Eddie leaned in to get a closer look. "He hit you? What would make him do such a thing?"

"I called him a louse," Bethany snickered and covered her mouth to conceal the laughter. Smiling, Eddie put his arm around her waist, realizing it would be the last time he'd ever do it. It felt comforting, familiar. Eddie savored the moment and for the first time, he didn't take it for granted.

"I have to leave. My footprints will surely lead them straight here. When they arrive, could you tell them I was never here?"

"I will."

Removing his hand from Bethany's waist, he said, "I suppose I'll hitch a ride on one of those fancy new trains far away from here."

Bethany smiled. "There isn't enough money in New York to get me on one of those death traps. It just seems so unnatural."

Eddie stood and looked solemnly at Bethany. He didn't say a word as he walked to the door and opened it with a quick jar, allowing the blizzard winds to swirl past his cheek and into the living room where Bethany remained seated. After looking back at her one more time, he closed the door behind him and paused on the top step for a brief moment, glaring out at the fallen snow, listening to the winds whistle through his ears.

A streetlamp flickered in unison with each wind gust as the distinct horse gallops and muffled voices sounded far away. Eddie estimated the snow to have accumulated to approximately five inches, which accounted for the desolate streets. But he needn't think twice about who or what dared to brave this harsh weather. They were looking for only one thing, and Eddie knew what it was. He'd already come too far to give up now.

Jumping the entire set of steps to the pavement below as only a young man could, he began to sprint as fast as he could down the empty street, never looking back.

As Eddie fled Bethany's cottage, another man approached. He stopped at the bottom of the porch steps, taking a brief interest in the stranger running down the snow-filled streets ahead.

Bethany remained on the couch in a daze. Her head filled with thoughts of Eddie and Charlie and the dark apparition that had appeared to her. Finally, she stood and rushed to her front door and threw it open.

"Eddie, wait!" But what stood on the other side was not Eddie. This man was pale, gaunt, and he looked almost demonic in appearance.

"Did you miss me?" Charlie asked. "So that was Eddie I saw down the road? I thought that pile of shit was in prison?"

She ignored his question. "What are you doing here? I thought I told you I never wanted to see you again." Charlie took a step closer to her and rested his hand on the doorframe.

"That's far enough," she insisted.

"Oh come now, I know you still have feelings for me."

"You're delusional," she snapped, stepping away from him. "I meant what I said about staying out of my life. I want you to respect my wishes."

"Nonsense, you say you want me out of your life, but yet you allow *him* in it? You're a liar and bitch, my dear." Charlie restrained himself no longer. He pushed his way into her living room and grabbed her by the hair, whipping her head backward with a quick snap. She exhaled a painful scream and clawed at his hands, digging her fingernails into his flesh.

"I'll show you what happens to people who betray me!" he yelled, pushing her against the wall. The impact caused one of her prized oil paintings to crash to the floor, detaching from its frame. He ignored her protests and wrapped his pale hands around her throat, squeezing with inhuman rage. He could see the flesh color begin to drain from her face, and her eyeballs transitioned to bloodshot pellets. She continued to scream a gargled breath, clawing at his chest in a vain effort to break free.

As the room grew dark, Bethany caught the recognizable glimpse of a large black phantom standing at Charlie's side, controlling him like a puppet. The room grew dimmer as she felt the air leave her lungs and her life evaporate.

"Don't move!" A coarse voice sounded out. Charlie released his grip and turned quickly around while Bethany collapsed to the floor, coughing and gasping for air. Two police officers positioned themselves at the open doorway, pistols drawn, hammer's cocked.

"This isn't what it looks like, Jonathan. I was simply trying to—"

"I said, don't move!" the officer commanded. "And don't call me by my first name, you miscreant. Now slowly, put your hands up where I can see them." Charlie rolled his eyes and raised his hands in the air, casually.

"This is ridiculous. If I would be allowed to explain."

"Now, turn around and put them behind your back."

"Make me!" Charlie blurted out. "You stink of cheap booze and failure. Who do you think you're fooling?"

Both officers blinked and looked at each other. "What did you just say?"

"You heard me. Now get back in your carriage and gallop off a cliff."

Both officers charged toward Charlie and gripped his arms, forcing them back while he continued to hurl insults at Jonathan. He was beginning to enjoy his altered nature and newfound knowledge. As he struggled to break free, they slammed him onto the floor next to Bethany. Holding him as still as possible, the officers placed archaic-looking handcuffs around each wrist while he gnashed his teeth and hurled foul-colored sputum onto their uniforms.

Bethany watched the situation unfold through weak eyes, concentrating on the dark beast that remained at Charlie's side—controlling his thoughts, his actions, his speech.

She noticed the officers lift him off the ground and escort him through the doorway and out of sight. The frigid air continued to aggressively blast squalls of snow into the living room, extinguishing the once emblazed fireplace, leaving her alone and cold.

Outside, officers Andrews and Jonathan escorted Charlie to the carriage while a third officer waited at the horse reigns.

"Hey rookie," Jonathan said, catching the officer's attention. "Get down here and open this cell!"

As the officer searched for the appropriate key, they questioned Charlie, asking his name, why he was there, and what his motives were. With each question, his only response was, "Fuck you," leaving the officers with more questions than answers.

Finding himself imprisoned in the back of their carriage did nothing to affect Charlie's demeanor, nor did it influence his judgment. No free-will remained. No emotion. No conscience. Nothing he did or said was his intention; his identity now lost. His appearance had shifted so drastically that even a once trusted friend such as Officer Jonathan had been unable to identify him. Jonathan assumed he was nothing more than a stranger, possibly a vagrant wandering the streets breaking into defenseless woman's homes to rob and torture them for his own sick amusement.

When Jonathan returned to Bethany, she was crawling helplessly across the white marble surface toward the fireplace.

"My apologies, ma'am, let me get you off that floor," he said, rushing to her side. The color had returned to her face, along with the air in her lungs. She was shaken, but ultimately fine. After setting Bethany gently on the couch, the officer took a seat next to her and nodded in the direction of the doorway. "May I ask who that man is?"

"He's Charlie Wilcox," she said then sighed, putting her hands over her face for a brief moment.

"Well, that can't be right. I know Charlie very well, and that man outside is certainly not Charlie."

"Believe me, it is," she replied, just as the front door unexpectedly flew open and the other officer entered quickly, massaging his upper arms as he shivered.

"I'm questioning our victim," Jonathan said. "What is it, Andrews?"

"It's our prisoner, sir. He says the escaped convict was already here tonight. He also told me that he saw him leaving and knows where he's headed." Jonathan turned to Bethany but spoke only with his eyes. She decided to keep her promise to Eddie.

"I haven't seen anyone tonight other than Charlie. He has to be lying."

"You're probably right," Andrews said. "But we should at least see if his story checks out, Jonathan. Remember what the warden told us, leave no stone—"

"Unturned, yes, I know," Jonathan interrupted, turning back to Bethany. "It might only be the ramblings of a madman, but we have to follow every lead. We'll be back to check on you as soon as we can."

"No, wait, I don't want to be alone right now," she said.

Jonathan stood and gazed into her glassy blue eyes. "I think it's better if you stay here for now. This is a matter for the police. You do understand?" Bethany sank lower into her seat and closed her eyes, forgetting her troubles for just a moment.

"Are you sure you'll be fine here by yourself?" Andrews asked.

As Bethany gently rested her head on the pillow, she replied, "It doesn't look like I have a choice."

Twenty-Seven

Richard and Alice continued to watch the situation unfold through each of the tiny eyeholes of their iron maidens. Since he arrived in the basement, Stockton had been playing with his victims the way a small boy with a mean disposition would play with his toys. He threatened many times to pull the lever, which would cause the pendulum to sway, degrading them as they lay unclothed and vulnerable, accusing them of adultery and an array of other misdoings.

The side of Mrs. Stockton's cheek had been sliced apart, along with her breasts and torso. Her vagina had been sewn shut with a dull needle and dirty thread, creating a pool of blood on the table directly between her legs. Stockton had been careful, however, to cause just the proper amount of wounds to prevent her from fully bleeding out.

Grant, on the other hand, had not fared quite as well. He wasn't dead. That would've been a blessing. On the table next to his head was a small pile of bloodied teeth that had been extracted with a pair of pliers. His body had also been lacerated, but other mutilations occurred too. Set neatly in a row, next to the teeth were an assortment of butchered fingers, toes, and partial pieces of his hands and feet. Richard had never heard a more soul-shaking scream than when Stockton began to carve Grant's fingers with a rusted amputation saw leftover from the Colonial era.

Blood had erupted across the pale room, painting Mrs. Stockton's naked flesh a bright shade of red as each finger plopped to the crimson-stained floor. He begged for Stockton to stop, pleaded with every moral fiber he could muster. But it did them no good.

Standing alone and quiet, Alice slowly reached her terror threshold. She prevented herself from screaming several times by simply closing her eyes and turning off the horrid visions, but even then, the shrill screams of Stockton's victims drilled her imagination. With each swipe of Stockton's knife, she bit down harder and harder on her fingers to keep the screams at bay, drawing blood from her cuticles and knuckles until it dripped down her elbows and onto her shoes.

She almost gave herself away when Stockton revealed the secret object he'd been hiding in the brown woven sack. When he pulled his valet's severed head from its resting place, her outbursts were shrouded by Mrs. Stockton's shrieks and Grant's ear-piercing obscenities. It was the only thing that saved her.

But with no willpower left and her nerves extinguished, she instinctively opened her tearstained eyes at the sound of Grant's harrowing protests, instantly regretting the decision. What she saw was Stockton hovering over Grant with the old rusted bone-saw placed strategically onto his genitalia, threatening his manhood.

Alice then belted out a penetrating scream which rung her eardrums within the confined space, startling Stockton and causing him to turn to its source.

The room became eerily quiet as all eyes focused on Alice's iron maiden. Even Grant stopped shrieking long enough to glance over.

Slowly, the door of the torture device creaked open, and Stockton's eyes darkened when he saw the weathered yet beautiful woman emerge.

"You," he said. "I remember you."

While clutching her handbag, she slid out of the contraption and stepped softly onto the basement floor, her head held high.

"Let...them...go!" she demanded. Stockton looked at her and began to chuckle. "I said, let...them...go!"

Stockton's laughter quieted down, and he gave her a curious look. "Wait a minute. You're serious?" he asked. "I must admit that you do have a fiery spirit. I remember that from the first time we met. Yes, I do believe you called me an asshole, if I'm not mistaken."

"And I told you to go fuck yourself," she clarified, walking closer to him.

"Be careful, Alice," Richard mumbled from his hiding place.

Stockton raised the bone-saw and proceeded slowly towards her, keeping his eyes locked on hers. "I think someone needs to teach you a lesson."

"Let me know when he shows up," her voice quivered as she rapidly closed the distance between them. She kept her hands concealed and fingered an elongated device inside of her handbag. As Stockton raised the saw, she swiftly dropped her bag to the floor and lifted the canister to his twisted face. She pressed down on the release button of the pocket-sized bottle of mace, expecting it to spray its blinding contents directly into the monster's eyes. Nothing happened. Not even a drop expelled from the canister.

She frantically pressed again as Stockton hobbled closer, but when his face hit the torchlight, her reflexes tightened from the shock of his disfigured appearance. She continued to press the plunger, hoping for something to happen, but the window of opportunity had closed. Stockton gripped her wrist and twisted the mace from her grasp, causing it to drop to the floor and roll out of sight. She kicked his shins and clawed at his face, but her feeble actions only fed Stockton's amusement. His smile said more than any words.

Gripping her other arm, he sandwiched her onto the table between Grant and Mrs. Stockton.

"Let go of me before I—"

"Before you what? You'll do nothing," he replied, clasping a pair of large shackles around her wrists and securing them tightly. "If you don't stop squirming, I'll have to resort to more extreme measures. He held out his hand and said, "Now, where is my basement key?"

"What are you talking about?" Alice asked.

"How else could you have gotten down here? Where is it?" he demanded.

"The door was already open. I don't have it."

"You're a terrible liar. Fine, have it your way."

From across the room, Richard watched his companion, feeling helpless. After securing Alice's shackles with a small metal key, Stockton retrieved the canister of mace that rolled under the table. After eyeing it for a moment, he held it up and asked what it was.

"It's a butt plug," she replied. "You can stick it up your ass."

From her sofa, Bethany watched the heavy snowfall outside her window. The throbbing in her throat had subsided to nothing more than a dull ache. Still, she was unsure if Charlie had done any permanent damage to her windpipe. Her breathing appeared normal, but it seemed difficult to swallow any of the brandy she had poured.

Out of disgust, she set the lead cup onto the wooden table next to her and opened her front door to get a better view of the snow. As far as she could tell, the drifts along her front steps had accumulated to close to one foot. She thought about Eddie caught by the cops, the same cops that saved her. It just didn't seem fair to make her wait at home after she insisted on accompanying them.

She couldn't sit around any longer.

After walking down the first step, she watched her right foot sink past her ankle into the untainted snow, inducing an instant numbing sensation. She continued down the steps, leaving tiny footprints behind her. By the time she reached the sidewalk, her stroll had turned into a light jog, and then a full out sprint that could turn any Olympic hopeful a pale shade of green. Fueled by adrenaline, she propelled down the center of the vacant streets, kicking up fluff, following the carriage tracks, and hoping she would reach her destination before hypothermia set in—even if it meant giving herself away.

Richard could hear his ex-wife in his head, encouraging him to be a man and rescue Alice.

Open the door and be the hero for once in your life!

Even though she wasn't there, he agreed with her. Wiping the nervous sweat from his forehead, he took a deep breath and carefully avoided the sharp spikes, placing both hands on the front of the door. He wanted to wait for the right time to pull his Harry Callahan act, thinking there might be a lull in Stockton's judgment that could allow him some leverage.

He continued to hesitate while Stockton examined the bottle of mace, poking at the nozzle and shaking the canister next to his ear. Confused with the strange device, he walked over to Alice. "Tell me how it works," he demanded, holding up the bottle.

"I already told you how it works," Alice replied, smiling. Stockton didn't respond, he simply grimaced and shook his head. After placing the mace onto one of the tables displaying the various bone saws and bloody rags, his interest shifted to the vibrant Emerald stone earrings that Alice wore.

He quickly faced his wife. "Do you remember these, dear? They were an object of my one-time affection for you," he said, ripping them from Alice's earlobes. Alice screamed, her head shaking as droplets of blood flecked into her hair. "I apologize to you, young lady, but I already gave you the chance to hand them over once before. This time, I'm taking them back myself." He placed the earrings in his pocket and stood in front of his three captives. "I will see you all in the morning, as I am exhausted and cannot stay down here any longer. As for Grant and my cheating wife, please do your best not to bleed out overnight. I would hate to think I'd be unable to observe your blank faces as the pendulum slices you in half. But in the meantime, I will give you something to ponder in my brief absence."

Stockton proceeded to the lever that operated the pendulum. With a hefty pull, he activated the rusty contraption, triggering its swaying motion.

"I won't lower it until morning, but I want you to gaze at its hypnotic sway on the last evening of your lives." He turned to the stairs, pausing at the first step. "Since we have a big day tomorrow, I'm going to get some sleep. Have a good night!" He placed the valet's severed head on the table next to them, then turned as he and the dark figure disappeared up the winding staircase.

Richard shook off the tension, feeling as though he'd failed Alice and the others. As Stockton's footsteps faded in the distance, Richard quietly pushed on the rusted door, causing the hinges to screech as it opened, revealing an unobstructed view of the room. For a moment, he kept his breathing shallow, listening, almost anticipating the return of footsteps.

"Richard?" Alice whispered.

"Yes," he replied, sneaking silently across the stone floor to the table, gagging as he noticed the piles of bloodied teeth and severed fingers.

"I'm sorry I took so long," he whispered between dry heaves. "Just hold tight." Richard examined the cuffs and the attached chain links. "Alice, I think the locking mechanism requires a—"

"Well, go get it!" she whispered. Richard stared blankly at her. "The key, Richard, get it."

"Right, I'm on it."

Glaring at the emblazed stone wall, Richard mustered his courage and grabbed one of the brightly lit torches.

"The key rack at the top of the staircase, you should check there first," Alice said.

Richard looked back one last time. "Wish me luck."

Twenty-Eight

Richard hurried through the open steel door and brightened the dusty wooden shelf with his torch.

Shit. It was bare.

Other than the fiery torch, the house was dark and silent. He didn't know which was worse, especially since he was out of options. He knew that waking Stockton and asking him politely for the key was out of the question, so he figured he'd just have to force it from him.

He worked up his courage, stepped lightly across the threshold towards the grand staircase and peered up into the ominous darkness. His heartbeat increased as he anticipated his actions. After grasping the iron railing, he began his ascent up the marble steps when a loud click rang out from the front of the room, followed by the creak of an opening door.

Richard stopped and watched the front doorway open, revealing the backlit shadow of an unwelcomed visitor. The man silently entered the mansion, bringing whirlwinds of snow along with him.

Richard didn't move as he watched him close the door and lightly brush the snow off his sleeves and shoulders. He proceeded further into the room and cautiously looked around. The low lighting made it impossible to make out his features, but he moved with a familiar walk and a blank innocent charisma. After pausing for a moment, the man began heading in Richard's direction.

As he closed the gap, it looked as though he were dressed in an officer's uniform but appeared unarmed. Realizing it would be only a few moments before the stranger noticed him, Richard decided to announce his presence first and worry about the consequences later.

"Stop right there," he instructed the stranger. The man gasped. Richard walked out from the stairway, holding the only source of light in the room, and proceeded toward him. As the ominous man's face came faintly into view, Richard almost lost grip on the torch. "Eddie," he whispered, keeping some distance between the two of them.

"Richard? Eddie replied. "What are you doing here?"

"I should ask you the same thing. I thought you were in jail? And why are you wearing a prison-guard uniform? And how did you even get in here?"

"It's a long story, but to answer your last question, I know all of Timothy's hiding spots," Eddie said, holding up a front door key. "You just have to know where to look."

Richard winced, thinking back to the ladder and his struggle through the second story window. "It figures," he grumbled.

"Anyway, I'm just here to retrieve my suitcase, and then I will be on my way."

"Oh, thank God. So you know where it is?"

"Of course I do, why?"

"Well, to be honest, I'm here for the same reason. You told me you had money in there, so I came back to retrieve it so that I could spring you out of that hellhole. But I've come across a little more than I anticipated. We need to help them, Eddie."

"Help who?"

"They're in the basement. Listen to me. We need to go to the police and get help immediately."

"Are you mad? The last thing I need to do is to go to the police. I'd be locked up the minute I walked in. Now, I would love to stay and talk about it, Richard, but I'm afraid the cops will catch up to me sooner rather than later if I stick around."

"Good, let them," Richard replied. "That's why I need to talk to you. I can prove your innocence. The evidence is right in the—"

"If you would be so kind as to light my way with your torch, Richard, I would be ever so grateful," Eddie said as he began to walk across the room." Just follow behind me,"

"Wait, I said I could prove your innocence."

"No time for that now," Eddie replied. He hurried to a corner of the large room located next to the darkened kitchen, followed closely by Richard.

"Right here, cast some light," Eddie instructed, pointing to a dark section of the floor. Richard relocated to the corner and shined the torch onto a small iron handle, attached to a well-camouflaged trap.

"Hold it steady now," Eddie commanded with the diligence of a desperate man. After getting a grip on the handle, he gave it a pull and slowly hefted the door, prompting the rusted hinges to shriek as he rested it gently on the floor.

"Could you slow down for a moment?" Richard asked. "What I have to say is very important."

"Give me some more light," Eddie said.

"Are you listening to me?"

"Please, give me some more light."

"No, not until you hear me out!" Richard replied. He reached his threshold as he grabbed Eddie by the arm, turning him away from the trap door. "Listen to me! They're in the basement."

"How about you listen to me? I don't know if I buy your story about trying to help me out of prison by stealing my suitcase back, but right now I am getting what I came here for, and I am getting the hell out of here before I run into Stockton or anyone with a badge and pistol. Do you understand?"

Richard shut up for a moment and watched the flames of the torch bounce in all directions. "Fine, have it your way." He directed the light over the gaping sanctuary as Eddie crawled onto the ground and reached inside. From his viewpoint, Richard could see the multitude of insects and spiders that laced the walls of the underground crypt, inducing a sickening sensation in the depths of his gut. And then, a shimmer of light gleamed off the handle of what appeared to be a suitcase—Eddie's suitcase.

"I think I have it," he announced, pulling it from the depths onto the floor next to him.

Confused, Richard asked," How did you know it was down there?"

"It's the only place Stockton would've put it," he replied, clapping the soot off his hands. "He thinks I don't know about his hiding place, but he's as predictable as a spooked horse."

"So, it's his storage area for useless junk?" Richard asked.

Eddie stopped brushing his coat sleeve off for a moment and thought about the question. "I suppose so."

"Well, I wish I'd known this was down there earlier, it would've saved Alice and me a great deal of trouble."

"You and Alice? What are you talking about?"

"Yeah, that's what I've been trying to tell you. She's in the basement." Richard started to explain everything when the unmistakable sound of a horse-drawn carriage approached the front of the mansion, infusing terror within Eddie.

"Wait, do you hear that?" he asked, grabbing Richard by his coat-sleeve. "Quick, I have to hide."

"What? Why?"

Eddie threw the suitcase back down the shallow crypt. "Just as I feared, they've found me."

The gallops from outside ceased as a carriage silhouette came into view through the wavy stained-glass windows. The faint sound of voices and footsteps could be heard through the walls as Eddie quickly jumped into the cold darkness of the pit.

"Richard, get down here," he stage-whispered. "You're going to give me away."

The door swung open, revealing two ominous figures positioned in the gaping archway. Richard gasped and quickly positioned himself over the crypt, handing the torch down to Eddie.

"Here, now move out of the way," he instructed as he grasped the trap door's handle, jumping inside. Eddie lowered it over top of them with a dull thud.

The crypt was disgusting. Richard almost wished he hadn't seen the assorted creatures that shared the small space. Both men bordered on childish actions as they squirmed from the crippling sights. Three-inch centipedes and various colored spiders crawled upon Eddie's back and shoulders. As Richard watched, he wondered what unknown crawly was simultaneously attaching itself to him.

The black smoke from the torch swept up and licked the underside of the trap door, distributing its toxic aroma to the confined space, allowing oxygen to deplete quickly. The nauseating scent stung their eyes and charred their nostrils as each breath became more strained. While brushing the insects from Eddie's back, Richard fought asphyxiation, and asked, "Can I see the torch for a moment? The fire is eating up the oxygen. We need to extinguish it."

"I think something is wrong with me," Eddie said softly. "I don't feel right. My head is swimming."

"Well, we're breathing more carbon dioxide than oxygen, so we either…blow out the torch, or we open…the trap door where you'll immediately be discovered."

Eddie chose the torch.

***

The two visitors above ground slowly headed to the kitchen area and stood directly on the trap door. "We should find Mr. Stockton and inform him that we're here," a raspy voice instructed.

Across the room, in front of the dim fireplace, Stockton rested in a blissful trance that began to lift slowly. Seated in his favorite chair, he listened to the dull voices carry on a conversation, practically unaware of the distraction. His eyes and ears eventually opened, now aware that more than one uninvited guest had joined him.

He sat up and grasped the firm arms of the elegant chair, digging his long unnatural fingernails into the thick wood, harvesting his anger for its intended targets. For he knew anyone foolish enough to snoop around in the cellar would soon have to join his growing list of permanent houseguests.

As he stared deeply into the extinguished fireplace in front of him, the subdued orange glow began to take form. It grew brighter, casting its essence upon his face, illuminating inhuman features.

His pointed ears and pale green skin hung off his skull like a wet washcloth on a rusty metal rail and his eyes flared red in the darkness. Only a few sprouts of hair remained upon his flaking scalp, hanging limp and seizing the space that his once ravishing crop of hair formerly occupied.

The glow of the fire billowed higher and further until it erupted out, prompting a blaze that spilled over the fireplace wall for a brief moment, casting its rays upon the menacing painting that hung above. Eternally gone was the tranquility of the masterpiece, replaced permanently with a portrait of sadness. As the fire ignited in a resounding display, the two frightened visitors quickly turned their attention to the incredible exhibition.

"Welcome!" Stockton announced, rising from his throne like a corrupt warlord, arms outstretched, smile blemished. His guests stumbled back at the sight of his presence.

"Oh, I apologize," one of them said. "I was unaware anyone was here."

"It's quite all right. Come in here. Don't be shy."

The guests looked at each other and proceeded over to where Stockton lingered near his fireplace. As the visitors approached, they glimpsed his mangled features and abruptly stopped.

"Mr. Stockton, are you feeling all right?" the visitor asked. Stockton turned away from the hypnotic dance of his fireplace and took a few steps toward them.

"I feel fine. Why do you ask?"

The same visitor noticed his gleaming eyes but remained subtle. "No reason," he added. "You just don't seem yourself."

Richard and Eddie listened to the muffled voices above while trying their best not to choke on the lingering smoke.

"This is it, they've found me," Eddie said. "I might as well slap the cuffs on myself and save them the trouble."

Richard cupped his ear to the door. "I still can't make out what they're saying, but I think I hear Stockton."

"Does it really matter?" Eddie asked, holding his hand over his mouth to curb an impending cough.

"Yes, it *does* matter. You should see what he did to the people in the basement. His wife and business partner are shackled to a table underneath that fucking pendulum he showed us the night of his party. And..." Richard hesitated a moment. "As I mentioned earlier, he also has Alice."

Eddie lowered his hand. "My God. Why didn't you say something earlier, Richard?"

"Well, I was trying to, but someone ignored me."

"Who ignored you?"

Richard rolled his eyes. "Just forget it."

"No, we need to help them. What can we do?"

"Well, I think the cops are up there talking to Stockton now. Like I said earlier, we can prove your innocence, and also save them. I owe it to Alice. She tried to intervene against that nutcase and now she's in just as much trouble." Richard thought for a moment. "Of course, I had the opportunity to rescue her while I was down there, but I froze up. I can't make that mistake again."

The guests continued to analyze Stockton's altered appearance.

"I apologize for the late arrival," one of them said, "but the storm slowed our travel time significantly."

"Nothing to worry about, I had simply forgotten that I was expecting patrons tonight," Stockton explained. "The upstairs rooms are mostly unoccupied, so you'll have the pick of the litter." The visitors kept a considerable distance, holding hands. The bride's rapid pulse spread outward to her fingertips while the groom held his top hat directly over his heart. They were both attractive, neither one more than nineteen-years-old. The bride still adorned her white lace wedding gown and flowing veil, its train cascading ten-feet behind.

Stockton nodded in their direction. "I can imagine you've both had a long day. And, I do believe congratulations are in order." Stockton's smile evaporated as he glared at the groom. "A word of advice to you, my good man," he continued. "Don't let her out of your sight for even a moment, lest she stab you in the back, betraying you, failing you."

The newlyweds momentarily glanced at each other. The groom spoke up. "Mr. Stockton, I apologize for my candidness, but when I was here last month reserving the room, you *appeared* much different. Forgive me for bringing it up again, but has something traumatic happened?" Stockton extended his fingernails and took a few steps forward. "No matter," the groom replied, noticing the apparent threat. "It's not important. We shall retire to our room now if it's all the same."

A loud screech from the trap door bounced off the far walls, causing the newlyweds and Stockton to flinch as it hit the floor. Richard was the first to emerge. He quickly got to his feet and headed toward the congregation. "Officers," he called out as he closed in, followed closely by Eddie. "You need to arrest this man immediately. I have physical proof of the horrible crimes he's committed."

As they approached the three shadowy figures, the warm light from the fireplace cast itself upon their faces, subtly revealing their identities. Both Richard and Eddie stopped immediately at the sight of the groom and his bride. A lump formed in Richard's throat and his heart almost stopped.

"Jesus Christ!" Eddie exclaimed at the sight of Stockton's new form. "What in God's name happened to him?" For a few moments, no one said a word. The only sound was that of heavy breathing induced by panic.

The groom, feeling uneasy, asked, "Is there any truth to what he said, Mr. Stockton?"

Stockton didn't return an immediate answer. Instead, he pulled out his pocket-watch and examined it. It was the bride's voice that cracked the awkward silence. "If it's all the same, I think we should be heading out now. The snow seems to have eased up, and we don't want to burden you any longer." Stockton leaned against the fireplace mantle as he closed his watch and peered up.

"I wouldn't hear of it," he wheezed." On the contrary, I think both of you will be here much longer than you anticipated."

"Don't listen to him," Richard whispered to the couple. "Just get out of here."

"It's quite beautiful, if you think about it," Stockton interrupted. "They both begin their future life here, and also end their life here."

The couple slowly stepped back, expanding their distance. After noticing their fear, Stockton asked, "You're not trying to leave, are you?" The couple ignored his mockery and continued to step back until they joined Richard and Eddie, leaving Stockton alone next to the fireplace.

"What should we do?" Eddie whispered to Richard.

"Why are you asking me?" he shot back.

"I thought you were leading this rebellion!"

"Right, well, I think we should do nothing, for now."

"Is that your advice?" the bride interrupted. "I most certainly am not staying here another minute." After gripping her husband's hand, she pulled him across the large living area toward the exit.

"Where do you think you're going?" Stockton asked, gliding to them like a paper airplane. You're not allowed to leave."

"No, please," the bride responded. Her emotions took over. Releasing the groom's hand, she ran toward the safety and freedom of the outside. As she reached for the door handle, a muffled voice from the other side caught her attention. The door opened, and three surprised police officers blocked her escape.

"Whoa, slow down a minute, ma'am," officer Jonathan said, holding her by the shoulders. "Why are you leaving in such a hurry?"

"Hello, Jonathan!" Stockton announced. "And Andrews, it is nice to see you as well." Stockton pointed at the third officer. "And you...I don't know who you are."

"Oh, yes, my name is—"

"He's a rookie," Jonathan blurted. "Warren is his name. Rookie Warren, we like to call him."

"Is that so?" Stockton reacted with more of a statement than a question.

"Uh, yes, sir. Sometimes they do," the rookie answered. Stockton's teeth gleamed as he broke a crooked smile, glancing at the bride.

"Don't worry about her. She is simply a homesick houseguest with wedding night jitters. Never got laid before tonight, I assume."

Eddie was grateful for the dim lighting of the room, which shrouded his identity, realizing the officers might've already shot him dead before hearing him out.

"We apologize for bothering you at such a late hour," Andrews said. "But may we come inside for a moment?"

"You are always welcome here," Stockton replied, waving the officers on. "Come in, please." The three officers walked inside, looking into the void that spread in every direction. "And may I ask what brings you all the way here tonight?"

"Do you remember the man we arrested?" Jonathan asked. "The murderer?"

"You arrested *two* men, if I recall."

"Yes, an Edgar A. Poe and Richard S. Langley. Earlier this evening, Edgar attacked a prison guard and is now missing. But thanks to the snowstorm, we've been able to track him." Stockton turned in Eddie's direction. "We kindly ask your permission to search the house and its grounds, as we cannot leave any stone unturned."

"No need, gentleman," Stockton smiled and stepped aside. "He's cowering over there in the corner." Eddie felt his body go numb at the sound of his betrayer's voice.

"It's all right," Richard whispered to Eddie. "When they see what's in the basement, you'll have nothing to worry about."

"Right here," Stockton announced, while walking over to Eddie and gripping him by the arm.

The bride and groom watched in shock, both of them seeing through Stockton's façade. He pulled both Richard and Eddie from their shadowy solitude, luring them to the front of the room where the officers awaited with pistols drawn. Neither man put up a fight. As Eddie stood sternly in front of the three officers, he maintained eye contact with Stockton, still taken aback by his brash appearance.

"So this is where the uniform disappeared to," Jonathan chuckled, noticing the dimly lit details of Eddie's wardrobe. He cocked the hammer of his gun and asked, "Do you have anything else you'd like to say before I put a bullet in your head?"

"Wait a moment," officer Andrews spoke up, "I thought we were simply going to arrest him?"

"You thought wrong, my good man. I do believe we'd be doing the entire justice department a favor if we were to finish the job right here on the spot."

"I agree," Stockton chimed in. "Just shoot him and get it over with."

Richard panicked, realizing his whole mission was collapsing. He didn't know what exactly would happen if Eddie were to be killed before he could finish his life's work, but he knew it might cause a disastrous ripple effect, possibly for centuries. Either way, the outcome would either be outright cataclysmic or, it might just mildly suck, but he didn't want to take that chance either way.

"With all due respect, sir," Andrews added. "I don't think this is a good idea. Shouldn't we just cuff him and bring him back with—"

"He assaulted and humiliated a prison guard. I'm the one in charge here, and what I say goes!" Jonathan continued to stare down Eddie. Eddie continued to stare down Stockton. Rookie Warren said nothing but looked as if he were about to lose control of his bodily functions.

"Now, you look me in the eye, *Edgar*!" Jonathan shouted. Eddie ignored him.

"Wait!" Richard called out. "I have some information that might be of some interest to you."

Jonathan slightly lowered his gun. "And what do we have here, another jailbird? Yeah, I remember you. If anyone asked, I'd say you deserve to get one in the head too. A thief is what you are, breaking into homes and taking what isn't yours. And there's something odd going on. You don't talk or act like anyone I've ever met before. It leads me to believe you have something to hide. Is that it? You have something to hide?"

"No, sir," Richard calmly replied. Slowly, he turned his head and extended his finger, pointing in Stockton's direction. "But *he* does."

Stockton's nostrils flared at the marvelous thought of ripping Richard's head from its spine and then reveling at the sight of it rolling down his basement staircase.

"It's true," Eddie added.

"I don't believe I was talking to you," Jonathan sounded, raising his pistol to Eddie once more.

"Wait," Richard said. "If you would just take a look in the basement, you will see Stockton's true nature."

"I've never heard of such nonsense," Stockton replied. "Can't you see these men will say anything to save themselves?"

"Down there, you will find his wife—also, her lover, and my friend, Alice, shackled to one of his torture devices."

"It's nothing but lies, Jonathan," Stockton said, walking a few steps in their direction and into a beam of outside light which brightened his disfigured face. Officer Andrews took notice, his eyes widened. "You've known me long enough to understand what they say is untrue."

Putting a hand on his holster for security, Andrews remembered their prisoner waiting outside behind bars. He recalled the same disfigured features and a similar feeling of dread.

Andrews spoke up. "Jonathan, maybe we *should* check out the basement, if only to put this silly accusation to rest."

Lowering his pistol again, Jonathan glanced at Stockton with a similar concern and replied, "Fine, we'll have a quick look if it makes you feel better." Richard felt a small amount of relief and a tiny glimmer of hope. Eddie was not as optimistic. He hadn't seen the basement for himself and could only hope that Richard's story held weight.

"Officers, these men are trespassing without my permission," Stockton said. "I demand you arrest them immediately, or shoot them. Whichever gets the job done." He looked at Eddie and Richard and his smile was black as midnight.

"I wouldn't do that officer," the young bride's small voice rose up. You didn't see the way Mr. Stockton was acting before you arrived. It was frightening. Why do you think I was trying to run out of here so quickly?" Stockton shot the bride a scornful look, warning her with his eyes.

Blood-trails streaked from the bottom of the basement steps to the top of the entryway. It took more than an hour for Grant to slide his stumps through the shackles and crawl his way up the narrow stairs. With Stockton being so preoccupied with revenge, he hadn't considered that an amputee would have a more accessible escape method.

The floor felt colder than usual due to his substantial blood-loss, but Grant pressed on, relying mostly on his elbows to pull his bodyweight. He was unsure as to where he was going, but he quickly noticed, while through the wooden doorway to the living area, that he was not alone. The echo of voices across the room drew his attention to the police officers and various guests that engaged in conversation. Without knowing it, he released a sob of anguish, alerting everyone to his presence.

They turned quickly to witness the dim silhouette of a mangled man attempting to get to his feet.

"What in God's name is that?" Eddie blurted out. The bride let out a scream and grabbed her husband's waist, hiding her face behind him. The officers stared at the abomination as it gained footing and proceeded to stagger toward them, its naked body gleaming with fresh blood that covered every area. The man's genitalia swung with each stilted step, mocking the onlookers. The mortified faces of the officers elicited no response.

As the pitiful man stumbled to the floor, Jonathan pulled his pistol and aimed it at Stockton's head, cocking the hammer as sweat beaded down his cheeks. The gun shook from his frazzled nerves, and he felt his pulse beat through his fingertips.

"Timothy, you're under arrest. Put your hands high above your head," he calmly instructed. Stockton paid no mind to the instructions and remained unresponsive as he glared heavily into the large painting above the fireplace mantle. His eyes flared with anticipation as he witnessed the ripples manifesting around the edges of the large wooden frame. "I will not ask again! Put your hands above your head!" Jonathan instructed.

The painting slowly began to animate with images of a vast burned-out hillside, engulfed by fire and thick smoke. A horde of shapeless entities materialized within its confines, fornicating with the unfortunate victims portrayed in the painting. At the same time, puss oozed from their lesions and the demonic figures raped their gaping wounds.

With each thrust, blood and bodily fluids dripped down the canvas and over the cherry wood frame of the painting. It splattered the top of the fireplace mantle and onto the marble floor at a rapid pace. A smile broke across Stockton's face as he turned to confront his guests.

As he raised his hands above his head, the row of extinguished torches which lined both sides of the wall began to burst into flames one by one as if an invisible force took a flamethrower to them. The group of guests huddled together at the baffling display, cowered away from Stockton and his mysterious power. The room, now brightly lit, brought its own terror. No longer shrouded in darkness, Grant's body laid sprawled on the cold marble floor, bleeding crimson red against ivory white.

The painting now visible to the guests, struck another chord, prompting a different emotion in each. Jonathan's nerves expired, causing him to drop his pistol. The bride blacked out and fainted into her distraught groom's arms, and in a panic, Andrews fled through the front door and slipped on the icy outside steps, causing him to topple down the stairs, landing directly on his lumbar.

Jonathan attempted to follow his partner but when he approached the open doorway, it slammed shut before he could make it. He witnessed the impossible; the bolt lock sliding mysteriously into place, as if an invisible hand placed it there, trapping the occupants inside. Jonathan attempted to pull the latch and handle but neither budged. It was as if they were welded shut. Rookie Warren remained frozen in place, pissing his pants and creating a puddle as he watched everyone scramble.

Jonathan turned and faced Stockton who remained in the center of the room. The torches continued their fiery eruption, engulfing the area in a dazzling orange glow. The phantoms portrayed in the rippling painting began to animate from the canvass, materializing in front of the fireplace.

The room soon became full of shadowy specters. They floated in a row, a few inches off the floor, resembling a Civil War marching line. Richard, now very familiar with the apparitions, counted twenty in total. Jonathan howled at the impossible sight and nervously continued his fruitless effort to un-jam the door lock. As he screamed and pleaded for his life, he appeared more like a frightened child than a courageous police officer. Richard could have sworn he called out, "Mommy!" at some point.

Upon losing his patience, Richard yelled, "Stop!" startling the officer. "We're obviously not leaving anytime soon. Get a grip on yourself." Jonathan released the lock and turned to Richard, but avoided eye contact.

Lowering his arms, Stockton glided a few feet in front of his terrified guests and abruptly stopped. A grand organ in the far corner of the room began to play, "I'll Be Seeing You," a song that wouldn't be made famous for yet another hundred years. Richard instantly recognized its beautiful melody and began to hum the soothing tune to ease his panic.

Lost in the moment, he barely noticed the horde of specters floating toward them.

"Fuck!" was all he said.

Twenty-Nine

On the other side of the door, officer Andrews continued to seethe from his painful fall when he noticed the holding cell that had imprisoned Charlie was gaped open and the lock that secured it rested in two pieces on a snowdrift.

Andrews wanted to stand, but when he attempted to roll on his stomach and grasp the side of the carriage for support, nothing happened. He tried again, and neither his arms nor his legs responded to his commands.

He attempted to scream, but again, nothing happened. The blistering wind struck his face, causing a burning impact across his cheeks and lips. However, all sensation below his neck had ceased. He attempted to move his arms and wiggle his toes, but they were completely unresponsive.

Unable to feel his body, he opened his mouth in another attempt to scream with the same horrific results. Behind him, the sound of footsteps meshing against fresh snow temporarily deterred him and a glassy voice sliced the silence.

"Hello, officer. It's a rather pleasant night, wouldn't you say?" Andrews looked up and saw the blurry outline of Charlie standing over him like a triumphant gamesman. After crouching down to the fallen officer's level, he casually glanced over him.

"I bet you would very much like to be enlightened on the matter of my escape?" he asked. Only a few garbles left Andrews' mouth. "I'll take that as a yes. It was rather simple, actually. According to the way you burst out of the house like a startled kitten, it appears as if you are more than aware of the situation occurring behind that door and if you had any doubt before, let me assure you that your chances of making it out of here alive are quite slim." Charlie laughed, shaking his head a little. "Just a few days ago, I was like you, weak and broken. But now, I am enlightened to the real world. The dark forces of the universe are wondrous and powerful beyond mortal comprehension, and I am now on a different tier. I'm a celestial being! And you..." He bent down close to Andrew's ear and whispered, "...are nothing more than an insignificant worm."

Andrews wished he could speak. If only to tell this piece-of-shit what he really thought of him. He imagined reaching for his pistol and placing it on Charlie's forehead. *Who's the worm now?* Andrews thought.

"It's still you," Charlie blurted out. "Oh, you can fantasize all you like, but it's not going to change anything." Charlie pulled Andrews' pistol from its holster and pointed it at his face. "This is what you want, isn't it? What do you think? Should I just shoot you between the eyes right now and put you out of your misery, or should I let you lay here like a head on a stick?" he asked, pausing for a response. "Well? What's it going to be?"

Andrews mustered all his energy, and still, nothing worked. "Hmm, I suppose I'll decide for you. Here, take your gun back," he said, throwing it at the officer's side. "It's not like I need it anymore. It's a shame you're going to miss the party."

Charlie stood and peered down at the pathetic sight. In the foggy distance, the faint outline of a person struggling through the desolate streets gradually crept into Andrews' view.

The line of phantoms grew closer. "Mr. Stockton!" Richard called out. "All of this for one man? It seems a bit extreme, wouldn't you agree?"

Stockton laughed at the accusation and pushed the few strands of hair he had left from his forehead.

"All of this is *not* for one man!" Stockton replied in an ethereal voice. "I rather enjoy my newfound abilities, so I find no shame in putting them to use and dealing with said man in the process."

Eddie looked at Richard. "Who is this man you speak of?"

"That would be you."

Eddie frowned. "Me? What are you talking about?"

"I'll explain later. Just do me a favor."

"I suppose."

"Don't die," Richard replied.

Stockton briefly assessed his reluctant guests. The groom was still tending to his unconscious bride, her back propped against the wall while he caressed her golden locks. Richard and Eddie stood their ground directly in front of the doorway. Grant lay dead on the floor, still bleeding out, while Jonathan crouched by the exit, still clutching the door handle like a frightened kindergartener that shit his pants on the first day of school.

The handle began to jiggle and the locks popped without human contact, prompting Jonathan to release his tight grip. The door abruptly swung open, and Charlie walked in, gazing at the alarmed group. A childlike smile swept across his altered face at the sight of

Stockton and his minions. Richard and Eddie backed away from Charlie as he casually strolled over to Grant's corpse.

"What happened here?" he asked, lifting the lifeless head off the floor. "I see you started without me."

After dropping the head back onto the ground with a hollow thump, he walked to Eddie and stood in front of him, glaring into his soul. "So, you're the one who is causing all this fuss. Let me ask if I may...who is the louse *now*?"

Eddie stared back. "Still you," he replied, cringing from the foul odor that reeked from Charlie's decayed lungs.

"Excuse me, your highness," Richard said to Stockton, "but why not let the rest of us go? None of us has wronged you in any way, not to mention the innocent woman shackled to your basement table, which I would very much like to see alive and unharmed."

Stockton smiled. "I'm sure you would. Your fondness for her is...painfully obvious."

Charlie walked to Stockton and stood by his side. "Let us do them a favor and end their lives right now."

"Just one moment," Stockton said, raising his hand in the air. He snapped his fingers sharply and cocked his head. "The woman's shackles have been released. Go to the basement if you wish to see her, time traveler, and bring her back. I will not offer this opportunity twice."

Richard's breath fell short as everyone in the room focused on him. "So you know?" he asked, shocked that Stockton was aware of his secret.

Richard stepped across the marble floor and carefully avoided Grant's mutilated body. A blast of stale air struck his face as he proceeded through the large oak doorway to the basement. Every torch was now lit, making his path easier to navigate. He anticipated seeing Alice again, unchained and free. As he reached the bottom of the winding staircase, he noticed Alice sitting up, rubbing the area of her wrists where the shackles once confined her. Blood still trickled from her torn earlobes to her bare shoulders and emerald gown.

"Alice!" Richard called out. "Are you all right?" She quickly turned at the sound of his voice and smiled weakly.

"Of course I am. But it seems like that nut job's shackles are faulty. One minute I was trapped, and the next, they snapped open."

"They're not faulty. Stockton did that with a simple snap of his fingers," he replied, mimicking the act. Reaching up, Alice touched her ears and winced in pain.

"Did you retrieve my earrings by any chance?"

"It's good to see you too," he said and grinned. "I wasn't aware that—"

"You don't understand. I need to get them back."

Richard shook his head. "I don't think either of us is getting anywhere near Stockton. You'll see what I mean when we get upstairs."

Alice jumped off the table onto the cold cement while Richard pulled the contraption's lever, slowing the pendulum's swing to a standstill. Mrs. Stockton's shackles still secured her tightly as she lay unconscious.

"We need to do whatever it takes to get my earrings back, Richard. They're more important than you realize."

"Look, Alice, trust me when I say he's not in the mood just to hand them over. Whatever sentimental value they might have, I can completely sympathize, but it's just not worth getting killed over."

"They hold no sentimental value whatsoever. But they're the only way I can get home. Without them, I'm stuck here forever! Just like you would be without your book. Just try getting home without it, I dare you."

"I've already tried, it doesn't work," Richard said.

"It will when the time is right." Alice looked flushed, nervous. He grabbed her hand. It was cold and clammy yet still pleasant to the touch.

"Come on, it's now or never," he said. They proceeded up the winding staircase single file. As they approached the top, the echo of discontented moans rung out. Alice stopped a few feet from the doorway and looked at Richard with a glare of defeat.

"Stay strong," he whispered.

"I'm always strong," she replied.

Thirty

Bethany stopped at the side of the police carriage, freezing and exhausted from the long journey on foot. But she quickly forgot her misfortunes at the sight of the officer's lifeless body that lay discarded in the bloodstained snow.

After vomiting more than once, she slowly glanced at his faceless corpse. Bethany couldn't imagine who or what could have done such a thing. It was as if someone had taken their boot and smashed his face into oblivion, scattering pieces of brain and skull across the virgin snow. He was altogether unidentifiable since nothing remained other than a cavernous hole where his face once existed.

Resting on his chest was a shiny pistol and an oversized raven perched on his hollowed-out cranium, pecking at his remains. Bethany winced and retrieved the gun, briefly studying it.

She caught her breath after a moment and gripped the railing for balance, beginning to regret her impulsive decision to chase after Eddie and the police. But now, her only options were to enter the house or freeze to death. Grasping the icy handle, she pushed on the wooden door. The lock on the other side immediately shot open by a phantom hand, allowing her entry.

As she stumbled into the living area, the large black raven swooshed past her head and landed on Eddie's shoulder.

"Shoo!" he cried before noticing Bethany. "What in the world are you doing here?"

"What do you think? I've come to save you."

"Well, you shouldn't have come," he whispered, hoping Stockton and Charlie wouldn't hear him. "Nothing about this situation is good. Just take a look around."

Across the room, Richard and Alice nervously exited the basement door just in time to see the front door slam shut on its own, relocking, while a swarm of dark spirits swooped down and held the groom against the wall, ripping into his flesh and tearing away his extremities as he stared dully at them.

The man appeared in shock. His blood painted the bride's face and torso, causing her to curl in a ball and scream uncontrollably. His left arm departed from its socket, detaching in a fountain of gore. His right arm followed, and both were hurled chaotically through the air, landing in different areas of the room.

The shocked spectators watched the man's face begin to glow bright orange, as if someone were heating a piece of steel over a roaring fire. It grew brighter and brighter until a burst of flames erupted through his eye sockets and engulfed his entire head, swiftly melting his features away.

While screaming for help, the limbless groom flailed on the floor, unable to extinguish the flames. As his screams intensified, a thick black substance began to drip from the ceiling and down the mansion's walls. It reminded Richard of something he'd seen in an old Roger Corman flick.

As the flames slowly extinguished, the groom's movement ceased and all that remained was a charred skull that replaced his human appearance.

Bethany swallowed hard at the sight of Charlie and the dark spirit that floated next to him. It was bigger than the others, and it carried the familiar pike in one hand and the golden urn in the other. Sitting atop the pike was the severed head of Officer Jonathan, his horrified expression forever frozen. A silver essence rose from the groom's corpse and traveled to the urn, entering it from all sides. Richard and Alice remained in the shadows as Charlie walked over to the groom's body and stood above it.

"I guess congratulations are in order," he said to the bride with a smirk. "How about you give me this dance, malady?" Holding his hand out, he laughed between the woman's muted sobs.

"Let her be," Eddie said, stepping forward. Behind him, the distinct click of a cocked hammer rung out, and Bethany slowly lurched forward, aiming it between Charlie's eyes.

"What do we have here? Two former love birds trying to make a stand." Charlie laughed and put his hands in the air to mock them. "I suppose I'm under arrest!" Bethany kept the pistol on Charlie's head while he tapped his foot to the ghostly organ music. "Well shit, you want to play cops and robbers, sweetie? It wouldn't be the first time you've had me handcuffed."

Richard turned to Alice. "Do you know what's happened to him?"

"He's weak-minded, and so is Stockton. It takes a strong mental state to resist its influence. You were able to do it, and thankfully so was I."

The pistol shook nervously as Bethany stared down the barrel.

"Oh, please don't shoot me," Charlie mocked. "Try and remember all the good times we had, when I used to ravage you like a whore."

A burst of anger surrounded Bethany and she squeezed the trigger. The bullet exited the barrel, tearing the air and rapidly closing on its prey. Before they could blink, the bullet stopped mid-air approximately two feet from Charlie's face, suspended in animation.

Lowering his hands, he reached out and plucked the bullet from its hovering state and briefly inspected it.

"Catch!" he called out, tossing the bullet at Bethany's chest, where it softly bounced off and hit the ground with a sharp ring.

"I should've killed you when I had the chance," he said softly. "But then again, this might be more fun." Richard wondered where the other half of Jonathan had disappeared to, as his torso was nowhere to be found. After quickly surveying around the room, he got his answer.

Attached to the ceiling high above them was the officer's headless body. His arms were outstretched, and his legs remained together. The four daggers that pierced his limbs resembled the crucifixion. A puddle of blood formed below him that collected each drop from his neck as it fell to the floor, mixing together with the black ooze, pulsating with a thrum of energy.

"What do we do?" Richard asked. But Alice was distracted by the auras of the deceased and the living, and Richard's dazzling gold was the brightest of them all.

"Alice?" he said while waving a hand in front of her face. Still, she didn't respond. It was the first time that everything became thoroughly clear to her. The auras and visions abruptly ceased, and she felt momentary relief. This was a situation not unlike the last time she traveled, but at least her experience had served her well. It was a matter of connecting the puzzle pieces. She turned to Richard.

"You need to—" she stopped after realizing he was walking briskly across the room. "Wait, Richard!" she shouted. "I know what we need to do!"

But he was too focused on his intervention to hear her. While stepping in front of Eddie and Bethany, he faced Charlie directly and stared silently.

Stockton noticed Richard had returned to join Charlie and the King Spirit.

"Leave them alone and take me," Richard said to Stockton and Charlie.

"We don't want you, time traveler," Stockton said with a sneer. "We don't want any of you. You're nothing but a bonus."

"But you," Charlie growled, pointing his pale finger at Eddie, "...we want."

"That's not going to happen," Richard replied. "Your assumptions of me are correct. I'm not from this period, but I'm also aware of my reason for being here, and I'm fully ready to carry out my obligations."

"Are you?" Stockton muttered, noticing Alice by the basement archway. "Come join us, Alice!"

She did as he instructed and walked over behind Richard, and secretly anticipated what she was about to execute. It had to work. If it didn't, they were all as good as dead.

The King Spirit raised the urn and glared forward. Its hollow face sent chills through their veins as they waited for what came next. Stockton took one step forward and looked at Eddie. "Are you ready to die?" he asked softly, keeping his eyes locked on Eddie's.

"Not particularly."

"Master of horror, isn't that what they call him in your time period?" Stockton asked, glancing at Richard.

"Some people do. He's created some of the best-written works ever put to paper, and his name is legendary two centuries later." Richard said this for Eddie's ears only. He doubted their survival and at least wanted him to know what he would've accomplished.

Eddie didn't know what to make of what he'd just heard, but somehow, everything Richard had told him earlier began to make sense.

Alice approached Richard and wrapped her arms around him. He wondered if it was for comfort or another reason. Either way, he savored her touch, which temporarily eased the heaviness of his impending demise. Lost in the moment, he almost didn't hear the soft voice whispering in his ear. "Hold still."

Stockton and Charlie moved forward with a clear focus on Eddie. Knowing she only had a few moments, Alice focused on the gauze that wrapped itself around Richard's wound. She quickly grasped the bandage and whipped it off his head. Throwing it to the ground, she exposed his ruined eye to both men at once. Stopping quickly, they glanced upon its icy blue appearance without reaction.

She began to think her plan was ineffective when not much happened. But then, something did. Stockton's expression turned dark. He held out his arm, stopping Charlie from proceeding any further, sensing the fire in his own eyes extinguish. His upper lip furled as the pain intensified, and his insides constricted and ruptured, causing him to collapse to his knees.

As Stockton wondered about his mysterious affliction, a broad smile broke across Alice's face as she witnessed him flounder on his marble floor, grunting in pain as his guts twisted.

Regardless of his torment, he remained transfixed on Richard's mangled eye, completely unable to look away. Although confused by Stockton's apparent downfall, Charlie's self-assurance took over, and within seconds had ignored Stockton's disgusting display.

"Pathetic," Charlie said as he kicked his curled body. "Get up!" Alice took a deep breath and whispered in Richard's ear once more.

"Look at *him* now," she instructed, pointing in Charlie's direction. "Look hard!"

Switching his gaze from Stockton to Charlie, Richard stared intently as Charlie halted his movements and began to moan softly. It quickly intensified, causing his volume to rise to an agonizing howl. Slowly dropping to his knees, he held his hand in the air as if to block Richard's malicious stare.

He fell on his side and joined Stockton, who still wailed uncontrollably while spouts of thick white foam protruded up their throats, spilling out of their gaping mouths. Alice released Richard's shoulders and spun to Eddie. "Quickly, go retrieve the painting," she commanded. Eddie remained frozen in shock. "Hurry! Do it while they're still down!"

Her demands snapped him out of his transient state. He gave her a nod and made his way across the room, past the torch-lined walls and medieval relics, only looking back briefly to see if the situation had changed.

Charlie and Stockton remained floor-bound, still screaming like cranky infants. Even at this distance, Eddie could hear their cries pulsate off the high walls and ceiling. The dark spirits continued to hover beside them, but their black appearance had changed to a pale gray, and it seemed as though a few had disappeared entirely.

As he approached the painting, he noticed two faded spirits out of the right corner of his eye, rapidly closing in on him. Eddie picked up his pace and headed straight for the fireplace, keeping his focus on the painting. He quickly ripped it from the wall and kept it at arm's length, looking over to Alice for advice.

"What are you waiting for? Throw it in the fire!"

The spirits closed their distance. Having no interest in seeing what they wanted, he stepped back a few feet until the mantle of the fireplace stopped him unexpectedly. The two spirits approached and glared into his eyes.

They were so close that he would've felt their breath if they'd had any. He sensed a tightness around his throat while the air was sucked from his lungs. As he attempted to breathe, the tightness intensified while his windpipes constricted.

After he kneed the floor, he scrambled to retrieve the painting that had escaped his grip while his face began to turn an icy shade of blue. As the invisible force pulled him across the marble floor and further away from the painting, he knew he had been beaten. Being the young man that he was, he hadn't entertained the thought of death frequently, but it was here.

According to the fogginess in his mind, he figured he had roughly one minute or two before death slipped in. The floor became cloudy as he struggled to retain self-awareness as long as possible before slipping into the void.

Just as he was about to close his eyes and surrender, the faint outline of a shapely woman came into view and spewed muffled demands that he couldn't interpret through the ringing in his ears. The woman gave the painting a swift kick, causing it to slide across the floor and land back in his arms. He wrapped his weakened fingers around the frame while he struggled to hear the woman's instructions, but he didn't need to hear them.

He already knew.

Mustering the last of his strength, he grasped the painting and flung it sideways into the roaring fire, changing the red and orange flames to a bright sapphire. The gold decorative edges of the cherry wood frame began to char black as the fire consumed it. Eddie couldn't help but crack a smile as he watched it incinerate.

The dark spirits that hovered above him began to dissipate. With each second that passed, Eddie felt his breathing and senses return to normal. He was so relieved that he barely noticed the helpful hand outstretched to him.

"Come on, buddy. Up you go," Alice said, taking his hand and lifting him to his feet. "Are you all right?"

"I should be fine," Eddie said, looking back at the fireplace.

"Sorry you had to go through that, Alice continued. "But you had to be the one to do it. It wouldn't have worked if it was anyone else." Eddie nodded as he continued to watch the blue flames erupt from the fireplace. She grasped him by the arm. "Come on," she said. He accompanied her across the large living area towards Richard.

As they approached the middle of the room, Stockton and Charlie, still writhing on the floor, combusted into two large balls of fire, followed by bright beams of light that flashed through their eye sockets and mouths.

The beams struck the high ceiling and walls, creating an intense light show for the remaining viewers while Alice and Eddie hurried to Richard's side. After taking a few steps backward, Richard shielded Alice from the unnatural display.

Chunks of their flesh melted away as their anguish echoed through the room. Stockton's left ear oozed to the floor while Charlie's nose crumbled off like dried cake. A loose eyeball rolled out of Stockton's socket a moment later, causing a distinct squishing sound as it hit the marble.

Alice grabbed Richard's waist and buried her head behind his back, squeezing him harder with each passing moment. Everyone closed their eyes tightly, remaining that way until the billowing screams slowly subsided.

An eerie silence fell over the room as the last gasp for air was heard. With caution, they reopened their eyes to see that Stockton and Charlie were nothing more than two large mounds of grayish goo that bubbled wisps of smoke, emitting the nauseating scent of rotten fruit.

A single pair of emerald earrings, a golden pocket watch, and a large steel key sat around the edges of the melted remains. For a moment, the only amount of energy they could muster was to stare at the horrific aftermath.

Alice's arms remained clenched around Richard's waist, and he could feel her hot breath on his neck. It felt good.

Eddie ran to Bethany who was crouched by the front door, and laid his hand on her shoulder. "It's all right," he assured her. "Everything's going to be fine now." She looked up at him and smiled. "Let me help you up," he continued, offering his hand.

Richard took a moment to assess the damage. The whole living area looked as if Godzilla had just strolled through. The headless corpse of Jonathan still hung tightly against the high-ceiling, and Grant's mangled body lay where it fell, as did the groom's.

The bride's fresh gale of tears landed on the shoulder of his tuxedo as she clung to his lifeless arm. Sharp bursts of embers continued to erupt from the fireplace, emitting clouds of black smoke. Richard was about to walk to the fireplace to witness the painting's demise when he noticed Alice still had her arms around him. He wondered if he should touch her skin or maybe hold her hand. Her embrace was comforting, but he didn't want to sour the moment. Instead, he remained trance-like as he studied the trepidation surrounding him.

"This is something you don't see every day," he said. "I still can't figure out what happened."

"I do," Alice replied. "It hit me while we stood by the basement steps, almost as if someone whispered instructions in my ear. It was the last piece of the puzzle that Eddie needed. If this event never occurred, there'd be no *Pit and the Pendulum*, or *Tell-Tale Heart*, or anything else, for that matter. But I knew that once I ripped your bandage off, exposing your wrecked eye, Stockton and Charlie would lose all power over us. It wasn't the act itself, just what it represented."

Richard nodded. "That's a lot of pressure. I'm nothing more than a divorced man who was fired from his teaching job."

"But there's one more important thing we should probably note," she said. "As I was saying earlier, everything Eddie writes for the rest of his life will be a result of previous events, these events here, and I'm sorry to say, but that also includes what's about to happen."

Richard looked to Eddie, then quickly to Alice.

"*What* is about to happen?" he asked.

Over the faint sobs of the distraught bride, a thunderous boom from the rafters diverted their attention, followed by the sound of wood splintering. As the guests gazed to the ceiling, chandeliers began to sway, and the walls shook and rumbled as if a level five earthquake had just arrived. It intensified to deafening levels, causing Alice to release her grip from Richard and cup her hands over her ears.

A collection of paintings and relics fell to the ground, crashing in multiple pieces, leaving debris scattered in all directions. The torches shook violently from the rumbles, prompting them to fall one by one to the floor. Some landed on the marble floor while others ended up on long flowing tapestries and curtains, generating an eruption of flames.

Richard looked at Alice. "Never mind. You don't have to answer that last question." He understood the clock was ticking, so he walked over to what remained of Stockton and Charlie, bending down to study both piles of goo. "Fuck both of you." He reached into Stockton's slimy remains and retrieved the emerald earrings. As he examined them, he noticed something gleam next to Charlie's puddle of sludge...

Eddie's pocket watch.

He promptly wiped the residue onto his jacket and slid the earrings into his pocket, taking back the timepiece from Charlie. He stood and spat a ball of phlegm directly into the mound of mush.

"What's happening?" Bethany asked. Eddie clutched the front-door handle and pulled at the lock. As he struggled, Bethany's attention was with the bride. She remained on the floor next to her groom, gripping his arm, seemingly unaware of the rubble that cascaded around them and missing her delicate frame by inches.

"I got it!" Eddie called out, turning the handle and throwing the door open. Officer Warren was the first to exit, holding his hands over his legs to conceal the embarrassment of pissing himself. Eddie moved aside and grasped Bethany's arm, attempting to pull her out of the doorway, but she resisted.

"We cannot leave her here like this!" she called out over the deafening roars of the house. "We have to help her!"

"There's no time! We should—"

"No, I'm not leaving her there!" Bethany insisted.

While Alice and Richard moved toward the exit, one of the massive pillars collapsed where they'd stood, producing a large cloud of dust.

The walls splintered and cracked. Broken glass shattered, and visibility became impractical. They stopped between the doorway when they noticed Bethany and Eddie making their way through the smoke to the opposite corner of the room.

"Where are you going?" Richard called out to them.

Alice noticed the bride on the floor. "Wait here!" she instructed him.

Bethany quickly arrived at the bride's side and grasped her under the arm. "You'll die if you stay here! We must go!" The bride looked up through teary eyes and shook her head.

"I cannot leave him," she said, looking over at her groom. "He would've done the same for me."

As Alice approached her companions, more pillars collapsed around them. Eddie grabbed Bethany around the waist and pulled her away. Alice extended her hand to the bride. "No! I cannot leave!" the bride repeated.

"She wants to stay," Eddie said. "We must leave her if that is her wish."

"You don't have much time," the bride said. "I am content right where I lay." The bride broke eye contact with Bethany and bowed her head. Alice retracted her hand and turned away.

Eddie grasped Alice and Bethany's wrists and reluctantly led the way through the littered rubbish to safety. While they navigated the perilous room, the thunderous roar of the collapsing structure rung through their ears. Eddie laced his fingers around theirs, feeling comfort in the contact. As they approached the doorway, Richard still attempted to locate them through the thick clouds of smoke.

They were only yards from the door when another intense rumbling echoed through the air and a large chunk of ceiling fell to the floor, clipping the back of Alice's leg, grounding her. Caught between the door and the front part of the collapsing mansion, she quickly released Eddie's hand when the pain coursed through her lower body.

A second chunk fell to the floor, lacerating the middle of her upper back and neck, opening fresh wounds. Eddie knew if he didn't act fast, she'd be buried alive. He and Bethany tried lifting the chunks of ceiling off her as pieces continued to fall, pounding their shoulders.

Richard stood by the doorway, a sinking feeling in his gut. He called out to them again, hoping for a response. And then he heard Alice's shattering screams. His stomach fell further. He quickly entered the wall of smoke and followed her voice, holding his jacket over his mouth and nose. The screams intensified as he approached, noticing the pale outline of three struggling shadows. He hurried to them, avoiding floor wreckage in the process. As they became identifiable, he witnessed them attempting to free Alice. He quickly ran to their side to assist them.

"Alice," he said. "Hang in there, please."

She looked up at him, her eyes pleading. "If I don't make it..."

"On the count of three!" he shouted. "One, two—" It took every bit of strength to move the heavy chunks that trapped her, but with Richard's extra help, they were able to remove the debris. "Alice," Richard said, lightly tapping her cheek when she didn't reply. She was free, but injured and unresponsive. "We have to hurry," Richard said to Eddie. He gripped her under the arms and lifted her upright while Eddie took hold of her legs. The two men retraced their steps to the front of the mansion, carrying her out the front door and down the steps to the snow-covered walkway. They all noticed Officer Andrews' corpse along the pavement, but no one remarked.

Richard eased Alice onto the icy sidewalk, examining the wounds on her face and neck while Eddie and Bethany remained silent. They were busy looking up to the crumbling mansion, mesmerized by its swift deterioration. Officer Warren stood behind them, watching the balls of fire spew through the stained-glass windows, hurling shards onto the outside snow. A succession of explosions followed, causing the front wall to buckle, sending layers of brick and concrete to the ground, missing them by inches. They hardly noticed.

The horses bucked and reared, triggering a fast evacuation of the police carriage. While galloping down the distant road, the backside jail-cell erratically swung open and closed. Richard only glanced up from Alice once, just in time to witness the walls collapse, taking the ceiling and the rest of the mansion with it. The familiar raven appeared through the smoke, flying through the front door to the open street and landing safely on Eddie's shoulder.

As the explosions subsided, the last section of a once majestic ceiling fell to defeat, joining its counterparts. All that remained of the mansion were large piles of rubble and a thick cloud of toxic aftermath. They gazed upon the spectacle for a moment, awaiting another horrific incident to occur. But everything now appeared calm.

"We need to get her to safety," Richard said.

After glaring at the bride and groom's carriage, Eddie jumped the platform and peered inside. "Hmm, this is an exquisite design. But the absence of any valet leads me to believe the honeymooners lacked the required wages to hire such a service." He jumped down and grasped Alice by her ankles as Richard hoisted her upper body. "No need to worry," he continued. "I've had considerable experience in the driver's seat, and can assure a safe trip with myself at the helm."

They gently laid Alice on one of the red velvet seats. Richard took off his jacket and draped it over her chest and arms, noting her shallow breathing.

Richard turned. "Where can we take her?"

"My cottage isn't far," Bethany suggested. "We can sufficiently tend to her needs there."

With the stairs extended to street level, Richard and Eddie helped Bethany into the back of the mid-sized wooden carriage. She took a seat across from Richard and Alice while Rookie Warren climbed in next to her.

Eddie relocated to the front driver's seat. "Are you ready?" he asked as he whipped the partially-frozen reigns, prompting the two stallions in motion. The carriage jerked forward, startling the passengers. It steadily gained momentum, plowing through the accumulated snow as best it could.

Richard stared out the window and watched the familiar landmarks pass. The Majestic Hotel came and went, as did the Skinned Calf and Town Square. His anxiety peaked as the seconds ticked on, realizing that if something happened to Alice, he'd be unable to forgive himself.

Regret flowed over him. He could've pulled her out the door when he had the chance but instead, he let her join Eddie and Bethany in their rescue attempt. And now she was mortally wounded, and it was his fault as far as he was concerned.

He watched the sky. The snow had stopped falling and the clouds parted, revealing the bright twinkle of the winter stars and the moon's full luminance reflecting off the snow-laden streets. It was the only thing comforting him as he stroked Alice's clammy forehead.

Thirty-One

The carriage halted in front of Bethany's cottage, kicking up melted slush from under the spoke wheels. Eddie jumped from the first platform and quickly threw the passenger's side door open, assisting Richard. With one arm over Richard's shoulder and the other over Eddie's, they carefully pulled Alice's dead weight up the ice-glazed steps while they waited for Bethany to unlock her door, but Richard noticed something missing.

The billows of mist that emerged from their lungs were absent from Alice's breathing. Her face was a pale blue, and her lips cast a light shade of purple.

"Hurry up!" Richard yelled, his pulse quickening in a sudden panic. A click was heard as Bethany pushed the door open. She stood aside as the men rushed Alice into the living area where they rested her down on a large sofa next to the cold fireplace. The raven abruptly left Eddie's shoulder and flew to the mantle.

"Bethany," Eddie instructed. "Get some fresh wood and get that fire going! We can't see a damn thing!" He stumbled to his feet and darted into the kitchen area, returning a moment later with several worn rags.

"We can soak the bleeding with—" He stopped mid-sentence at the sight of Richard kneeling over Alice, pushing on her chest and breathing into her mouth. "What in God's name are you doing to her?" he asked. Richard ignored his inquiry and continued with the CPR, trying to remember each step precisely as he was taught.

He only used it once during his short stint as a medic after high school, but it was something he'd never forgotten. He dreaded the same outcome, however, because this time, it was personal, and it needed to end differently.

The fireplace sparked to life as Bethany tossed in another piece of wood, casting a pleasant glow around the room. Richard's resuscitation attempts appeared ineffective as Alice's face changed from light blue to dark purple.

"I do believe you are making it worse," Eddie said, standing over his friend.

"Please, Eddie! I need to concentrate!"

Bethany finished fanning the fireplace and placed the bellows back on their holder. She avoided the space where Alice lay and joined Eddie. As he watched Richard execute the unfamiliar procedure, Eddie felt Bethany touch his hand and grasp it securely. "Forgive me for speaking up," Bethany said, "but I do fear she might need the care of a local doctor."

"I agree," said Warren. "As an officer of the law, I believe professional medical expertise would be beneficial."

"No," Richard replied. "I'm more knowledgeable than they are. She's better off with me."

As the minutes passed, Richard understood that his actions were now in vain, but he somehow refused to accept it. He could no longer ignore the simple fact that Alice was entirely unresponsive to his best efforts. After one last pump of her chest, he slowly eased his hands off and sat upright, gazing down at her lifeless form.

"I am greatly sorry for your loss," Eddie spoke up, "She seemed like a fine woman."

Richard nodded. "She was." He looked up to Eddie. "We can't leave her on the floor like this."

"You can rest her on the grand-sofa for now," Bethany replied.

The three remaining men lifted her body off the ground and carried it to the comfort of the velvet sofa where they gently placed her. She reminded Richard of a sleeping angel.

Richard held back the tears and reached into his pocket, retrieving the pair of emerald earrings that Stockton had ripped from her ears. He placed them gently into her left hand and closed her finger tightly over them. Her skin felt cold, lifeless, and he quickly retracted his hand from her icy touch. It disturbed him more than he thought.

"I'll leave in the morning and take her body to the morgue," Richard said to Bethany. "If it's okay with you, I'll use the newlywed's carriage for transportation."

"Keep it," she replied.

Warren took a seat on one of the wood-carved chairs and addressed Eddie. "I apologize for everything you went through," he said. "Being falsely imprisoned is a grave injustice, and I will personally see that your good name is cleared of all wrongdoing."

"Thank you," Eddie said.

The four of them sat for minutes, listening to the crackling of the fireplace. It warmed only a small area, leaving the rest of the cottage frigid. Richard noticed the piano across the room. "Would you mind playing something for us?" he asked. "Something to calm my nerves, maybe some Mozart."

Bethany began to play Sonata 11. It soothed Richard's troubled mind as he sunk lower in his seat, closing his eyes. Eddie approached and sat in the space next to him.

"I am surprised a man such as you would know of such a composition. I'd assume it long forgotten where you come from."

"No, Mozart isn't forgotten," he replied, looking at Eddie. "Just like you."

"Forgive me for asking, as I understand this is not the most appropriate time, but I would like to have more information about this mystery that surrounds me. If what you say is true, then I feel I need to know."

"Just keep writing," Richard replied. "Do what comes naturally. Pull off of your life experiences, and you will be great." Richard smacked him on the back. "And Eddie, a small word of advice—stop eating and drinking from the lead-based tableware."

"What do you mean?"

"Just don't do it," Richard replied with a shudder of laughter.

"All right then, who am I to argue with a future man?"

"Oh, I almost forgot." Richard slipped Eddie's gold watch from the inside of his vest. "I believe this is yours. I took it from Charlie as we were leaving."

Eddie's eyes brightened as he recovered the timepiece. "Richard, I never thought I would see it again!"

"You almost didn't." Richard turned to Alice, where his smile quickly fell away. Bethany continued to play as Richard reached inside his coat and retrieved his book of poems. "I'd like to thank you for signing this for me."

"The pleasure was mine."

"But there's one more thing I need to do. Could you please get me a pen?"

"A pen?"

Richard smiled ruefully. "I'm sorry. I mean a quill."

Eddie stood and left the room. A moment later, he returned with a feathered quill and a small glass bottle. After handing them to Richard, he walked over to the piano and sat on the bench next to Bethany. The raven on the mantle stared back at him.

Richard opened the book and flipped to the last page. It was blank. Grasping the quill, he dipped it into the dark-sea of ink and scribbled a message. He blew on it a moment to dry it out before examining the words closer.

It read: *To my Emerald Lady, I will never forget you. 1831.*

Slowly, he closed the book and placed it on Alice's chest. "If you can't leave, then neither will I." He slid further down on the sofa, putting his arm across her chest and over her shoulder. It was cold but soft. He listened to Bethany's tranquil music as he closed his eyes. Tears welled up as he felt himself drift away.

Thirty-Two

Sunlight streamed through the window, hitting Richard's face and invading his slumber. He licked his lips and squeezed his eyelids tight to shield the sudden brightness of the room. With last night's vivid memories still flooding his mind, he prolonged opening his eyes to an unfortunate reality. After scratching his head and yawning, he rolled on his side to avoid the blast of sunlight.

Half asleep, he reached out to touch Alice but caught nothing. He reluctantly sat up, expecting to see the familiar surroundings of Bethany's quaint cottage. What he saw instead was the alarm clock, the television, and the computer desk. The calendar on the wall read: *January 20th, 2021.*

Next to him was the book. It once again looked tattered and worn. While his eyes adjusted to the rest of the room, he struggled out of bed and peered out the window. Snow littered the streets and sidewalks, but the sky was blue and inviting. A few pedestrians strolled up and down the walkways while a yellow cab passed at a snail's pace. Richard figured the snowfall to be around four-feet of accumulation.

As he pulled the curtains over, his bladder made its presence known. After another yawn, he shuffled to the bathroom with squinted eyes. As he hit the switch, the bulbs sparked to life, engulfing the room with irritation. He squinted further, glancing into the mirror in his zombified state. What he saw caused him to jump backward. His bodyweight hit the glass shelves, causing them to fall to the floor, taking all contents with them. Decades-old cologne bottles and hairspray and pain pills littered the tiles with expired contents.

But Richard didn't flinch.

He was too interested in what he saw in the mirror: the same white shirt, black vest, and overcoat that Eddie had loaned him. He looked down and examined the outfit for himself. Everything checked out. They were the same clothes that came from Eddie's suitcase.

"Alice."

A ping of guilt hit him as he recalled his failed attempts to save her life. The flesh wound on his eye had disappeared overnight. He examined it further, but no trace remained.

He glared into the mirror, brushing his fingers through the greasy unwashed hair on his head and sighed. He was happy to be home, but the sting of losing Alice sliced through him. She was all he thought about as he bowed his head and leaned both hands on the white porcelain sink.

He decided to go about his usual morning routine as best he could. While pouring the milk over his first bowl of corn flakes, his apartment buzzer sounded, startling him and causing his hand to flinch, spilling milk onto the kitchen table and missing Eddie's book by inches. He breathed a sigh of relief and set the carton down. In the back of his mind he couldn't help but recall the way he originally acquired it. Just the thought of running from the store with it under his coat made him cringe. He felt terrible, even though it wasn't his fault.

This might be payback time. No use in delaying the inevitable, he figured. After removing the book safely away from his spilled breakfast, he quietly entered the small living room.

The buzzer sounded again.

He took a deep breath and peered through the eyehole. But he only saw the vacant hallway. Apprehensively, he shot the lock aside and threw it open. Standing there was an older woman, probably in her sixties with shoulder-length gray hair that flowed out from under a blue wool hat.

Her bright pink lipstick detracted from the puffy white coat that caused her to appear larger than she was. "Hello, Richard," she said.

Her eyes were dull, yet reflected an appealing blue tone. The pink scarf wrapped around her neck matched the lipstick and mittens she wore with apparent coordination. As she smiled, the crow's feet and age lines around her eyes and cheeks crinkled, showing her wear.

"Yes, can I help you?"

"I believe you can." She opened the top of her tan purse and rummaged through. Richard shook his head slightly.

"Do I know you?"

"You're still the same as I last remembered," she replied. "I've waited forty years to thank you." After examining her closer, he began to recognize some features.

"Oh my God, Alice!" he said. She didn't respond. She only smiled. "But I saw you die. I wasn't able to save—"

She pushed her finger to his lips. "Because of you, I awoke in my room, in my own time, holding these." Opening her palm, she revealed the pair of emerald earrings and placed them in his hand. He smiled as he curled his fingers around them. "And check it out," she said, unzipping her coat to reveal a faded Ramones tee-shirt. "We never got to see them together, but I bought this at their Palladium show in New York. Best. Concert. Ever!"

"I'm sure it was," Richard agreed, laughing.

"You have no idea." She smacked him on the shoulder and said, "Now, let's go get some breakfast."

He nodded and held up his copy of *Tamerlane*. "Sure, but first, I need to return this to a dear friend." They walked out together.

About the Author

Phil Thomas is an author and screenwriter from the suburbs of Philadelphia. He is a member of the "International Association of Professional Writers & Editors," and he currently writes for Cultured Vultures, moviequotesandmore.com, and is a staff writer at Hardcore Droid. He is also the co-host of "What Are You Afraid Of?" a weekly horror and paranormal show, available on iTunes, iHeart Radio, Stitcher, and airs on Para-X radio on Friday evenings at 9:00 pm. You can find the complete episode list on the show's website at www.whatareyouafraidofpodcast.com

There you'll find interviews with wonderful guests such as Lloyd Kaufman, Katrina Weidman, Joe R. Lansdale, Grady Hendrix, Greg Bear, Daniel Krause, and many more.

You can get in touch with Phil on his website at www.philthomas.net.

You can email him at extraordinary117@gmail.com.

Follow him on Twitter at philthomas@filmauthor1 and Facebook at facebook.com/phil.thomas.50115

The Poe Predicament is his first novel.

More from Foundations Book Publishing

Where is Gabriel Clay?

The search is on for missing twelve-year-old, Gabriel Clay. Few know Gabriel has a secret. Dangers are built-in with his secret. Seasoned detectives, Ben Schwartz and Al Di Natale have joined the rest of Boston in what many call a fool's errand. The Boston area the boy and his grandmother live in is plagued with drugs and violence.

In order to solve this case, the two detectives must risk their lives to uncover the secrets. Otherwise, there will be more empty doorways unfilled because loved ones are never coming home.

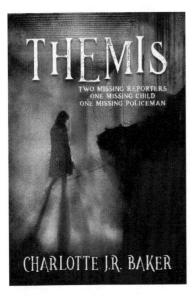

Where do the lines blur between justice and sacrifice?

Run by the beautiful and charismatic woman known only as Bow, Themis is an organization created with the sole purpose of doling out justice—justice that picks up where the law fails. When fifteen-year-old Liberty begins questioning the very essence of what she'd been taught all her life, those who have nurtured her are faced with the decision to either continue to give her the protection she has been allowed or seal her fate within its walls.

Foundations Book Publishing

Copyright 2016 © Foundations Book Publications Licensing
Brandon, Mississippi 39047
All Rights Reserved

10-9-8-7-6-5-4-3-2-1

The Poe Predicament
Phil Thomas
Copyright 2021© Phil Thomas
All Rights Reserved
ISBN: 978-1-64583-047-4

No copy, electronic or otherwise, in whole or in part may be reproduced, copied, sold in physical or digital format without expressed written permission from the publisher, pursuant to legal statute 17 U.S.C. § 504 of the U.S. Code, punishable up to $250,000 in fines and/or five years imprisonment under 17 U.S.C. § 412. Not for sale if cover has been removed.

Made in the USA
Middletown, DE
03 November 2022

14057888R00141